WHEEL and SERPENT

By E.A. STEWART

LEGENDS OF VALERÓS SERIES
Wheel and Serpent: 1
Traitor: 2
Hero: 3

ACCIDENTAL HERETICS SERIES
Book 1: *Bone-mend and Salt*
Book 2: *Trebuchets in the Garden*
Book 3: *Crux Lunata*
Book 4: *Song of Valerós*
The Mad Woman of La Catalane: A Novella
The Blue Door… and More Accidental Heretics Tales

RAIN CITY INCIDENTS SERIES
(as Annie Pearson)
The Grrrl of Limberlost
Artemis in the Desert
Nine Volt Heart
The Pirate King

WHEEL *and* SERPENT

LEGENDS OF VALEROS: 1

E.A. STEWART

Jūgum Press

Print ISBN 13: 978-1939423887

Published by Jūgum Press
505 Broadway East #237
Seattle, Washington U.S.A.
www.jugumpress.net

For Jacyn, who always wants a story to read.

'It is an heretic that makes the fire,
Not she which burns in it.'
— William Shakespeare, *A Winter's Tale*

'When they return to that land,
they will remove all its detestable things
and all its abominations from it.
And I will give them one heart,
and put a new spirit within them
And I will take the heart of stone out of their flesh
and give them a heart of flesh...
But as for those whose hearts go after
detestable things and abominations,
I will bring their conduct down on their heads.'
— Ezekiel 11

WHEEL *and* SERPENT

In 1213 in the Languedoc...

AS A RESULT OF THE European crusades in the Outremer, the area that we now call the Languedoc in southern France became quite wealthy, first serving as the departure point for crusaders intent on recapturing Jerusalem, and then benefiting from the trade, improved agriculture, and science the crusaders brought back to Europe, spawning an early renaissance.

Historians continue to debate the nature of a form of Christianity that became widespread in the Languedoc in the twelfth and early thirteenth century. Dubbed a dualist or Manichean heresy by the Catholic Church, the extinct sect is now often called Cathars. Whatever these people might have believed, however they might have prayed, these Christians were deeply embedded in the rich Troubadour culture of the region.

In 1209, French crusaders descended upon the rich southern lands between the Rhone and Garonne rivers, with a charter from Pope Innocent to restrain the heretics in what became known as the Albigensian Crusade. The crusaders' leader, Simon de Montfort, made himself viscount of Carcassonne after early military successes. Pedro II, the king of Aragón, sought to establish peace through a diplomatic relationship with Simon, promising his young son Jaimie in marriage to Simon's infant daughter and putting Jaimie under Simon's care for his education.

In 1212, Pedro joined with the kings of Castile, Navarre, and León in a decisive strike against the Almohad caliph in Iberia, defeating the Moorish forces at the Battle of Las Navas de la Tolosa. As a Reconquista hero, Pedro came to the Languedoc in 1213 to support the southern lords in their resistance to Simon de Montfort's aggression—and from there, the tale in *Wheel and Serpent* begins.

1
The Weasel and the Jay

A holm oak forest in the Languedoc
Monday, September 16

"IF WE WERE WORTHY KNIGHTS of Valerós, we'd be in Cahors by now, eating good bread. Drinking good wine. Instead, we're two days late and freezing in the wild woods."

Taresa hauled another linsey-woolsey shirt from her pack, shivering in the *montanha negra*. A warm September had descended to false November over the past day. Her two companions lounged under a sweet chestnut tree. Their horses browsed sun-yellowed grass.

"If Pedro wanted knights to perform his chore, he wouldn't have asked us to do it." Yusuf, her scholarly, too-pretty brother-in-law, grabbed the last dried apple just as Qasim reached for it. "You'll find a solution, Taresa."

"Except, don't think we can ride harder and faster. We lost two days with a lame horse, *Tarrr-ezzza*." Qasim, the family's bodyguard, spoke her name with a burr hanging off the R and a bee buzzing over the S, his accent revealing that he'd once been a Mozarab dock-boy in Valencia. Dressed as a warrior now, he'd groomed a grand beard, except it didn't cover the dimples that exposed him as an essentially happy man.

At Qasim's insistence, they'd again rested the horses alongside a mountain trail that led north from Toulouse to the Frankish territories, and then to Paris. Her travel plan had gone awry; however, she couldn't prevent either lame horses or the frequent need to dash off the trail to avoid French soldiers who roamed the countryside in search of heretics and rebels.

Yusuf sat on a granite boulder, his black clothes a sharp outline against the chestnut tree's grey, deeply furrowed bark. His stark figure was softened by a dark yellow aura, the color-cloud Taresa had seen around other scholars, though few were as serious as Yusuf. Lost in thought, he stroked his carefully crafted, yet thin goatee. Yusuf looked out of place, exotic and cosmopolitan in the wilderness. And ever since they'd left Toulouse, he seemed twitchy, nervous, on the verge of illness.

Qasim said, "We make a plan and follow it. Worry won't get us to Paris faster."

He imitated what Taresa said whenever either of them questioned her plan, then stuffed a too-large hunk of trail-biscuit and sheep's cheese in his mouth. When he spoke again, his voice lilted like a priest chanting mass.

"And, therefore, we continue to pray to you for mercy, O *ma dòmna* of our travel fortunes."

Before she could respond, his attention flitted elsewhere. Qasim pointed to a jay that lingered on a chestnut branch in hopes of scraps to steal, the azure stripe on its wings flickering when it hopped to a closer branch.

"Look, Yusuf! Your bird-brother from a previous life wants you to share your breakfast."

The last cottager who sold them food, a merry old healer woman with a sky-blue aura, had called Yusuf a wild jay, insisting he'd sung from the branches of oak and beech trees in a former life. She'd been kind to them and pleased to meet Yusuf, because he'd once been her brother, generations before. Yet Taresa learned long ago that women floating in a sky-blue aura are always kind, whether Christians of the Catholic faith or the goodwomen who agreed with the Cathar teachers.

"I shall call you *gai sauvatge*." Qasim used the goodwoman cottager's words.

"How do you say 'mute weasel' in French?" Yusuf asked Taresa, but he used a Castellano slur they'd heard last year in Iberia: *comadreja de silencio*. "We're supposed to practice our French, aren't we? For when we come to Paris?"

"Let me think." It wasn't a phrase her tutor had drilled. "*Belette muet*. Sounds rather pretty for an insult."

"It's perfect." He tapped Qasim's boot. "I shall call you after your own brother from a previous life, *ma belette muet*."

"I'd rather have a *nom de guèrra* than a heretic's pet name," Taresa said, using words she'd heard from Catalan mercenaries when she traveled in King Pedro's baggage train the year before—the journey where she'd first met Yusuf and Qasim, when they escaped from Andalusia.

"*Pastor de cabras*," Yusuf said in the local tongue, calling her the shepherd of goats.

"Not poetic enough." Qasim pondered it. "*Cavaller de cabras?*"

"She's the knight and we're the goats? Suits her, since Taresa is on a noble mission." Yusuf teased, which was how the three of them rubbed on together. "She hopes shepherding us to Paris will earn her a place among the *bonfraires*."

Taresa ignored their teasing, though she did indeed hope to be made a member of her husband Sebastián's secret brotherhood of knights, the *bonfraires*. She'd married into a family of warriors and intended to be worthy of their loyalty.

"Sebastián told me," Qasim said, "that only one woman has ever been made a member of their *bonfraires*."

"That's why she steals our clothes to travel in disguise," Yusuf said. "I shall compose a song, like the troubadours." He sang, making an ancient *cançо de guèrra* into a children's song.

> I'm a *cavaller* in chainmail,
> and here's my steely blade.

> I don't seek your magic Grail.
> Be a knight! That's all I prayed.

> Unlace my rusty aventail,
> and see if you're dismayed.

Qasim applauded him, but then argued. "*Ai, gai sauvatge*, but our Taresa dresses as a man because she's too distracting otherwise. That's what Sebastián, her lord and master, says."

"Don't laugh at me," Taresa said for the tenth time since they'd left Toulouse. Yusuf served as scribe to Pedro, the king of Aragón.

And Qasim had trained with Sebastián's knights for the past year. Yet she still had to prove her worth on this adventure. "And Sebastián is my husband, not my master."

"But you do hope to be made a knight as a consequence of our adventure," Yusuf said.

"Òc." She said *yes* in the Languedoc tongue. "It's why I accepted Pedro's request to travel with you this season, instead of staying with Sebastián." She twitched like you do when dozing off, then she felt a tickle, squeezed her nose to stop it, but still sneezed. A burnt sugar-apple odor filled her nose, the way it did whenever the familiar haunting sense came over her, that she'd already lived this moment.

"*Et beneeixi!*" Qasim blessed her for the sneeze, since he believed that your soul leaves your body for one heartbeat when you sneeze.

"*Aiieee!* Did you see the future, *bruixa?*" Yusuf called her sorceress, never granting credence to her claim that sneezes always led to the vision of an already-lived moment. "I believe the French call it *déjà vu*. Is my French improving?"

"I saw you lost and starving because I left you here alone in the wilderness. Wolves gnawed your bones." She prevaricated, not telling about the false memory of bandits brought on by her sneeze. Taresa caught the musty folds of her second-best shirt to drag it over her head. Hands seeking sleeves, her face buried, she paused when a hoarse voice squawked behind her.

"Your silver, or you die!"

Tugging her shirt down, Taresa didn't see bandits from a previously-lived time. Only barefoot, starving children gone wild in the woods. Like lost dogs.

The tallest boy, who'd clear the top of her shoulders if he stood on tiptoes, held a rusted knife at Yusuf's throat. Yusuf froze, his small book in hand, seated on that boulder. Two filthy children held sharpened sticks to Qasim's neck. One turned and ran toward her, stick aimed at her heart.

"You wizened brats!" Taresa roared, her heart folding into a fist at the sight of Yusuf threatened. She knocked her little attacker to the ground.

Whipping her dagger from its baldric, Taresa advanced, intent on the boy with the knife. He wavered when she shouted, and at the same moment Qasim swept his leg across his attackers' bare shins. Both little ones scrambled to rise from the slippery leaf mold and humus on the forest floor. Qasim tossed a horse blanket over them, then he snatched up their stick-swords and pitched them deep into the underbrush.

Yusuf knocked the knife from his distracted attacker's hand, then shoved the boy's sternum with the base of his palm. The boy fell on his skinny ass, clutching dirt to keep from skidding.

Taresa grabbed the boy's hand and jerked him to his feet. When she touched the boy, an image appeared in her mind, as if it were her own memory, a distraction she'd lived with since she was a child.

> A dozen scrawny, unwashed children huddled in a cave, stinking of piss and worse, miserable with hunger. A baby cried. No, not crying, screaming in pain and fright.

Her stomach cramped as if the boy's hunger were hers, the memory she'd eavesdropped far more frightening than being threatened with sticks.

"Take the food and this silver." Taresa tossed the purse tied to her belt at the feet of the smallest one. "Run. Now."

The little ones snatched up the purse and scampered into the brushy rockrose undergrowth.

Still holding the boy's arm—in her year traveling in the army's baggage train, she'd learned how to handle attackers—she dragged him to where their travel gear was piled. Fishing out the leather pack that held their food, she thrust it on him, so the boy again fell on his bum, this time tumbling into their gear.

While the boy struggled to stand, Taresa continued to berate him for thieving, yet threw that horse blanket over the boy's shoulders. He stumbled, then righted himself, the horse blanket turning him into a much larger demon who tumbled off into the woods.

"There's a Church farm down the trail!" she called after the boy. "They'll feed beggars but not robbers."

A hoarse squawk echoed from deep in the woods. "They don't feed goodmen or their spawn!"

"Goodmen don't threaten to kill people!"

Unsatisfied with her shouted argument, Taresa stuck her dagger back into its baldric, the pretty embroidered one her husband Sebastián gave her, her favorite present from him.

Yusuf was laughing. "Great practice if we're attacked again."

"As long as it's only children." Qasim was talking to the horses, calming them after the ruckus, since he loved the horses more than anything else in this life. "I spent a year learning to fight with steel, and two infants pin me down with sticks."

"They're starving." Taresa rubbed at the sharp pain in her belly, inherited from the memory of hunger she'd seen, once more disliking the flashes of others' memories that came to her, unbidden. "I saw it when I touched him. There's a batch of children in a cave farther up the hill. Refugees from Simon de Montfort's heretic hunters."

"Those are the goodmen souls that Simon claims will destroy Christianity?" Qasim said. "That Pedro d'Aragón hopes to save from Simon's ambitious crusaders? Or rather, one of the weird dreams you have when you touch people?"

Inside Yusuf's shirt, wrapped in a waxed packet, he carried letters from Pedro to Philippe of France, begging that king to intercede with the pope and Simon de Montfort to stop the heretic hunters who were ravaging the Languedoc. Meanwhile, Taresa's husband Sebastián traveled with Pedro, leading an army to stop Simon from laying siege to Toulouse.

"Should we wear our chainmail?" Yusuf asked. "To protect ourselves from ferocious children?"

"I like having a noble mission," Qasim said, ignoring Yusuf's tease. "But I also like knowing what's for supper. Taresa gave our food away."

"*Jhezu del tron!*" She swore, standing up from searching their travel gear, knowing her two companions would tease her for the rest of the day. "That wretched boy stole my sword."

Yusuf jolted as if struck. Her men's clothes didn't bother him, but her swearing a man's oath did. Qasim reached out to calm him, the same way he calmed the horses. "*Pax, gai sauvatge.*"

"We just earned a *nom de guèrra* as victorious warriors who stick together. We'll call ourselves *los tres amics*." Taresa christened them the three *amigos*.

"Striking fear into the heretic hearts of feral children everywhere," Yusuf said. "However, *los tres amics* need food, even in victory. We need to find another cottager who'll trade *mongetas e carròtas* for a silver penny."

"Beans and carrots," Qasim repeated, miserable. Their campfire cooking attempts had proved tragic. They hadn't even managed to cook decent trail biscuits. So, they'd committed to buying food from cottagers, most of whom in this country were goodmen, who therefore provided neither meat nor cheese. "Heretics' marrows and mushrooms. I'd sell my soul for a hot rabbit stew."

"Do *belettes muet* eat meat?" Yusuf asked. "Assuming a weasel has a soul that can be reborn into a hungry horse-lover."

"Let's travel," Taresa said. "We're now more than a day late for Cahors, and we need to ride hard to make up for it."

"*Òc, lo mieu comandant!*" Qasim saluted her in the local tongue.

"We're supposed to practice our French, my dear weasel." Yusuf saluted Taresa. "*Oui, mon commandant!*"

2
The Falcon and the Shrike

THE TRAIL NARROWED FOR AN extended passage between granite outcroppings, not a true gorge, but bare of bushes and trees and so constricted that they had to ride single file, Taresa leading the way. It was impossible to imagine a merchant's wagon passing this way, which caused Taresa to worry that she'd taken a wrong turn, though she wasn't about to voice her worries.

"When we get to Cahors," Qasim asked, "do we sleep past dawn? Let the horses rest for a full day?"

"Probably." Yusuf knew the plan for a rendezvous in Cahors, while Pedro had shared with Taresa an imprecise explanation. "We shall find a French lord, a friend of Pedro's who'll go to Paris with us."

"Is the French knight rich enough that he can offer more horses?" Qasim asked. "We can't keep riding our three horses into the ground every day."

"Maybe," Yusuf said. "Maybe the guards that Pedro is sending for us will have more horses."

They rode north, which meant that it wasn't possible to stay lost for long. Fear of getting lost absorbed Taresa's thoughts as the horses trod through the corridor, so narrow she could reach out to touch either side of the passage. More than a day behind in their travel plans, and it seemed as if the harder they rode, the more time was lost.

When Taresa emerged from the deepest shadows, a shriek echoed, so near that Taresa ducked in her saddle. A red-backed shrike landed in a wild rose hedge. A pretty bird with a grey head, a ruddy back, a pinkish lower belly, and a handsome black stripe through its eye. The bird bent its head to snack on a lark that it had impaled on a thorn, as if lunching from a convenient larder.

"Butcher bird," Qasim said from behind her. "Lucky guy, getting meat for its dinner."

Her horse lurched, stepping sideways, backing her knee and thigh against the left granite wall.

A wild boar stood pawing alongside the trail ahead where the earth was soft beside the trail, under a holm oak, perhaps seeking fungus or tender roots. The wind blew the wrong direction, or perhaps the right direction, for the boar wasn't looking their way. Instead, its attention turned to a viper in the path. It ripped the snake with its hooves, with no regard for how the viper bit at the boar's thin legs.

Then the snake was dead.

Taresa's horse whinnied its dismay. The boar looked around — weren't these beasts famous for being nearly blind? It sniffed the air, but the wind blew the stink of boar their way, so its nose didn't detect who shared the trail.

The boar pawed at the ground again, deciding whether the noise coming its way meant enemies, preparing to charge.

Taresa didn't have a sword. Throwing a dagger would be futile. Qasim carried their sole javelin, and he was behind Yusuf, still in the narrow corridor.

Were you supposed to look a charging boar in the eyes? Yell at it? Throw things? She didn't know. Before she could decide, the boar decided that the whinnying beast on the trail was an enemy. It squeaked and huffed, and then began to trot their way. Her horse screamed as if already struck.

The boar rapidly advanced, but then a stray flicker of sunlight caught a flash of a bird in flight, its silver wings shimmering. A silver hawk descended on the boar, claws out, wings hissing. It ascended after one attack, and then came down again from behind, ripping at the boar's eyes. The boar screamed in pain and anger, turning back in the direction from which the hawk last struck, the bristles on its back up in anger, ready to charge.

A silver-haired man blocked its way.

He flung a javelin that struck the boar in its already bleeding eyes. He strode up the path, short sword out, and even though the boar writhed and squealed, he stepped up and plunged the sword into the boar's throat.

Blood gushed.

The boar fell to its knees, snorting and choking on its own blood. Then it heaved over, gore running over the trail, down the ruts that would fill with rain in a storm.

"It's all right, gentlemen." The man spoke French, repeated the same words in the local tongue to be sure they understood. "I'm sure your horses took a greater scare than you. Lead them around to where they can't smell the blood. It will make it easier to convince them all is well."

Qasim took Taresa's horse and walked with Yusuf down the trail to calm the horses away from the stink of boar and blood. Taresa hung back to thank their shining savior.

He had long hair, as silver as his hawk, so until she approached him, she guessed him much older than he was. Close enough to greet each other, he proved to be no more than forty. Beside silver hair, his teeth gleamed when he smiled, and the stray rays of sunlight that broke through the clouds lit him like the statue of a saint in a cathedral. Around him, a rose-gold aura glowed, the color Taresa saw around sensitive, trustworthy people. He wore a white deerskin vest over a pink shirt, less clothing than she'd choose for a chill damp day. And finer clothes and boots than men might choose to wear in the wild woods.

"*Merci*, monsieur."

"*Bon jour*." He held out his hand in a French greeting, a lopsided smile that was both friendly and wry. She touched his hand, and consequently shared his enjoyable memory.

> A romp between two young men hunting with merlins in a meadow, spring flowers all around, laughing, daring each other to feed their hunters without gloves. The sunny happiness washed over Taresa like dunking in a Barcelona bathhouse. A musical voice calling out, "*Trust. Power. Which is most important?*" And more laughter between two adolescents. "*If only we could fly like merlins!*"

He released her hand. "What are you fine young men doing out here in the wilderness?"

"We're…" Taresa hesitated, still savoring his memory of a romp in the sunshine. "We're on our way to Cahors to visit family friends. And we thank you for your hunter's skill."

"It's nothing. This is an adolescent. He stood still so long like a squeaker does, hoping not to be seen."

"What's a squeaker?"

"What we call a baby boar. You were never in danger—but you knew that, didn't you?"

"I've never seen a wild boar before."

"Yet I saw your eyes," he said. "You never gave one thought to fear, too busy considering options. I salute you."

He glanced up, and Taresa followed where he gazed. The sky was deep grey, black on the horizon, threatening dire weather.

The man bent and sliced a morsel from the dead boar, and then looked up again, whistling. That silver hawk flew to his gloved hand, and he fed it from his bare fingers. The bird gobbled it, chirping soft *chup* sounds until done. Then the man hooded the silver bird.

"I've never seen a bird like yours before, monsieur."

"It's called a gyrfalcon. It came to me many years ago from a North Sea captain."

"In every story I've heard," Taresa said, "men hunt boar in teams, with packs of dogs and bows and lances. I'd claim it's you who's peculiar out here, alone, while we three travel together."

"I'm rather like this poor creature, a solitary pig. And I'm afraid of becoming too soft and comfortable in life. There must always be a challenge on the horizon, don't you think?"

"Me, I haven't known a time when there wasn't a challenge," Taresa said. "Thank you again. We have to ride on. We need shelter and food, and don't expect to find either between here and the monastery at the river ford."

"Bartomeu, a cottager, lives half a league north. Peek for the path that leads to his door. It's just past three tall chestnuts."

"*Merci.*"

"Now, I also must get to work. My cooks will have my hide if I describe killing a young boar but don't field-clean and haul it home."

"Should we help you?" Taresa heard the stupidity of that offer as she spoke. She wasn't prepared to gut an animal, and neither were her two friends.

"No, young friend. Lead your friends to food and shelter. And give my greetings to Bartomeu when you find his cottage."

"*Adieu*, monsieur."

She returned to join Qasim and Yusuf, but the man called her back with a question.

"Do you believe in the sanctity of the *domus* and the holiness of paratge?" The man spoke of the famous ways of the Languedoc: the extended family household, often as large as a village, and the southern ideal that meant more than honor and nobility—what your soul owed your *domus* and grandparents far back into dark history. "Do you young gentlemen believe the future lies with Aragón? Or Simon de Montfort? Or the counts and viscounts of the Languedoc?"

"We're not from here," Taresa said, having more than sufficient sense not to discuss such topics with a stranger. Such a question was the beginning of judgment, whether they prayed Roman prayers or sought goodmen's blessings. "Our future lies north in Paris."

She returned to where Qasim and Yusuf stood with the horses. Musing aloud, she said, "That was interesting."

"Taresa liked that handsome seigneur," Yusuf said when she joined them, "because he's not filthy, while we—" he pointed between Qasim and himself "—wear half the dirt of Languedoc."

"But we smell like horses," Qasim said. "That's good, isn't it?"

"I didn't smell him," Taresa protested. "And you were both on the other side of the clearing. People with a rose-gold aura like his are always trustworthy." Neither Yusuf nor Qasim answered; they stared as if waiting for her explanation. "My ancient uncle claimed some people take from everyone, while others are always giving. You have to judge quickly, even before the first hello. The cloud of color that floats around people, their auras, shows what kind of person they are."

"What do you think the silvery seigneur smelled like, Qasim?" Yusuf didn't respond to her assertion about judging strangers' auras.

"The flower of southern knighthood," Qasim said. "Sandalwood wrapped in silk and fine wool. How did he kill that boar without getting a speck of blood on him?"

Ready to ride, they glanced back to wave *adieu*, but the man was busy heaving on a rope to suspend the trussed boar from a tree. The red-backed shrike landed on the thorn bush again, snatching another morsel from its speared, dead lark.

"The butcher bird." Yusuf noticed this time.

"*Mongetas e carròtas!* I'd kill a rabbit myself if someone would cook it. Stick a spear through its roasted carcass and gnaw on it while we ride." Qasim complained again—*beans and carrots*—about the stew-and-bread fare that cottagers had sold them. "Is every cottager in the wilderness a goodman heretic?"

"The goodmen don't swear oaths. They simply don't eat meat. If you catch a rabbit, I don't think I can find a cottager to cook it for you. We should be at the monastery soon enough."

"Can you promise me that Christians will feed us a rabbit? A chicken? Even oily, aged mutton?"

"No. The sole promise we have is that twenty Aragónese guards will be waiting there for us. Maybe they'll feed you meat."

Yusuf wasn't listening. "I wonder where Taresa's boyfriend hid his horse."

"Maybe he's a djinni," Qasim said, "and flew here from his crystal castle in the desert."

"There are no such things as djinn."

"The man said there's a cottager half a league down the way." Taresa wanted them moving along while they argued. "Let's go buy food so I don't have to listen to you complain."

¤

When they started down the path that led past three tall sweet chestnuts, a dog greeted them, a snow-white Great Pyrenees. It must have been trained to guard something other than this trail, because it greeted Qasim as a long-lost friend. Qasim slipped from his horse to fondle the dog and sugar-talk dog-love with it.

"*Que és un bon noi?*" Qasim asked the dog over again, *who's a good boy?* After a bit, the dog seemed satiated with affection from Qasim and loped off to explore a noise in the underbrush, which smelled strongly of sage and thyme, which sent Taresa into a sneezing fit. A flush of songbirds burst into the air, scrambling in the sky, seeking direction, and then winging southward. Not a flock, since it was a fleeing mass of birds of various sizes and colors. Orioles, redstarts, black woodpeckers, larks. A pair of red kites.

Los tres amics hobbled their horses off the trail in a holm oak grove and crept up the trail to a rise above the cottage where they hoped to buy food. It was the usual whitewashed stone hut with a red tiled roof—but smoke rose from the cottage, a blaze visible inside the open door. Seven armed men were battering and badgering an old man, who cried out, "*Per l'amor de Déu!*"

The old man's pleas rang through the vale that held his cottage.

A dog came racing past them, the Great Pyr that Qasim had stopped to pet further up the path. It leaped to attack one of the armed men, but another interfered, jabbing a sword into the dog's throat. When the Great Pyr fell to the ground, the attacker pulled out his sword and then jabbed it into the dog again. When the man faced the direction where Taresa and her friends hid in the undergrowth, his crimson surcoat flickered in the light, revealing a dancing white lion, the colors of Simon de Montfort and his relentless heretic hunters. Too far away to see him clearly, Taresa noted long locks of honey-and-grey hanging from the open aventail of his chainmail. The smaller man next to him, who moved like a younger person, wore the white robe of Cistercian priest under a rusty coat of chainmail.

"They killed the dog." Qasim shuddered at Taresa's side, weeping. "You don't kill a dog."

Yusuf whispered, "We need to go."

They stole through the rockrose-and-Artemisia brush, as silent as any other animals that had fled the massacre, dodging among boulders and trees to stay hidden. When they reached the oak grove, Qasim whispered to the horses, begging them to be quiet. *Los tres amics* had mounted, ready to ride, before voices down the trail shouted in French, "We have visitors!"

Then a volley of French commands:

"*Arrêtez!*"

"*Attrapez-les!*"

Qasim and Yusuf understood enough of the language that Taresa didn't have to translate. They kicked their horses into motion, hurrying along the narrow path back to the three sweet chestnuts.

Taresa pointed north. "On to the monastery. We're safe there."

"Are we afraid?" Yusuf asked, though he didn't seem panicked.

"No." Taresa attributed the strong beat of her heart to the extra need for caution. "We haven't done anything to bring heretic hunters down on us."

"Maybe that old man didn't either." Qasim had passed through grief for that dog. Instead, his face was inflamed, burning with anger.

"We need to make up time anyway." Taresa again pointed north. After all, she carried the letter of safe passage from Pedro that identified them as messengers on the king's business. Not the unwary prey of heretic hunters. "Let's just ride hard and pretend the devil isn't chasing us."

The wider main trail was smooth enough in some places to gallop. They rode on, unsure whether they'd escaped their pursuers.

"Wrong place. Wrong time. Not your battle."

Sebastián's voice plagued Taresa, more like a bad conscience than reasonable advice. The three of them couldn't have done anything to save that ancient cottager. But Taresa felt failure and cowardice burn in her belly, like coals left to smolder in a campfire that had been defeated by rain.

"It's the world we live in now."

That voice rang in her ears, too.

Until she realized it was the murmured comfort Yusuf tried to offer Qasim.

3
Earth to Cloud

AFTER RIDING THE HORSES RAGGED (Qasim claimed), *los tres amics* hung back in the trees, letting their horses rest a moment while they surveyed the valley below where two streams met, roaring together into rapids. On the arrow-head of land that jutted between the two rivers, a manse and great barns sprawled, serving a monk-managed farm that produced food for other monasteries.

On the flat hill that rose behind the monks' farm, a trifling stone castle stood modestly, too small to shelter the people or animals living below, a relic of a former Languedoc seigneur who'd rendered his castle when the French crusaders came south four years earlier.

Twenty wicker hives sat in the monks' bee yard, safe from the rain in their wall-less huts. Grain sheaths stood along the farm-yard's wooden picket wall, waiting to be winnowed in the great barn and then the stalks stashed for winter fodder. The threatening weather promised mold if the threshing didn't commence the next morning. The local people required more golden weeks of September to prepare for winter. Yet the wind of the coming storm blew the kitchen smoke sideways. Across the fields, three harrier hawks swooped low, seeking one more chance for prey before the storm began. Then they caught the updrafts and disappeared into the mountains.

The monastery's gregarious abbot was known to open his great hall to travelers. In the courtyard of the manse, four gaudy mer-chants' wagons huddled, animals unharnessed and penned for the night. Smoke wound up from what must be the kitchen chimneys, since it was not yet autumn, too soon to be lighting fires for comfort.

However, the manse's courtyard did not contain what *los tres amics* expected. Pedro promised to send twenty guards to escort them to Cahors to meet a French lord who would take them to Paris. Their escort, like *los tres amics*, should have arrived at the monastery yesterday.

"Pedro's men aren't here." Eager to ride with an army again— On a mission! Couriers for a king!—Taresa smothered pangs of disappointment over the missing escort. She was the leader and so had to decide what to do next. "Let's go on, toward Cahors. If we ride hard, we'll get there some time tomorrow."

"We need to take shelter. We can't ride at night in the weather that threatens." Yusuf hunkered within his night-black wool cloak.

"Our horses are too tired," Qasim said. "And we need to beg supper from the Churchmen, since—"

"I know. I gave away our food store." What she didn't say, because any thought of it had depressed their day's rapid ride: the cottager they'd hoped to buy food from had been killed.

The wind cried, an inhuman shriek echoing in the forest.

"It would be nice to sleep on dry straw," Taresa said. For the journey, she dressed like Qasim, but the wind threatened to pierce her two shirts and quilted surcoat and freeze her bones.

"And hot food," Qasim said.

On the late-afternoon horizon, streaks of white light angled through the jagged fissure between heaven and earth until thick grey clouds rolled down, closing off sunlight like a shutter. The tiny hairs on Taresa's arm stood on end, waiting for the storm. Muscles jerked awake.

"It looks like the end of the world. Like in a song by a sad and lazy troubadour." Yusuf shrank deeper into his cloak. Since they'd left Toulouse, a vague illness had dampened his usual boldness. Taresa reached to touch him, to check for a fever. His hot skin burned her cold hand.

Yusuf shied away, his horse prancing sideways.

"Don't try to read my mind, witch-girl. Don't go around eavesdropping on people's private regrets and torments."

"Not a witch. Not magic," she said. "And I'm older than you, so not a girl."

"You make up stories, to be mysterious." Yusuf covered his eyes with his gloved hand, pretending to hide. "What do you see in my memory this time, O seer of secrets?"

"The same as every time I touch you. Books and scrolls in a language I can't read." Except she lied; she saw a memory Yusuf didn't want to talk about, awakened by the swirling wind.

> A wild storm. Waves washing overhead. Gulping salt water, swallowing it. Gut-searing, choking need to vomit. Voices shouting in terror. Screams that tasted of bitter salt and bile.

Which caused Taresa to choke back bile, her own belly aching from that memory; Yusuf had once survived a shipwreck where everyone else was lost in the storm. However, it wasn't polite or kind to invade. When Taresa first told Sebastián about seeing people's memories, he insisted that she ask before seeing his. Since she couldn't control when or whether she saw anything, she'd practiced blocking such flashes, like shutting one's ears to noisy voices in a crowded room. However, she seldom found any value in others' memories, which were usually as boring as men's after-battle bragging.

"My aunt reads memories," Qasim said. "She scared the ifrits and marids out of me." He patted his horse, which skittered, uneasy in the coming storm. "Not real demons. I mean—"

"As Yusuf says, there's no such thing as demons and magic," Taresa said. "He enjoys ruining the pleasure we seek from scary tales."

The wind shrieked again, racing its way through the forest.

"You can read my memories. I don't mind." Qasim offered his hand. Usually, when she touched Qasim, she saw the last good meal he ate and felt pepper exploding on her tongue and lips, or saw a trek he'd made with Yusuf, sun burning skin and eyes, the air too hot to breathe, heart beating in excitement, his hands in the mane of a sweet-tempered horse. Which meant that Qasim liked being on this journey, free of Pedro's court, as much as she did.

"Don't need to touch you, Qasim. You're remembering a rabbit potage and that you don't like being cold and wet in these strange black mountains."

Qasim agreed. "The air's thick as a sopping horse blanket."

Taresa twitched, then sneezed. She smelled burnt sugar-apple, which promised the sense of an already-lived moment.

An eagle screeched overhead, diving into the cover of dark trees whose spines jutted like skeletons along the steep hillside. The darker shapes of the *montanha negra* were lost in a murky veil.

That eagle's cry sharpened her mind, so it came to Taresa that the scene below evoked merely a depressing memory. Last year, on the army's journey back from Andalusia, they'd paused above a view like this. Pedro, *el rei d'Aragón,* patted his horse to calm it from the pending storm, and said to her, "I dreamed last night that you saved Aragón." Then he'd laughed so hard he almost fell off his horse. "Serena Taresa, runaway senhóreta of Girona, the hero of Aragón."

"*Jhezu del tron!*" She swore aloud at the memory. The king of Aragón had laughed at her. She resented it down to her finger bones.

Fat forks of lightning flashed on the horizon, shooting from the earth to the clouds. Her muscles juddered in a way that felt like fear, even though she wasn't afraid of lightning.

Yusuf shuddered too. He almost fell off his horse, but was caught by Qasim.

"It's only lightning, mon amic. All is well. All will be well." Qasim reached to quiet Yusuf's horse, speaking softly as if to also calm Yusuf. When did the warrior Qasim turn comfort-sister for Yusuf as well as for his horse? For that matter, when did her bold and brave brother-in-law Yusuf turn twitchy? Had that scene at the cottage unhinged her friends' usual tranquility?

She pointed to the trail that led down into the valley. "We'll take shelter at the monastery and leave before dawn for Cahors."

¤

The deep black heavens opened upon them just as they arrived in the courtyard of the monastery's huge manse and barns. They could ride no farther that night.

"Get inside," she said, motioning for Yusuf and Qasim to hand over their swords and horses for her to manage. Taresa once more asserted her place on the journey. *Cavaller de cabres.*

"We have to say our creed and beg priests because you gave our food to feral children." Yusuf groused, but she knew he didn't like sleeping on dirt and rocks any more than she did.

"You promised Pedro that you'd say your creed when asked and that you'd speak only in a Christian tongue." She chided him in Catalan.

Yusuf spoke in a tongue she didn't know, though she caught *Aristotle* and *Averroes*.

"Pedro meant don't speak Arabic." She guessed.

"It's Latin," Yusuf said. "The Churchmen's own language. After all, I'm a traveling scholar."

"And I'm his ill-bred Mozarab bodyguard." Qasim spoke in *valencià*, his own dialect. "You're a squire who longs to be a knight."

"*Silenci!* Pedro asked me to come with you, because I know people's ways in this part of the world." She'd repeated this too many times. "Which you've only read about in books."

"I mastered the Aragón dialect this winter," Yusuf said. "And Catalan when I first came to Christendom. I can speak the local tongue as well as you."

"Except with an accent that makes you sound like—"

"An Aragónese scribe with mysterious parents." Qasim came to Yusuf's defense, but in a thick *valencià* accent.

Yusuf said, "Don't treat us like we're your children."

"You are the smartest, bravest men I know," she said. "And I can't be acting like a mother. I don't even know what mothers do."

"*Òc.*" Qasim agreed, in the local tongue. "For example, my mother can cook."

"Don't talk to people inside till I join you."

"To make sure no one mistakes us for Saracen invaders?" Yusuf, willing to soak in the rain in order to tease her, waved one narrow hand, still ink-stained from scribe's work.

She shoved Yusuf toward the manse doors. *And because you look too exotic for this part of the world.* She didn't say it aloud because she didn't want to explain what she'd seen of exotic Iberian men while traveling to Andalusia last year with the army's baggage train.

Under the eaves of the manse, four armed guards lounged, eating stew from bread bowls. The young, innocent kind who hired themselves out as mercenaries and, from Taresa's experience, the kind that Churchmen like to keep when traveling. Innocent, pale, unused, the light around them murky pink, unstreaked by experience. And all of them dressed in fustian dyed a deep, deep woad. They glanced at her, but a mid-sized squire in a plain surcoat proved uninteresting to them.

Trailing three horses on the way to the monastery barn, she once more let her excitement rise, fluttering in her heart, over the promises for the journey. The rain didn't matter and, though their Aragónese escort hadn't arrived yet, she'd gotten *los tres amics* this far. Tomorrow they'd be on the next leg of their journey, carrying messages to Paris from Pedro. Once again she'd get to ride in the heart of a small army, this time as a member instead of an escorted wife, like last summer, struggling home across Iberia.

At the huge doors that opened into the barn, two drovers from the merchants' train squatted where it was dry, near the single lamp permitted in the barn. Their backs to the woad-clad guards, the drovers tossed dice, one nudging the other when Taresa passed.

"*Hola*, freckle-face! Join us after supper!" one called, speaking the local tongue in a backstreet Toulouse accent. He had a nose like a radish and seemed to be perpetually amused with the world.

"*Gràcies!*" She exaggerated her Catalan accent. What better opportunity to learn about the dangers of this road than a conversation with drovers? "We will, mon amics. Backgammon?"

"With two strong boys and their pretty friend?" The second drover laughed in his fist. "Bring your silver pennies, young squire, and we shall see."

Amid the green, nose-tickling scent of silage in the barn, Taresa sneezed and then again felt that already-lived sensation, as if she'd been enveloped in just this way by the friendly odor of warm animals and fodder. But of course, she had. She'd married into a family that cared for its horses, finishing every day's travel by ensuring the animals' comfort. In last year's journey home from Iberia, she'd often ended dry days and wet ones like this in the barns that local lords lent to the king of Aragón. After she and Sebastián finally sealed a real marriage, she'd tumbled in the straw with him several times, her nose confusing the smell of horse, fodder, and her sweating, energetic husband.

Here she was, having the journey she wanted, while Sebastián was with Pedro, preventing the siege of Toulouse, as they'd agreed.

However, she hadn't planned to miss Sebastián as much as she did. She'd never missed anyone before. She couldn't reach out when she wanted him, like she had for the past year. Missing, like her lost sword. Then again, she didn't want to be a knight because she wanted to fight wars, but because she wanted to be part of Sebastián's confraternity of knights, not merely his wife.

She settled their horses in a large stall, pulled off saddles and packs, and began to wipe down the wet, tired animals. A sob echoed from a nearby stall, rousing her sense of an already-lived moment, though there'd been no tears when she and Sebastián found moments alone in the hay. She followed the sound. Two stalls over she found a young boy weeping in a pile of straw, his face and hands blotchy with cold and grief, chaff caught in his dirty hair. Taresa didn't know much about children, guessed the lad was five or six compared to those she'd met in the baggage train last summer.

"Why the tears, *fadrin*?" She used the term of affection she'd heard Yusuf's father call his son.

"God has left me." He got a few words out, and then coughed, which built to a racking blast that matched the night's thunder.

"Oh no, *fadrin*. Doesn't the priest say Jesus cares for the little ones?" Not raised where prayers were said outside mass, she wasn't prepared with bromides to calm a child's fears.

"My grandmother ran away. No one here knows me."

"Where are you from? Can we take you there tomorrow?"

"From the cabbage farm in the valley. But we can't go there. Simon's crusaders came."

"You must be lonely. The monks here will care for you, won't they? Did you ask?"

"I can stay if I muck out the stables." Again, a cough.

She meant kindness, but then, this wasn't a kind world, even if the abbot allowed a sick, sad boy to work in his stables. "Why did your grandmother run away?"

"Because the king is dead."

"You mean Pedro of Aragón? He's not dead." She patted his barn-dirty hand, having no idea how little boys are best comforted. "I saw the king a few days ago."

"You know Pedro the king?"

"I fought with him at Las Navas del Tolosa." Not a total lie. "He's alive as you and me."

"No." A determined shake of his head sent snot flying. The child pointed to the gambling drovers near the barn door. "Ask them."

She called to the drovers. "*Hola!* What have you heard about Pedro of Aragón?"

"*Ai,* that bastard Simon killed him at Muret day afore yesterday." That red-nosed drover flushed even redder.

Her blood turned to ice. Her heart couldn't beat.

"We're in hell now," the other drover said. "No one kills a king in battle. Anointed by the pope himself. Only a serpent like Simon would dare."

"The world's gone mad," the first drover said. "Simon's heretic hunters are chasing Pedro's army all over the Toulousain, slaughtering them like rats in a grain barn."

"*Mercé.*" A reflexive thank-you, but she couldn't make her voice work for them to hear.

The crying child sat in the straw, shivering, wiping at snot and tears. Taresa knelt by him, her knees hitting the hard dirt floor instead of straw. She whispered, "Is your grandmother hiding from heretic hunters?"

"*Òc.* Simon de Montfort is on his way to kill us all."

"The abbot here won't give you to the hunters, if you say your creed." Clenching the boy's hot, frail hand and hoping offer comfort, she heard his memory of a woman's voice, like a lute playing a sad song.

> "*Hide in straw, fadrin.*" Skirt smelled of kitchen fire and funk and fresh bread. The straw is sneezy and promises rot. Tears run down the stalks. Then voices chat in French, casual as merry servants on holiday.
>
> "*You seem happy.*"
>
> "*Oui. By this hand, my very own, we stopped Aragón. That bastard king is dead. We are heroes to God and Simon.*"
>
> "*Aiieee! You did the deed? When is killing a king God's will?*"
>
> "*We're forging a new kingdom. God can follow along. We shall find grace and joy in burning the devil's own.*"

Taresa parsed the French slowly to be sure of what the child overheard. He'd begun sobbing again.

"Dead!" Sebastián shouted. *"We're all dead! Dead!"*

Behind her? Nothing. No ghosts. Sebastián wasn't here with her. She'd seen spirits rise from dead men, when her father and uncle died. And when she and other women from the baggage train searched for injured soldiers among the festering bodies on the killing fields, but she'd never seen ghosts.

She released the boy's hand, his grief now inside her like an icy stone lodged in her belly.

"Do you have a blanket, *fadrin?* You'll make yourself sick crying in the cold." She gave him her second-best surcoat as a blanket and promised him a silver penny if he slept near her horses for the night.

"Thank you, master!" The idea of a penny consoled the boy as much as the quilted surcoat. "I shall pray for your good end."

"Keep quiet about such prayers, *fadrin*. Stay safe until your grandmother can fetch you."

Pedro dead! And Simon's crusading knights were hunting Aragónese soldiers. Which meant they hunted Sebastián, if he hadn't perished in battle beside Pedro.

Of course, Sebastián had been right beside Pedro.

That stone in her belly pressed so hard, she couldn't swallow or get her breath.

She'd galloped for days with Yusuf and Qasim to join the Aragónese guards who'd ride with them to Paris. But those guards were being hunted. Or already struck down. Amid a hundred missed heartbeats, she settled the horses—Pedro dead! Sebastián hunted!— and then tugged on another shirt, borrowed from Yusuf's pack, so she looked more scholar than squire.

The boy had cried himself to sleep. Only soft animal noises echoed in the barn. In the dim twilight, Taresa stripped the Aragónese tassels from their horses' halters. She grabbed her braid to tuck back into her shirt, but instead gave in to the despair that gnawed ragged edges around that stone in her belly. She hacked off the braid with her dagger and stepped into the rain behind the barn to dump her coppery braid and the gold tassels onto the muck pile.

She trudged to the manse, lugging their weapons to be left with the doorkeeper, expecting to find heretic hunters and Pedro's killer inside. Her fingers curled as if clenching that stone of grief she carried.

Pedro dead!

And Sebastián—

4

Bread and Lentils

"DEAD AS A DOG!"

Riotous, laughing men, voices rising. Hot bread. Stale male bodies. A whiff of horse sweat and wet wool.

When she opened the heavy oak door, the clamor and stink hit Taresa as hard as the buffeting wind and rain did when she crossed the courtyard. Her friends huddled on a bench in the far corner of the great hall, lost in the shadows of the timbered ceiling and tree-sized poles propping the oak beams, smoke-stains overwhelming the whitewash on stone walls.

She crossed the room, her heart thudding, dreading what she had to tell, conscious of the knife she'd kept in her boot instead of surrendering it to the doorkeeper. She threaded her way among travelers on benches, around tables, propped against the stone walls. Someone in here had bragged about killing a king.

A half dozen French nobles gathered at one end of the great hall. Long curled hair. Silk coats. No chainmail in sight. None looking like he'd ever killed anything except a bota of wine.

In the middle of the room, a trio of priests in white surcoats sat at a table, their travel cloaks and chainmail piled on the benches where they sat, laughing, passing chunks of bread and cold meat on a board, so amused that you couldn't guess the world had just been dumped upside down, that a king had been murdered.

A French knight sat with the three priests, his back to Taresa. He'd draped his quilted surcoat so all could see the dancing white lion on a blood-red field. Simon de Montfort's coat of arms. Here were the heretic hunters the boy in the barn feared—the same ones they'd seen attack the ancient cottager. Which one bragged of killing Pedro?

Their words didn't carry far, but Taresa touched one of the priests as she passed, the youngest of them, the blond one, and shared a hot, fast memory.

> A ringed hand slapped mercilessly at his face. Twice. A bitten lip stung and bled. Burning tears. "*It's wrong! It's evil!*"

Yet the young priest, even while remembering this slap, threw his head back, laughing at whatever the French knight said. The deep scratch down the blond priest's face must have come from that slapping hand.

Did the hot tears she blinked back come from the priest's mortifying memory, or were they her own tears from failing to swallow grief? Blinking again, she was now close enough to see Yusuf's face under the shadows, with Qasim whispering in his ear. Taresa let go of the dread she carried, loathing what she had to tell them.

The rictus of Yusuf's smile held no joy, his eyes stared at nothing. Qasim watched Yusuf, his face pale, one hand hovering over Yusuf's, a sentimental gesture of comfort frozen, unfinished.

They'd heard the appalling news.

She collapsed on the bench beside Yusuf.

"*Jhezu del tron!*" She swore. Yusuf twitched at the oath, but why should he care? Neither he nor Qasim ever called upon Jesus in heaven for help. It occurred to her then that others in a room such as this might not appreciate the oath she'd adopted while practicing the swagger of young Toulousain men.

Feeling as if they were watched by every man in the room, Taresa checked her friends again. Did Qasim or Yusuf resemble Aragón knights (like Sebastián) that Simon de Montfort was chasing through the countryside? Yusuf, all in black, thin as a reed, carried himself like a scholarly noble. Qasim, after a year training in a king's court, could pass as a lord's bodyguard, no longer the scarecrow servant she'd first met. But he wore no signs of Aragón or Valerós service.

"Each man here is guessing who they can trust." Qasim spoke in a whisper, his voice like sand in the wind.

"Or who they can turn over to the heretic hunters." Yusuf motioned vaguely to that trio of priests. He twitched again, his eyes wandering as if he'd indeed taken sick after they'd left Toulouse. "I'm sure it's the same men who burned that cottage."

"You cut off your hair." Qasim came back from his misery to see her for the first time. "Why? You look enough like a man in Yusuf's clothes. Why would you—"

"*Silenci!*" She didn't want to speak of it.

"Out of respect. When others can't know you're mourning." Yusuf whispered the words, his dark eyes approving what she'd done. "It makes you beautiful, *sòr*." He rarely called her sister.

"And terrifying," Qasim said.

Taresa gripped her arms so hard, muscle tension warned that every man there must see how the wildfire coursing through her blood was heating the stone in her belly. She dropped her hands into her lap, shook her head the way Sebastián did when he argued.

"The whole world has gone mad." She too whispered. "But you know what we have to do."

"Yes, just what we were asked to do." Yusuf seemed sure of this, still staring bleakly. "Bring Pedro's letters to Paris."

Qasim nodded, but watched Yusuf, who bit his lip, his jaw quivering. Pedro had been their friend.

She needed to get them busy. Grieve later.

"We are scholars traveling to the university in Paris," she said. "Not Pedro's scribe with an armed guard, carrying secrets."

Qasim passed a bowl of lentils her way. "Eat. There's bread. Did you pay the abbot for a bed?"

"No. We'll sleep in the barn and leave before first light." She took a bite but could scarcely swallow. "And keep to ourselves."

Yusuf bowed his head, folded his hands, and did a fine imitation of a man at prayer. Qasim blinked twice and did the same. In this room, it was the best way to claim privacy. Where it was not possible to cry out in grief. But Taresa couldn't keep her eyes closed for long. She sought that trio of warrior-priests, one of whom might be the murderer-braggart.

One priest, broad shoulders straining his white cassock, was twenty years older than the other two. Thick lips, bulbous nose, pendulous earlobes, as if the parts of his face had overgrown their bounds. His dark brow hung as a growth over his small, bird-like eyes. Though he laughed, a muddy-brown, angry cloud hung around him. Not the aura of a soul who could be trusted.

The lank, blond priest who remembered being cruelly slapped was prematurely balding. The other was black-haired and thick as a tree. Both had thin grey auras and the unlined faces of young men who'd seen nothing, yet believed in their own unearned wisdom. She knew their kind from life in the army's baggage train last year. Before the riots in Toledo and the battle at Las Navas, she'd washed shirts for dozens of innocent, self-important priests in chainmail. Every one of them lost that look by summer's end, so it seemed that these two hadn't participated in last year's heroics in Andalusia. This must be their first adventure, out bringing infidels and heretics to the One True God.

Yusuf's words were strangled in grief. "We have to get to Cahors as soon as we can. If the guards don't arrive tonight, then—"

"Listen." She seized Yusuf's hand, but he jerked it away. "Simon is chasing Aragón's knights and infantry through the countryside. Slaughtering them. No one is coming. Everyone died at Muret." She tapped the table beside Yusuf's hand but didn't touch him. He'd turned pale as a blanched almond, his face scrubbed of expression, his eyes burning like a balefire. "Everyone, including…" She faltered, that fist tightening around the cold stone in her belly.

"You mean, Sebastián and Tomás are dead. Simon killed our brother and father." Qasim's voice sounded like it came from a tomb. Her husband was gone, along with Yusuf's father Tomás, who'd first hired Qasim in Valencia.

"No." Yusuf denied that with vigor, his color warming, anger replacing shock. "Sebastián and Tomás weren't at Muret."

"They must be dead." Taresa choked out the words. "What other two knights would be right beside Pedro in battle? No killer could get past them, as long as they lived."

Still shaking his head, Yusuf said, "Pedro gave them tasks like ours. Sebastián went to Rome with a dozen lords of Aragón. Tomás is on his way to Narbonne, carrying the same message as ours, for the viscount and archbishop."

The fist clenching the stone in her belly loosened its grasp. Sebastián not lost?

"We are—what?" Qasim's voice squeezed into a boy's shrill plea. "We're carrying a packet of diplomatic letters to Paris begging their king to stop Simon."

Yusuf seized a round of bread, as if to steady his hand. "More than that. We were sent to beg Philippe of France to help return Jaime to Aragón. That's what Sebastián and Tomás are doing, too."

"Who's Jaime?" Qasim seemed bewildered.

"Pedro's son." Taresa knew that much, but her mind spun in a whirlwind—Pedro was dead, but Sebastián lived!

"Pedro pledged the infant Jaime to marry Simon's daughter. He placed him in Simon's care. Like noble lords do." Yusuf pretended to nibble at his bread, his Adam's apple bobbing as he swallowed grief.

"As surety for shared promises." Taresa got words out, still deciding whether Yusuf was right, that Sebastián didn't die at Muret.

"Òc. Pedro asked for Jaime back when their parleys took a bad turn this summer. But Simon refused."

Qasim wrenched apart a small loaf but then couldn't take a bite. "And we sit here with heretic hunters laughing their heads off, happy that Pedro's dead—"

"Pedro sent us away—" Taresa just then understood "—to keep us out of battle."

"No, he sent us to warn Philippe," Yusuf said. "Simon wants to be king in the south. The Languedoc needs Philippe's help to stop Simon and return Jaime to Aragón. With Pedro dead—"

Qasim said, "Lower your voices, *mon amic*."

¤

They fell quiet again, and Taresa scanned the room, seeking the bragging voice from the barn. The abbot, who'd moved through the room greeting people, approached their table, and Taresa sat up, preparing for an interrogation. This abbot resembled a commanding Brabançon general she'd met once, bigger than a Pyrenees bear, hands the size of the hams hanging in his smokehouse; the forearms jutting from his robe were wide, muscled. The golden-amber color around him was familiar; it told Taresa that this was a priest who truly believed what he preached.

Instead of greeting Taresa and her friends, the abbot veered to the right and began an animated conversation with a noble lady in the corner opposite Taresa. The abbot stroked the hand of the lady while they conversed, as if offering comfort. But he kept hold too long after the lady wished to withdraw.

The woman with whom the abbot conversed talked with her hands, thin white fingers outlining whatever story she told the abbot. The woman swept the air grandly but then shook her finger at the abbot, upbraiding him. Playful or serious? Taresa wanted to see her face, but that woman seemed to know how to keep secrets and never once peeked out from the shadows of her hood. While chatting with the abbot, the woman twisted strands of her dark hair that had escaped her veil. Not like a woman twirls her locks at a lover. Like a woman disturbed in her core, anxious.

"Don't ask me to respect heretic hunters," Yusuf murmured beside Taresa. "*Ai*, they're bloodthirsty hypocrites, more eager to burn souls than save them."

"Pedro wanted to stop it." Qasim muttered in the same grief-clogged whisper. "He's the best ruler in Christendom. How could Simon—"

"It's much worse." Taresa spoke low while burning inside, wanting to run out into the storm to quench the fire. "In the barn, a man bragged about killing Pedro and saying what a joy it is to burn heretics. That murderer is in this room." Indicating her best guess, she pointed to the two priests. The French knight and the blond, slapped priest were now gone.

Yusuf gasped as if punched, then gnawed his lip again.

Qasim denied the idea with one curt shake of his head. "Those men were here when we sat down. No one else came into the great hall until you did."

"There's a lost child hiding in the barn. When I touched him, I heard the killer bragging."

"But you didn't hear him directly?" Yusuf crossed his arms and rocked on the bench, either for comfort or to resist what she claimed.

"No, but you can ask the boy what he heard." Except it was in French, which the boy didn't understand.

"No one kills a king," Yusuf whispered. "Your Old Testament times have passed. It offends paratge. Your pope forbids—" He choked back grief again.

"When we find that bragging man," Taresa sought words to help cool that stone that grew hotter in her belly, "we kill him. Pedro deserves justice."

"What?" Yusuf spoke too loud. Qasim tugged at his sleeve. Yusuf dropped his voice. "We aren't killers. We'll tell—"

That's when she discovered more fury than grief in her heart. "Tell who? Simon holds the new king of Aragón. These priests are overjoyed that Pedro's dead."

"We must use the law to deliver justice. Not our swords." Yusuf recited words as if from one of his indecipherable books.

Taresa and Qasim stared at him. Last summer, the pacifist Yusuf had killed a man to save Pedro from an assassin.

"Killing to stop a murder is justified." Qasim spoke up.

Yusuf nodded as if he read their minds. "But killing one man for murdering another isn't justice. It's revenge. We become savages."

"That's what the commandments say. But—" Taresa pointed to the chainmail piled beside the crusader-priests. "We saw what these men did today."

"If it was them. Or just another of their ilk."

The abbot's voice rang through the room. "My friends in Jesus Christ our Savior."

He'd stood from his conversation with that woman, and all the chaotic chatter ceased. In the silence, Taresa smelled unwashed men and rancid lamp oil.

Yusuf's hands trembled on the table. He jerked them into his lap. All emotion was gone from his face, unless you saw the tiny bits of dried salt at the corners of his eyes. Qasim's dark eyes, also damp, flickered to Yusuf. He worried, so Taresa did too.

"I am called Guillem and come here from the Templar house in Arville." The abbot spoke the local tongue with a Norman accent. "If you didn't know, the Knights Templar bought this farm. I'm here to build on the glorious work of the monks who toiled here for years."

This wasn't the gregarious Cistercian abbot they'd been told to seek. With the world turned upside down, perhaps this was better. The Templars weren't involved in Simon's quest to defeat heretics. In Andalusia, the Templars she'd met were real knights, not overly-proud priests in chainmail. Perhaps this warrior-abbot could help.

Sell them provisions. Provide a guard as far as Cahors. Listen to what she knew about the man who murdered Pedro.

"Let us pray."

The abbot's voice boomed.

"We shall ask God for mercy on the soul of Pedro d'Aragón, that he may at last be forgiven and then admitted to heaven. And we beg the Holy Spirit to guide our work to advance Christ's victory over evil."

Yusuf quaked so hard the bench wobbled. Qasim had to help him up when all the men in the room stood and bowed their heads in prayer, each checking every other begrimed, stinking traveler in the room.

5
Priests in Chainmail

TWO YEARS AGO, TARESA RAN away from evil, when a bad man bought her and her horse from her dying uncle. It was an ordinary marriage contract, but she'd been sold against her will. She'd sheltered in Pedro's baggage train and baked in the heat of Andalusia. She learned how to travel rough and how to protect herself. Those were happier days than she'd endured in Girona. She might still be living that life if Pedro hadn't made Sebastián marry her, making life far, far better than she'd known possible. Now she couldn't run away, because evil had overtaken the entire world. Yet she still knew how to travel rough and protect others. That's why Pedro asked her to accompany Yusuf on this journey.

And all they needed to do, amid this day's danger, was listen to prayers in a room full of silk-clad French lords, warrior-priests, and heretic hunters. Then rise early and ride to Cahors.

The abbot began with the creed.

"*In nomine Patris, et Filii, et Spiritus Sancti. Credo in Deum Patrem omnipotentem, Creatorem caeli et terrae.*"

If the prayers and creed were all to be in Latin, this was goodness. Taresa had, of course, learned the words in her cradle, and could mouth them alongside other believers. Glancing at Qasim, she saw with relief that he mimed the words. Behind the abbot, that noble woman's face appeared from within the shadows of her hood. Her eyes reflected the light of the rush-wick lamp on her table as she stared at Taresa, who fought against fidgeting. Did the lady see Taresa as a sister through the layers of shirts and breeches that hid her form?

The abbot finished the prayers and promised to protect Christian travelers on this road, the same way Templars protect travelers in the Holy Land. Taresa sucked in a deep breath and swallowed trepidation when she realized the woman stared at Yusuf. From three hundred days in the baggage train, Taresa recognized when an older woman sets her sights on a young man. This woman preferred the delicate form of a pretty one like Yusuf instead of the rough, manly bulk of a warrior like Qasim. The abbot's Norman-inflected voice interrupted Taresa's speculation. Templar master of this monastery, the abbot was a master of using his voice to force emotion.

"As the prophets of old taught us, by God's Will alone kings reign. When the righteous increase, the people rejoice. But when a wicked man rules, people groan."

Did the abbot mean Pedro? Yusuf's eyes widened, still burning from an inner fire. Taresa fought the urge to step in front of Yusuf, to hide him from examination. The fire smoldering in her belly grew white hot, spreading to her heart.

"Where's Milon de Breteuil, our comrade in arms?" The abbot surveyed the room. The abbot pointed into the midst of those chain-mail priests.

"Here I am, Monsenyor." The French knight held up a hand. The man who wore Simon's dancing lion on his surcoat.

"Master Milon, you were at Muret. Tell us what happened."

Milon joined the abbot, shaking hands with him in a way that meant they shared a warriors' connection. A wispy beard streaked with grey, long locks like city knights, Milon had the soft, elastic face of an infant, but now aged, his nose grown long. The light around him was grey with spidery threads of burnt umber. Milon smiled too much. Each started with a slow lick and ended with a pout, like a child charming his way out of punishment and into a sweet reward.

"South of Toulouse, Simon crossed the Garonne River to meet the Aragón army. With his usual wisdom, he divided his army into three units."

One of the chainmail priests called out, "Three is an inspired choice, like the Holy Trinity."

"For whatever reason, Pedro decided against the formation that succeeded in Andalusia." Milon offered his open hands, shaking his head as if not understanding a mystery. "But Pedro was so confused and weak at Muret, many say the stories from Andalusia must be wrong, that Alfonso of Castile alone led that victory."

"All victory comes from God." Another of the chainmail priests called out.

No, Pedro was strong when Alfonso wanted to turn back.

Taresa bit her lip, her cheeks, her tongue to keep from shouting the truth. She glanced at Yusuf. White lines appeared around his hard-set lips. Qasim shuffled, uneasy. One thing to expect people to say a creed whether or not they believe, another thing entirely to ask people to accept lies when they'd been in Pedro's camp before, during, and after the battle in Andalusia.

"That man was with Pedro's mercenaries a fortnight ago, camped on the other side of Muret." Qasim whispered. "I saw him there. Different surcoat."

Taresa put her finger to her lips, wanting them to avoid drawing attention.

"Don't believe me?" Qasim whispered. "Touch me and I'll show you the memory."

"It doesn't work like that." She too whispered.

Milon pointed to the ceiling, perhaps meaning heaven. "All victory comes from God, but men must still do the work. Many men loyal to Simon and God's True Church sowed discord and wrong news among the Aragón fighters."

"See," Qasim muttered. "I saw him."

"If you're on the wrong side of God," a priest called out, "the truth is invisible."

Milon nodded, as if these were sage words. "The final undoing was Pedro's alone. He's long been known as a disorderly man. He rode to the front in plain armor. No crown on his head."

Always. Pedro always does that, to thwart assassins.

Taresa had bitten her cheek raw to keep quiet.

"His force was so confused," Milon continued, "that Simon's first unit crushed the Aragón cavalry. Pedro lost his horse and was killed. The Aragónese panicked and ran." Milon shook his head, as if in sad dismay—but then licked his lower lip and smiled like a snake again. "I've never seen a Christian force behave so cowardly."

"When you know God is not with you," a priest called out, "you run for shelter."

Qasim whispered, "There was a retreat plan. Yusuf, you wrote the message for his generals. Why did they—"

Taresa reached behind Yusuf to poke Qasim into silence. Meanwhile Milon finished his story.

"When the militia from Toulouse heard that Pedro was dead, they left their fortified camp and retreated toward the Garonne."

Again, Qasim whispered. "Wrong direction."

Milon wiped his hands like a man finishing a chore. "Simon's army crushed them in the rout."

"I'm surprised." The abbot cocked his head. "Not about the rout. But did Christian soldiers indeed kill a king? Was there no one to protect him?"

Milon threw up his hands. "They say Pedro cried out, '*Je suis le roi! Ieu soi lo rei!*' Still, he was killed."

Je suis le roi! When the knight spoke those words in French, Taresa heard the voice from the barn. *J'ai tué le roi.*

Shards of ice flowed through her veins, stuck their sharp points in her heart. This man was Pedro's murderer. He knew Pedro was the king when he killed him.

"It's that man. He did it." She tugged at Yusuf's sleeve, nudged Qasim, but she couldn't look away from the murderer to see their response.

"At the day's end, Simon led his men in prayer," Milon said, "thanking God for this great victory."

The abbot, slow to respond, seem to ponder the surprise that Christian soldiers killed a king. At last, the abbot had his huge beefy hand on Milon's shoulder. "Thank you for your service."

Rei assassí. Tueur de roi. King-killer.

How could there be justice? She peeked at Yusuf, to see if he still felt that killing a murderer was savage, wrong. She couldn't read his face and glimpsed only a colorless void when she touched him. Gray veins muddied Yusuf's dark yellow aura. Qasim, however, flushed red with rage, fists clenched, ready to strike out.

Milon smoothed one lock like a girl, not seeming to notice that his loose, long locks hung greasy from handling. "I've traveled as a crusader for twenty-five years." He still smiled too much, pretending to be humble. "It is I who must thank you, for all the Templars do for pilgrims and crusaders."

He offered a gold coin to the abbot in his open palm. "Since returning from Constantinople, I've allied with my cousin Simon, offering the special talent God has given me."

Talent? To murder a king? When she shuffled, brushing against Yusuf, he too felt as cold as the ice in her veins.

Milon held the coin up between his thumb and finger, turning it so the gold reflected rush lamps in the great hall. "Our work now is to flush heretics from their nests, but also to recover their hidden treasures. Take this coin to help the work of the Templars."

"Heretics' gold, eh?" the abbot said. "Don't you need this to provision your men for their work?"

"*Ai*, Monsenyor, we discover more gold all the time. And like every aspiring knight, I keep thirteen coins—for the bride Simon will find for me among women of the south." Milon licked his lips, pouted his serpentine smile. "Those women know their price. Which is far below rubies."

Men around them chuckled at this. Yusuf squeezed his eyes closed, dismayed at Milon's joke. Taresa, insulted, glanced at the only other woman in the room, who had retreated further into the shadows of her cloak.

"We mint these for Simon from the hoards we find." Milon passed the coin to a priest at his right hand. "Take a look. Simon uses these to reward those who fearlessly do God's work among unbelievers and schismatics."

The abbot studied the coin and then passed it to the man next to him. While that flash of metal journeyed around the room, the abbot held his hands in the way priests do when they're done, when you hope to be free to flee in the next breath. But rather than finish with a benediction and a final amen, the abbot chose to preach more. People in the room shuffled. They'd all had enough.

"As the blessed St-Paul taught…" That Norman accent got under Taresa's Catalan skin, like a pebble caught in a laced boot. "…we are all in subjection to the governing authorities. For there is no authority except from God, and those that exist are established by God.

Therefore, whoever resists authority opposes the ordinance of God. They who oppose will receive condemnation."

Yusuf trembled so violently, Taresa reached out to brace him. At that touch, she saw his memory of the text the abbot recited, though she couldn't read the language in the book Yusuf saw. Qasim, pinch lipped, reflected Yusuf's distress.

"And so," the abbot said, "we call for judgment and blessings to fall upon us in the same way the Holy Spirit descends upon us like a dove."

Yusuf wheezed like a frightened cat. She touched him again.

An eagle descended, claws out to tear flesh, crying like the desperate boy in the barn. The taste of cold ashes.

She coughed, as if the ashes had turned to clay and clogged her mouth. An ancient tale from his books? She hadn't seen a book in that last flash of memory. Yet a winged creature flew at Yusuf and then—

"Amen."

The room echoed with amens.

One of the priests finished examining Milon's coin and handed it to Qasim for his turn. The flash of metal showed a snake embossed in the metal.

Yusuf fainted.

Behind Yusuf, Qasim grasped Taresa's wrist to brace Yusuf and keep him upright.

¤

"Do you need a healer?" The big-face white-robed priest was at their side in an instant. "Does he have the falling sickness?"

"*No és res.*" Taresa answered in Catalan, her own tongue, her own accent, claiming it was nothing. Then she switched to the local tongue, which the priest spoke. "He took a chill in the storm. We lost our food to bandits, so he's not as strong as you and me."

"Bandits or heretics?" The murdering Milon intruded where he was least wanted. The abbot stood at his side. Milon retrieved his coin from Qasim's hand.

Taresa's fingers again clenched, as if instead of that stone of grief she gripped a real stone.

"Bandits, not heretics." Yusuf answered, Qasim had jammed his hand and Taresa's into Yusuf's back, knuckling him awake.

"You seem familiar." Milon stood too close, studying her. "Did we pass you on the road today?"

"What are you young men doing alone on the road in the middle of Simon's effort to bring peace to the south?" The abbot pried.

"You aren't from a local household?" Big-face priest pressed boldly, tapping a finger on Qasim's chest. He meant a local heretic's house. "Part of the fleeing army of Aragón? Fighting for heretics is the same as heresy, as far as I'm concerned."

"We're going to Paris." Taresa answered the abbot, ignoring the priest's questions. The priest's eyes bored into Qasim, so she pointed to Yusuf. "Don Josep is joining the university. Our family sent Castor and me to keep him safe. I'm Tarek. From Girona." She held out her hand in greeting, the way she'd seen knights do.

"Alone?" The abbot might be certain in his faith, but he held grave doubts about these three travelers. He barely touched her extended hand.

"At Carcassonne, Simon de Montfort offered our guards more than we could pay to keep them. We set out on our own, keeping to trails in the foothills."

"All the way to Paris alone? You are bold young men."

"We have family connections in Cahors. So, just one more day to take care of ourselves."

The abbot pointed to the drovers. Those men are traveling north. Perhaps they'll let you join them in the morning. And ask Brother Jacques over there—" he next pointed to an ancient monk across the great hall "—for provisions. It's a long ride to Cahors."

She'd held her breath, like a fear-frozen child trying not to be noticed, but now nodded vigorously and answered him in French. "*Merci.* We appreciate the kindness."

With that, the abbot and the big-face priest lost interest and drifted away. Freed from interrogation, Taresa took a deep breath, then coughed from the overwhelming stench of horse sweat and men's funk when people in the great hall all stirred at once. Rush lamps flickered so the shadows on the walls, arcing up to the timbered ceiling, hunched over the crowd like descending demons.

Yusuf and Qasim got ahead of her, headed for the door, where men were retrieving their weapons from the doorkeeper and then lingering under the eaves to talk and laugh. She'd endured long moments in that great hall, and now men's laughter curdled the milk of kindness she kept in her heart. She bent to retrieve her dagger where she'd left it amid others' weapons.

She sneezed, and that already-lived feeling flooded over her. She smelled burnt sugar-apple. When she stood, a man bumped her elbow, hard. Pain radiated up and down her arm.

Instinctively, she said in the local tongue, *"Desencusatz-me."*

"Excusez-moi, joli garçon."

King-killer.

She drew her sword, pirouetting to jab it through the man, so his liver was pierced, her sword emerging from the back of his dancing-lion de Montfort surcoat. Blood poured from the dark cavern of the man's mouth, like demons gushing from hell. The smell of offal from the bastard's guts and the metallic tang of blood filled her nose.

"Vos llunàtic, Serena Taresa!" Sebastián shouted that she was insane, his breath hot and wet against her ear. *"Furiós* Taresa!"

Taresa whirled around.

No Sebastián.

No butchered murderer lay at her feet.

Her scabbard was empty. The wild boy in the woods had stolen her sword.

No smell of blood. Only the cloying scent of burnt sugar-apples. And Yusuf examining her, as if she'd left all sense behind.

6
Conflagration

THE FRENCH KNIGHT MILON—untouched, still alive—tossed his surcoat over his shoulder, showing off the dancing lion that meant he was Simon de Montfort's relative. He stood under the eaves with two of his chainmail-priest friends. He talked, that tongue snaking out, and jerked a thumb in the direction of *los tres amics*. His companions turned to stare at Taresa and her friends, dark questioning frowns clouding their faces.

Taresa forced her friendly smile, but didn't bow. Behind Milon and his priest-friends, the two drovers squatted under the wide eaves, throwing dice with the young guards in woad who'd ignored Taresa when she first arrived. Just inside the manse, the cloaked noble woman stood with her back to the door, surrounded by that passel of silk-coated French nobles from the far end of the great hall, men who had applauded Milon's story about Muret.

Brother Jacques, the ancient monk, returned with a packet of food that he thrust into Taresa's arms. He bid her, in French, to go safely with God, and she'd muttered *merci,* answering in his tongue. Her words cooked into steam from the fire inside her, the cloud hanging in front of her face.

Lightning flashed once more. Her grief-taut muscles jerked. She crossed the sodden courtyard. Lamps at the manse and the barn doors cast speckled white ribbons of light through the torrent that drenched her boots after a dozen steps.

"We sleep. We ride early for Cahors."

If she said it any more often, it'd become their private creed. Neither of her friends answered. Alongside her, grief poured from

Yusuf, as heavy as the rain, his face drained of blood, his eyes flashing fire, as if the lighting lodged there. Wild concern cascaded from Qasim, who never took his hand from Yusuf's shoulder, as if he guided a blind man. Yusuf reached up and touched Qasim's hand, a mute thank-you.

She didn't need to touch either Yusuf or Qasim to know what they felt. They'd embraced Taresa in the same way in Andalusia when her childhood friend Felip was killed, his pure spirit rising straight to heaven. Yusuf and Qasim embraced her then to comfort her, and they did it for each other now with that touch. Yet Taresa did not share the full portion of their colossal grief over Pedro, because inside, part of her celebrated that Sebastián wasn't dead. Yusuf knew Pedro's plans. Sebastián was alive and on his way to Rome.

At the barn's wide door, Taresa stepped out of the rain, determined to draw *los tres amics* back to practical tasks, repeating the plan.

"We'll sleep in the barn's loft."

"*Òc.*" Qasim, like a sleepwalker, stared past her as if into another world.

"We need to ride hard enough tomorrow to reach Cahors." Yusuf shrugged off Qasim's guiding grip, standing on his own, yet still shaken. "We're already late."

"You weren't worried this morning," Taresa said.

"But now..." Yusuf wiped damp hair from his eyes. "The French lord we're seeking is sure to be on the move. We can't afford to miss him."

"Why?" Taresa glanced over her shoulder, watching for eavesdroppers."

"Surely you see? With Pedro...gone...any knight who can sit a horse is either moving his family to safety, like ours did, or he's marching with allies, either to fight Simon or to rise in power under Simon."

"Why?" Qasim echoed Taresa's question. "If Simon's army is marauding everywhere, isn't it safer to stay home?"

"There is no safe place," Yusuf said. "That's why Taresa's family retreated to the hills when Simon prepared to lay siege on Toulouse."

"*My* family?" Taresa protested. "I hardly know them, except Sebastián. It's *your* family. Mine is dead and buried in Girona."

"We can argue that later."

"What happens if we don't get to Cahors by...when?" Qasim woke enough to enter into the planning.

"Tomorrow," Yusuf said. "Yesterday. We need this knight to come to Paris with us, to help beg favors from Philippe. We must be his first choice for action after he hears about...Pedro."

Taresa said, "We can go to Paris on our own. You have Pedro's letter begging for help. I have Pedro's document guaranteeing our safe passage."

Yusuf rejected that idea with an abrupt wave. "Philippe refused to receive the last two ambassadors Pedro sent. Said he was too worried about his own Christians to worry about Toulousain heretics. We need a French ally to convince Philippe to accept our message." He leaned close to her. "And I'm not sure safe passage is possible now."

Taresa repeated her private creed. "Then we get up before dawn and ride hard for Cahors, to make up for lost time."

"As hard as the horses can bear," Qasim said.

"And when we get to Cahors, how do we find this knight?" Though warmed by the idea that Sebastián lived, it gnawed at Taresa that Yusuf hadn't trusted Qasim or her with the full story of Pedro's task. "A dozen French priests, knights, and soldiers are here. And other French lords now hold every seized castle between Toulouse and Limoges. How do we recognize Pedro's friend?"

"Pedro gave me a question. Like a code." Yusuf's voice rasped, like a nail scratching steel. "I shall ask, 'Did Perseus slay Medusa?' Then the knight who is Pedro's friend will answer—"

"*Senhórs, perdon, se vos plai.*" The woman from the great hall called to them in the local dialect, inflected with a Provençal accent.

They waited under the wide arch of the barn door while the woman hurried across the rain-splashed courtyard to join them. She pushed back the hood of her cloak, revealing dark hair, dark eyes, a beguiling rosebud mouth. The light that shone around her—not from the lamp, but her own aura—was carmine, a deeper red than ever crafted in Girona's dye-works. Women from the baggage train whose auras shone dark-red were passionate and strong-willed.

The woman smiled. Her face had been perfected by Nature; but when she smiled, Heaven warmed her face so she appeared both tempting and welcoming, as if you'd shared precious secrets. At the end of her smile, she pressed her lips into a line, as if promising your secret would never be revealed. Her voice, warm and deep, was as beautiful as her face.

She pushed aside her waxed rain-cape to extend a hand to Taresa, revealing that she dressed in scarlet-dyed leathers, with a scarlet leather overskirt, ready to ride rough, yet elegant and voluptuous. A few dark locks strayed, framing her face, but most of her hair was captured in a gold-filigree net, like Taresa had seen on noble ladies enjoying Toulouse court-life. A gemstone hung near her throat, just above where her pulse showed above her breastbone. A garnet. Only an immensely wealthy person—a marquesa or a queen—would possess a ruby that large.

"Excuse my boldness, but I heard you gentlemen lost your guard. Mine has only me to care for. Perhaps we can journey together. Are you bound for Cahors?"

Qasim blinked as if struck dumb by beauty. Yusuf remained lost in grief and whatever illness gripped him. Taresa stepped up, ready to perform the duties for which Pedro had sent her on this journey. Shifting the packet of food to her other hand, she bowed the way troubadours did in counts' and kings' courts, and answered in the local tongue, deepening her voice to speak the way Sebastián might.

"*Ma dòmna beneït.* You are kind to offer. We cannot think to inconvenience a lady."

Taresa touched the lady's fingertips, the way a jongleur she knew treated court-ladies.

> Yusuf's face appeared in a close, hot room. Deep-red draperies and gold trimmings. Fingers warming the gemstone at her throat. Consumed with passion, eyelids fluttering in the heat. Searing, sweet breath. Pleading in the midst of most private...

Taresa jerked away from the woman's hand, embarrassed to intrude on such private memories. Two breaths later, Taresa felt annoyed that the woman had such thoughts about Yusuf.

"It's not an inconvenience," the woman said, as if she hadn't just remembered deep passion. She directed her words to Yusuf, who behaved as if he didn't speak her language. "I'm going to Cahors, too. Only—"

A quartet of men joined them at the barn door. The woad-clad guards. With an imperious gesture to those men, the woman made it clear that they belonged to her. When she asked them, "Are we ready to travel?" it seemed that yes was the single allowed answer. The woman returned her attention to *los tres amics*.

"You're quite welcome to come with me. I wish you would. Only we must leave tonight. Since the Templars have purchased this farm, they won't offer shelter to a woman." She laughed without humor, tipping her head back so her hood fell away. Dark tresses fell free, and under the candlelight at the doorway, her face as flawless and beatific as an angel's. "The Templars like pilgrims, but not women. No matter. I have a friend half a league away who'll shelter us for the night."

Taresa hesitated, unsure of such a grand invitation from a stranger. "I'm not sure our horses are rested enough."

"It's only half a league. Surely your beasts can manage that." The woman urged with kindness and warmth, which Taresa had missed while traveling alone with men. "I'm called Blanca. Blanca of Avignon. Tell me your names again. I confess that I eavesdropped in the great hall, but I didn't hear your names."

"I am Tarek from Girona," Taresa said. "This is Don Josep and Qa—Castor, my companions."

Qasim folded his arms, which meant he waited for Yusuf to decide. Yusuf bowed at the introduction, the way Castile lords do, and spoke the local tongue, with a Catalan inflection, though the vowels held musical notes of Cairo, if you knew to listen.

"Don Josep de Morella y St-Joachim in Aragón, *ma dòmna*. Though I understand Aragón is not popular in this part of the country."

"Enchanted." Blanca offered her hand for Yusuf to touch, while tugging at the hood of her cloak to hide her face.

While Yusuf kissed Blanca's hand the way a Castilian *caballero* would, Taresa couldn't forget the passion she'd witnessed in the woman's memory. Senhóra Blanca did not prompt her men to join in the introductions, and she seemed to assume that *los tres amics* had agreed to her proposal.

"Meet in the courtyard as soon as you're ready to ride."

Her guards were attending to their horses near the barn's front opening and drew Blanca into their preparations.

¤

"Senhóra Blanca is full to the brim with secrets," Qasim said as they walked toward the end of the huge barn.

"Any insights from touching your new friend?" Yusuf truly wanted to know, rather than finding an excuse to tease.

"No, nothing." Taresa wasn't about to reveal another woman's secret. "I can't make it happen on command." Then she felt compelled to admit her own secret. "However, I keep hearing Sebastián shout warnings at me."

"Bragging how Pedro gave him the easy task?" Qasim said.

"Don't jest. I hear his voice, as if Sebastián were here with us."

"Perhaps," Yusuf said, "since you are disinclined to doubt your impulses, you need Sebastián's voice to keep you from leaping into danger."

"You accepted the senhóra's invitation," Taresa said.

"Perhaps Sebastián's ghost-voice told me to accept her offer," Yusuf said.

"Did his ghost tell you to faint like an old grandmother?" Qasim asked.

Taresa interrupted their jests, repressing her curiosity about what happened with Yusuf. "Go grab the lantern, Qasim."

"The hostler said no lanterns in the barn."

"We can't harness the horses if we can't see." Taresa spoke with conviction, making them believe in her. *Los dos amics* still moved like wounded birds. "We'll go with Senhóra Blanca tonight, and then—"

Outside the stalls where their horses nickered, that poor child lay in the straw, now blue, gripping Aragónese tassels tied to a rusted short-sword. An azure wisp, like the cloud made by Taresa's hot breath, hung over the boy, who still wept as if it was the end of the world, so lonely for his grandmother. A dead priest—the young balding blond one from the great hall—cradled the boy, Taresa's surcoat tossed over the pair of them, crimson slashes where they'd been stabbed through the coat.

Her heart a fist, she felt that stone again, icy cold, sinking in her belly. Qasim whispered words that must be Arabic.

The dead priest clutched something in his hand, which rested on the boy's head. Taresa tugged at the man's cool fingers. A coin fell free, rolling across the packed earth to stop at her boot. Taresa snatched it up, not needing the lamp light to see, instead feeling the embossed snake with her fingertips. Heretics' gold.

Yusuf said, "What do your visions tell you, Tarek of Girona?"

"That we should—"

"Leave now." Blanca came behind Taresa, so near that she felt the woman's breath on her neck. Blanca knelt to untie those tassels, handing them to Taresa. "These shouldn't be here. And that surcoat? Stolen?"

"I gave it to the boy. He's—"

"He's no one, *mon amic*. Take your surcoat. Prepare to ride."

Taresa didn't want the torn, blood-stained coat. "We need to tell the abbot. If we run away, they'll think we did this."

"Those heretic hunters will smell blood, no doubt. Especially given how you all behaved during prayers." Blanca fiddled with the fastener on her cloak, as if deciding what to do. "Truly, you're safe with me if you're Pedro's men. You are, aren't you?"

"No," Yusuf said. "We're traveling to Paris. To study law."

Blanca pressed her finger against Yusuf's lips. "It's bad form for a woman to ask any man whether he's a liar or fool. You're too wise to remain here. Come along."

"*Òc, ma dòmna.*" Yusuf agreed, while Taresa still twisted that golden coin in her fingers.

Blanca turned to her men. "Help them prepare to ride."

While her men worked, Blanca stood with *los tres amics*. Taresa whispered the prayers she'd been taught for the souls of the dead. That azure wisp over the little boy flickered like a flame under Taresa's whispers.

One of Blanca's men called to her. "We're ready."

The beautiful woman said, "Our animals are out?"

"*Òc, ma dòmna.*"

"Go now." Blanca pointed to the rear door of the barn and then to Yusuf and Qasim, who accepted the reins of their harnessed horses from a pair of Blanca's guards. Qasim also led Taresa's horse. With a simple push, Blanca knocked the lantern from Taresa's hand onto the boy and priest in the straw. Her men ran for the rear door, and Blanca followed.

Her heart thumping, Taresa took her horse's reins from Qasim, who stood stunned.

"Fire!" At the other end of the great barn, men were already shouting and pulling animals from their stalls.

"The horses!" Qasim cried.

Taresa shoved him. "Go! They're getting all the animals out."

Taresa's horse didn't need urging to escape the fire. She and Qasim led their horses out the barn's rear door and mounted. Fingers tingling with fear, she followed Blanca. Her men rode in formation around her, also encompassing Yusuf. Blanca led them back to the manse's courtyard. Amid all the commotion—people rushing from the kitchens and outbuildings to form a brigade—one of Blanca's guards was shouting at the abbot. "Thieves stole two of our palfreys, riding north. They started the fire and ran when we came in."

"Santa Maria!" the abbot cried out. "This valley is a sanctuary. Thieves? Or heretics?"

The guard held his empty hands up to heaven. "Who can tell the difference?"

"We won't importune more tonight," Blanca said. The abbot was turning away to join the brigade. "Send word to the baron at Marais if you recover my palfreys."

Lightning flashed again, turning the beautiful lady into a scarlet ghost for one heartbeat. Taresa's horse skittered sideways, coming near Blanca's horse.

"Whoever murdered them—" Taresa couldn't get the words out, her lungs full of grief and heart filled with fury. "No one will ever know now."

"That's for the best," Blanca said. "There's no justice in this world. Only do what you must in order to be safe. In this case, let's put a half a league between us and the heretic hunters who would enjoy a conversation with you."

7

A Southern Castle

TARESA GASPED SEVERAL JAGGED BREATHS. After all that noise of the great hall and the tragedy in the barn, dark silence wrapped around her like comforting blanket. With tired, rain-cold hands, Taresa guided her horse, though it seemed to find its own way, following the other horses. Sebastián claimed horses see better in the dark than humans.

When the rain stopped, Qasim and Yusuf let Blanca and her men pace ahead of them a few horse lengths. Taresa kept looking back, listening for whether they were pursued.

"We had no choice but to go with that woman," Yusuf said, as if he guessed Taresa's complaints.

"You said we need to be in Cahors as quickly as possible." Unease fluttered in Taresa's throat. She was ready to cry *Beware!* But she didn't express her resentment that Senhóra Blanca had seized control in the barn and made decisions—starting a fire!—that forced them to depart. "We don't know where we're going or who that woman is."

"And she doesn't know who we are," Yusuf said.

"Explain my name, Tarek of Girona." Qasim interrupted, sounding offended. "Josep gets his same name in the local tongue. Why am I called Castor? How am I like laundry?" He used a similar word in *valencià* dialect, *colada*.

That was as good an argument as any to entertain while they rode wearily along a dark pathway, with no idea where they were going.

"From Perseus, the Greek hero. You know, Pedro's code to find Yusuf's French knight." Taresa felt fatigue settling into her backbone and knees, yet that flutter continued to warn her to beware. "Castor doesn't sound so—"

"Saracen?" Qasim challenged.

"*Òc*," she said. "Simon's men will kill any infidels they find."

"Castor is from the story of Theseus, not Perseus," Yusuf said. He too sounded exhausted. "Perseus beheaded the Gorgon. Theseus was the king who—"

"Never mind. If you don't like Castor, use the new name the priest gave you last year when he baptized you."

"Baptized?" Qasim repeated the word as if it came from a foreign tongue.

"*Aiieee!*" Why had Pedro sent these two other-worldly innocents out to cross Christendom? "Wait, you're teasing."

"I'm as righteous as any man." Qasim began to say the Roman creed. Even in the dark, Taresa could see that he held his arms aloft, wrists crossed, though he'd once claimed that where he came from, anything said with crossed wrists meant just the opposite. Qasim raised his voice at the third line.

"*Qui conceptus est de Spiritu Sancto...*"

A wildcat howled in the night, protesting the disturbance.

Yusuf cried out, as if in pain, struggling with his unlaced aventail, throwing back the hood of his surcoat.

And fell off his horse this time.

Qasim grabbed the reins of the prancing horse, leading it away so it couldn't step on Yusuf. Taresa went to aid her brother-in-law, who refused her offered hand and got up on his own.

"What is it, brother?" Worry gnawed her gut. "Not falling sickness, is it? No, you'd still be gnawing your tongue."

"I'm fine." Yusuf swiped at the sweat drenching his forehead. His eyes swept left and right like a frightened soul, the same as earlier episodes. "Flea up my aventail."

"*Jhezu del tron!* You scared the living soul out of me."

"Tarek of Girona swearing like a wrong-headed infidel is enough to upset any decent human." Qasim came to Yusuf's side, murmuring words of comfort in Arabic.

"She learned it in the baggage train." Yusuf brushed away mud and dirt. "They say laundry women are neither Catholic nor infidel. That's why they rely only on God to protect them."

Before Taresa could complain, the mysterious Blanca and her four guards had ridden back to wait for them.

"A flea got inside his aventail," Taresa explained, repeating Yusuf's lie. "Vermin are the true enemy of travelers in Christendom."

Qasim led Yusuf's horse back to him. The horse must have smelled Yusuf's perpetual fear of horses, because it pranced sideways, returning to Qasim, who every horse fell in love with, because he cared more for horses than he did most people.

On their way again, and after Blanca and her guards were once more several horse-lengths ahead, Qasim said, "When you ask the French lord, 'Did Perseus slay Medusa?' What's the answer supposed to be?"

"'Better still, he saved Andromeda.'" Yusuf's tired words wafted in the night with the horses' clomping on their dark-night trek. Taresa worried for him, but then, as women in the baggage train often said, worry won't get you to Toledo.

Tired as she was, she spoke her frustration. "Why didn't Pedro just tell you the knight's name? Why are we riding into a territory and town we don't know, asking for someone in a secret code?"

"Why did we ride lonely mountain trails out of Toulouse?" The familiar note in Yusuf's voice meant she'd wakened the teaching scholar that never hid far from the surface. "Why are goodmen heretics fleeing all the castle-villages? Why were those wretched children living in a cave? Because Simon de Montfort has people everywhere, looking for heretics under every rock."

"But we're seeking a French knight, not a heretic."

"In the borderlands, the marches, Simon has spies watching for any French lord or knight of Philippe's who might shelter heretics. He'll present them to the king of France as traitors."

Taresa liked to learn; she just didn't like to be taught. She didn't appreciate that Pedro gave her a map and a bag of silver, with instructions to guide Yusuf and Qasim through the Languedoc. But Pedro didn't share the mission; instead, he said, "Yusuf wants to see the university in Paris, so he can carry letters for me on his journey."

And he didn't tell her how to find the guide who'd take them to Paris. She resented not being trusted with the secrets that mattered for this journey.

"It's not as if we'd tell everyone we're seeking a French knight who's friends with Pedro."

"You know what happened to people in our family who were in the wrong place when the heretic hunters came." Yusuf meant Sebastián's mother, who'd been attacked by heretic hunters. "You can't answer the hunters' questions if you don't know. Codes keep us all safe."

"I never heard of Perseus," Qasim said, "even from Mozarabs who prayed to Jesus."

"His story is older than Jesus," Yusuf said. "Who knows which of the old stories are true?"

"Or if none are real at all," Qasim said. "Like magic."

"There's no magic, right?" Taresa said. "No demons?"

"Just tales from old men's nightmares," Yusuf said, "meant to scare children. However, many scholars continue to write about two kinds of magic, natural and demonic."

Curious, and hoping to keep Yusuf and Qasim from sinking into bone-weary grief, Taresa asked, "Then some demons are real? Is that why I see people's memories?"

She didn't ask about the azure wisp of spirit that hung over the dead boy's body, or the colors of auras floating around people that told her who she could trust.

"No," Yusuf said. "Your second sight is natural, not demonic."

"Natural magic? Like spirits that live in trees?"

Yusuf barked a laugh, though who knew what he thought was funny. "You want me to concede that spirits indeed live and can be contacted? No. What you experience must be what scholars have called *Sensus Naturae*. Which happens mostly with women."

"Scholars write about it?"

"Scholars today," Yusuf voice flagged with fatigue again, "claim *Sensus Naturae* comes from a woman's wish to know what her absent lover is thinking."

"Like when I heard Sebastián's voice tonight?"

"Exactly. You just miss your lover."

That didn't account for a lifetime of accidentally peering into people's souls. Taresa went along with his explanation, though, like how her horse jolted along in the dark.

"But she's the *cavaller de cabres*," Qasim said, "With a single desire in the world, to be a knight with the *bonfraires*."

"Now she wants more." Yusuf sang his annoying song.

> I'm a *cavaller* in chainmail,
> and I lost my steely blade.

> Get to Cahors and out of the rain.
> Bring my lover back from crusade.

> Keep me safe on this bad trail.
> And make me a knight, that's all I've prayed.

"You broke the song's rhythm," Qasim said as their horses plodded in the wet, dark night.

"Only because the list of Master Tarek's deep desires keeps growing."

She had, in fact, one more desire. "Yusuf, how can I use *Sensus Naturae* to bring Pedro's murderer to justice? Peeking into people's memories has never been worth anything until tonight. What good is magic if you can't change anything?"

"My scholarship on this topic is neither deep nor broad." Yusuf sounded weary to the bone once he stopped singing. "For justice, you need witnesses and a court to pass judgment. I don't see how a woman's magic can help."

"What do men use *Sensus Naturae* for?"

"The basics," Yusuf said. "Adultery. Theft. Murder for the sake of power."

¤

Their destination proved to be the small, forlorn castle on the plateau above the monastery farm. As soon as Taresa could see the tower in the dark, they were under attack by its inhabitants.

Torch light flashed at the arrow slits and at the gate.

Voices hurled Toulousain street-thug insults.

An arrow thwacked into the ground near Taresa, startling her horse. More thudding arrows, and the whine of frightened horses. Too tired to be afraid, Taresa backed her horse away, down the trail they'd just ridden up, out of range of the castle's ambitious defenders. She called to Yusuf to do the same.

Blanca called out, "*Misericòrdia,* Monsenyor! We are friends!" She kicked her horse, galloping away from her hired guards, reining in her horse in front of the castle gates. Only Qasim rode ahead, shield thrust out to defend Blanca.

"Ricart de Marais! *Senhór amable!* You once swore you'd know me in the dead of night in a blinding storm. Here I am, drenched in the dark!"

The night fell silent, except for the resentful nickering of frightened horses. The gates creaked open, the grating of iron on iron shrieking through the night, as if the decrepit castle were a living being, just barely alive, tortured to near death.

A short, emaciated man stood in the opening, arms lifted in greeting, his slim figure lit by torches that the armed men beside him carried. Perhaps he hadn't always been so thin, since his chainmail coat hung on him like a steel-mesh horse blanket. Given his gaunt face and thin white beard, he might be any age between fifty and seventy.

"*Ma dòmna!* You might have warned me."

"You aren't happy to see me, my dear, dear friend?"

Neither the lord at the gate nor her armed guard approached to help Blanca. Only Qasim stayed by her side, helping her from her horse.

Though Blanca didn't seem to need help with much of anything.

Inside the gates, after the lord of the castle had embraced Blanca in welcome, they were all sorted, which Blanca handled deftly. Her paid guard was sent off with a stable man to care for the horses. With her hand on Taresa's shoulder, Blanca introduced *los tres amics* as her companions.

"Baron Ricart, let me introduce my...cousin Tarek. From Girona. And his friends Josep and Castor. They are traveling with me to Paris."

Ricart didn't take his eyes from Blanca or acknowledge the introduction. "Tell me the truth. Are you instead running to your old friend Giles de Nully? I hear he's at his house near Cahors."

"No, it's Paris for us. Both for family business and to install these young men at university." Blanca didn't shrug off the baron's arm, which lingered at her waist, his hand wandering while she spun lies. "I'd have sent messengers ahead, begging your hospitality. But this was sudden for me. My family had planned to send my sister on this journey, but she fell ill."

Taresa admired Blanca because she was a great, commanding beauty. She also admired how readily Blanca prevaricated. Then wondered when to trust anything Blanca said.

"I'm sorry." Ricart sounded jubilant rather than regretful. He reminded Taresa of her late, unlamented great-uncle, the one who sold her horse to a bad man and smelled like wine turned to vinegar, coughing his words with a dusty, phlegm-plagued voice. "Your sister's misfortune falls to my good luck, *ma dòmna.* Come inside. As I've always promised, everything I have is yours. You don't have to ask. Only say yes."

Ricart ushered Blanca into the tower's great hall, still ignoring *los tres amics,* who followed along because Blanca motioned for them. Compared to the monastery manse in the valley below, the room wasn't large, the plaster in ill repair. But in the torchlight, the great hall retained what might have been southern glory a half-century earlier.

A pair of serving men stood waiting for instructions, as ignored as Taresa and her friends. Neither responded to greetings from either Taresa or Qasim. Their patched and worn clothes indicated a genteel country poverty, and the room's condition and odors indicated that no women lived there.

Taresa strayed from Blanca's side and surveyed the room while Blanca and the baron traded stories, their voices like the calm clopping of horses on the night road. Where had they ended up? Who were these people?

"I looked for you everywhere in Avignon last summer, *ma dòmna.* Where were you?"

"In Narbonne with my sister."

"Hunting a new husband, *ma dòmna?*"

"Ha! If a woman possesses wealth and respect, why would she take a husband?"

"A lover, then?"

"You are incorrigible, my dear baron."

The north end of the room held an enormous fireplace, the kind used for both heat and cooking in winter. Which meant this had been built as a working house, not the *casa* of people taking their ease in the country. The room's stone work imitated an old-style barrel-vaulted church, though the room itself was square, with rough joists overhead and the floorboards of the upper room showing through. A four-pane patchwork of windows sat high on one wall. A torch on a post reflected in the windows, each glass with inlaid color, though at night it was impossible to see the design. This was a working room, with a modest display of former wealth.

Qasim and Yusuf also studied the room, since no one had offered them a seat, or food, or acknowledged that they lived and breathed. Taresa shifted her attention to what caught her friends' notice: neatly arranged racks of lances, javelins, and swords.

"Not all mine." Ricart crept up on her unnoticed until his old-man's vinegar smell filled her nose. "Three were mine in the Holy Land. I rode with my namesake, Ricart, the Angevine king. That's Saracen blood that I drew when we took Acre." He glanced at Taresa, obviously wanting the praise every crusader she'd met believed was owed him. She nodded, resenting that it was required of her; she'd met much more noble crusaders than this old man. "The upper three lances belonged to my father, who rode with the first crusaders when they won Jerusalem."

Her eyes flitted to Yusuf, to see if he was applying the magic of *mathematica* to the timing of the baron's and his father's heroics. Taresa remembered the dusty voice of the oldest woman in the baggage train. *"If all men who claimed to be in Acre with Philippe and Ricart Cor de Lion were truly there, they'd of been mashed shoulder to shoulder all the way to Cairo."*

"The swords—" Taresa approached the wall, pretending to admire them. Half were pells, the edgeless wooden stakes that children use in practice. Two steel blades were corroded beyond salvation.

"That one slew infidels at Constantinople." Ricart was by her side again, too swiftly. He lifted a withered finger to point to a rust-eaten short-sword, then dropped his hand on her shoulder. "You'd be lucky, young man, to see such wonders performed in the name of our glorious Savior."

At his touch, Taresa didn't see glory.

> Bloody carnage filled a city square, women dead, men butchered, children shrieking and animals crying in terror, the stink of burning flesh.

Her heart beat too hard, but Taresa fought the impulse to run from the hideous baron. After a lifetime of peering into people's trivial thoughts, she'd endured a day of seeing horrors.

"My dearest Ricart." Blanca stepped between them. "I promise you can regale my friends with your stories come morning." She threaded her fingers up in the ties of the man's linen shirt. He responded by winding his skinny arm around her waist again. "But, Ricart, we've ridden far to be with you. My cousin and his friends need a bit of bread and a bed for the tonight."

Distracted by how close Blanca spoke into his ear, the baron smiled—like a ghoul, from Taresa's view—and motioned to one of the ragged serving men, who in turned motioned Yusuf and Qasim to a curtained alcove off the great hall.

"And you, *ma dòmna*, who have captured my soul, shall have my own bedchamber." He led her to a small door, tall enough for a slight man like him. The second serving man brought a rush lamp, revealing a narrow stone staircase curving up to the next story. He disappeared up the steps and made a great deal of noise preparing the bed.

"Ricart, dear heart, you offer too much. A pallet in any alcove will do for me."

"If I offer less," his hand rubbed her back, "my own heart would stop beating."

Taresa stepped back to escape the ridiculous tête-à-tête, but Blanca called out, "Tarek, my dear boy, would you fetch my pack? I dropped it in the courtyard."

When Taresa returned from performing that porter's task, the baron was gone. Blanca stood at the door that led to her borrowed bedchamber, waiting. Taresa handed over the travel pack.

"Why are you doing this for us, *ma dòmna*?"

"I believe that you serve Pedro, though you won't admit it. Therefore, I am an ally. I too care what happens next."

"What happens?" The fluttery warning in her throat kept Taresa from sharing secrets with this woman.

"Clever boy." Blanca traced a finger along Taresa's jaw. "Why won't you trust me?"

"For one, you're flirting with that...relic!" Taresa tried to restrain her indignation at the idea of this beautiful woman with that vinegary old man. "It's...obscene."

"Ricart? He's a friend from my former life. He flirted that way in front of my husband, the poor departed soul." Blanca waggled a finger, scolding Taresa for her lack of urbanity.

"Your husband was deaf and blind?"

"Let me say it brutally, for your offended sensibilities, dear Tarek. We need the baron to shelter us for a day or so."

"From—"

"From the same chaos and evil that killed Pedro." Blanca stroked Taresa's face again, the same flirting as with the baron. "From whatever evil caught up with you at the Templars' farm."

"That b—boy in the barn..." Taresa stammered. The scene in the barn overwhelmed her again, too fresh. "It had nothing to do with us."

"Someone made it look like you were involved, draping your Aragónese tassels over the bodies. They were yours, right? I can help keep you safe. It requires merely a little flirting."

"When you bat your eyes at the baron, I see you looking past him, wanting to eat Y—Josep body and soul."

Blanca tossed her head with a small purr of laughter, which grated on Taresa's bones. She didn't like being laughed at.

Clutching her pack, Blanca started up the narrow staircase. Taresa grasped Blanca's wrist and held her back. "Leave Josep alone, ma dòmna. He isn't what you want, is he?"

The sweet, warm memory that flowed through her touch differed from the first time she'd touched Blanca.

> Fingers stroked a man's dark hairline, tracing a scar on sharp cheek bones, dark lovely lashes. The good smell of leather and clean sweat. The warmth and peace of a sleeping man, his head in a velvet-clad lap. Warming her to the core with comfort. *Bien-aimé.* Beloved.

"Did he love you? *La siá amant francesa?*" Taresa asked, startling Blanca. "He was French, wasn't he? Your beloved, who laid his head in your lap?"

8

Gawain and the Fair Unknown

"HOW COULD YOU KNOW?" Blanca glanced around the empty hall behind them and then dragged Taresa after her, up the narrow staircase.

"Second sight." Taresa released Blanca's wrist. "I can see that you loved a man once. Deeply. Did he love you?"

"Yes. Too much." The corners of Blanca's lips twitched. Her eyes flickered downward, as if remembering again what Taresa had just seen. When Blanca looked back at Taresa, tears brightened her eyes, one trickled along her cheek, dropping from her jaw to get lost in her robe. "He loved me and I...I betrayed him. Now, in these desperate times, I see that I asked more than I gave."

"If you know now, can you—can he—will—"

Blanca wiped at the tears. "Surely you're old enough to know there's no going back. Or perhaps you don't. Have you lived even twenty years?"

"Twenty-five." Taresa lied, but it was a justifiable untruth. She'd seen more of the world than most women. "And I was at the battle against the caliphate in Andalusia last year. I have seen things."

"Whatever you learned," Blanca said, "traveling with an army on the other side of the world, I can't imagine you had much chance to learn about romance."

"I would argue that you're wrong."

"Then let's not quarrel." Blanca tipped her head, smiling up at Taresa. A smile that would make a troubadour promise fidelity and ridiculous heroics. Blanca fingered the ties on Taresa's jerkin. Taresa stepped back, trepidation warming her innards—liver, spleen, wherever faith lived and could be tempted into faithlessness. Blanca stepped closer. "As a man, you know that a woman gets one chance. If she's cheated him once, she doesn't deserve more. It took me twenty-five years to learn that."

"I've learned—"

Blanca grasped Taresa's jerkin and tugged her close, running soft hands up her neck as she stood on tiptoe and kissed Taresa's mouth.

"*Ma dòmna*—"

Blanca's tongue probed. Surprised, Taresa took a breath, kissed her back. Blanca nibbled Taresa's lip, holding her close, as close as in that flash of passion Taresa saw when they first met.

Taresa had kissed only two men, neither of whom had ever kissed another woman. And the women she'd kissed were jesting friends from the baggage train who insisted Taresa learn to kiss before trying it with a man, so she wouldn't be deceived when a man claimed to be the best lover. Now, with each breath Taresa took, Blanca forced a deeper kiss. And Taresa kissed as if she didn't know she was hungry until she tasted that rosebud mouth.

When Taresa dared open her eyes, she locked gazes with Blanca, whose dark eyes were hot with passion. Blanca's hand crept up Taresa's jerkin, feeling for the edges of her undershirt. Taresa stepped back, wanting to break the embrace. Blanca tugged at her sleeve, and that hidden coin fell out, hitting the floor with a loud ping.

"*Ma dòmna*, I don't want you to think—"

"I don't. And I don't have to guess any more about whether you're a boy or a woman." Blanca touched where Taresa had bound her breasts with a linen wrap.

Taresa covered Blanca's hand, holding it in place instead of pushing her away.

"You are a sweet one. What's your real name, my dear Tarek?"

Taresa didn't want to confess more here, with Blanca still flush from their kiss. All of Taresa's suspicion flooded back now that she was two steps removed from all that heat. "It's safer to travel this way. I learned as much with the army in Iberia last year."

Blanca knelt to pick up the fallen coin, with more grace than Taresa hoped to ever master. "What's this?"

"The coin that dead priest held. It's like what the French knight Milon passed around when he told the story about Muret."

"The dead priest?" She held it out to Taresa, her lips pursed, a moue of distaste. The coin flipped in Taresa's hand to the other side, not the snake. Blanca, startled, took it back again.

"Do you know it, *ma dòmna?*"

"I've seen...no, it's merely a coincidence." Blanca pushed the coin back into Taresa's hand, forcefully. Under lamplight, the reverse side showed an eight-spoke wheel.

"What does it mean?"

"It means," Blanca shrugged, "that someone made a mold and poured molten gold into it. Someone who wasn't a king or a caliph. I don't think it signifies more."

Taresa folded her arms, resisting the flood of feelings Blanca provoked, uneasy that she'd kissed back when kissed by someone who knew how. "It's true that I'm from Girona, and you must continue to call me Tarek. I'm traveling to Paris with Josep and Castor of Morella. One is a scholar going to university, and the other—"

"Fine, senhóreta—Tarek. I shall tell you what I'm doing." Blanca sat on the high bed. "I promised a dying friend that I'd make sure her son is safe. Now I'm riding more miles in greater discomfort than I've ever known, to protect a child I've never met. And I don't even like children."

"You must have cared a great deal for your friend." Taresa remained disinclined to reveal more. "What was she like?"

"Selfish, conceited, thinking more of herself than the world did." Blanca untied her scarlet leather jerkin, preparing to undress in the casual way that women do when alone with each other. "But I'm repeating what a man said about me once. My friend was fiercely devoted to any friends who stood by her. She was kind to me. She took me in when my husband died, when his title and land all went to another man."

"No children?"

"Do I look like anyone's mother?" Blanca shrugged off her jerkin and the scarlet leather skirt, leaving her white shift flowing over tight breeches. Under that, all of Blanca was as beautiful as her face. The flutter in Taresa's throat warned her to look away.

"Now, tell me what you're doing out in the wilderness," Blanca said, "with two men who never in their lives cared to have a woman for company?"

Taresa said, "Josep is going to study at the university. My... guardian asked me to travel with them. Dressing as I do, that was my idea."

"Your guardian? *Ai*, no father or mother would send a woman out with two men such as those."

"My father is long gone, and I never had a mother."

"It shows. What reward does your guardian offer for your service?" Blanca probed, but in the same seductive, eyelid-trembling way she'd used earlier.

"I'll be—" Resisting the seduction, Taresa owed one secret in exchange for what Blanca revealed. "I want to be a knight."

Bad enough to remember Yusuf's silly song when she said it, Taresa suffered through the look of disbelief on Blanca's face.

"I have unusual skills," Taresa added, "that make me worth more in the world than—"

"Birthing heirs for a lord in Girona?" Blanca seemed to understand. "Whose knight will you be? Ai, you did know Pedro!"

"Only because I traveled with the army of Aragón last summer, from Barcelona to the battle, and home again."

"Dressed as a woman or a man?" Blanca purred. "Only laundry women travel with an army. Cooks. *Putas*. And rarely, the wife of a general or commander."

"As I learned in Andalusia, more than one woman serves as a fighter in any army, either living alongside men without their knowing, or else protected by friends."

"Tell me, were you dressed as laundress, infantryman, or commander's wife?"

Taresa decided to stop sharing secrets. "I was using my unusual talents, like I am on this journey."

"*Ai*, Tarek of Girona. My dead husband was a warrior. I've lived in armed camps. There are no women knights." Blanca pointed to the staircase. "You'll find your companions in the curtained alcove."

While Taresa descended the stairs, Blanca called after her. "I promise to protect you as best I can, as long as we're travelling together."

"*Mercé, ma dòmna*. I'll remember your promise."

¤

From Taresa's experience, if someone makes a promise, the size of the promise tells you the likelihood of ever receiving any benefit from the promise. Most promises are made to end (or prevent) an argument. If you don't want to surrender, you say sincerely, "I'll remember your promise," while reserving the possibility of victory later.

In the same quick way that Taresa used people's auras to judge character, she also wanted to know at a glance whether a person in distress needed help. If they do, you shouldn't make them prove it. If they don't, you have no time to waste on them, because in this world, many other people truly need help. Blanca needed help from *los tres amics*—though Taresa couldn't perceive why—and therefore promised to protect them. How much protection could Blanca offer with four mercenaries in her traveling retinue? If they encountered Simon's marauding army, Blanca's promise meant nothing.

Blanca's protection was of little value for what Taresa needed most: to get Yusuf and Qasim safely to Cahors and on the road to Paris. The promise did nothing for what Taresa wanted most, to be a knight of Sebastián's *bonfraires* confraternity. And Blanca had laughed when Taresa expressed that desire.

Blanca's prevarications and seduction served as counterpoint to why Taresa longed to be part of the *bonfraires*. She left Girona with no parents, no siblings, no friends. She'd been taken into the warmth of the baggage train women. But that was nothing like the camaraderie Sebastián's knights enjoyed with each other. That's what she wanted: belonging among the best of the best, with promises, real promises, to serve and protect each other. Loyalty and respect, that's what mattered in the world.

Not a lightly given promise of "protection."

In the curtained alcove, a rush lamp on a ledge showed Qasim and Yusuf asleep in the narrow bed, leaving her a pallet on the floor. She sat on the pallet to pull off her boots, awkwardly, since the bench was piled with gear. She flung off the jerkin, but stayed in her shirt and breeches.

Keeping as quiet as possible, she found her saddle bags and rummaged to find the one thing she needed to sleep, then crawled into the smallest ball possible on the pallet, pulling a blanket and her surcoat over for warmth. She buried her nose in Sebastián's stolen shirt. Only a fortnight since he'd worn it, so it smelled strongly of what she'd sensed in Blanca's memory. Leather, sweat.

Except the scent she'd buried her nose in belonged solely to Sebastián. Which meant no betrayals. No loss of love.

Just absence.

The finest scent, beyond frankincense and myrrh.

What to do? She summoned her lover with a question, longing to hear him speak to her. You want justice served for Pedro's murder, don't you, Sebastián?

Sebastián's voice didn't come to her. Instead, Yusuf and Qasim whispered in the bed.

"Is she asleep?"

"Yes. Now tell me."

"Castor is a good name," Yusuf whispered. "A hero's name. It suits you."

"You've been like a man possessed since Toulouse."

"I'm not permitted to speak of it."

"You know I'm more than your brother. Tell me."

Yusuf whispered, "It's like a curse my grandmother delivered when we said goodbye last week. Just before the family left to take shelter in the upper hills."

A curse from his grandmother? The kindest soul in all of Christendom? And Yusuf didn't believe in magic or curses.

Qasim murmured more, but in Arabic. Then in Catalan, "So your life is held captive under this curse?"

"No, I mean yes. But you are more to me than any cursed creature under heaven." Then Yusuf yelped, like a man bitten or scratched.

Qasim laughed. Yusuf wrestled with him, covering Qasim's mouth to stop the laughter.

"It's not funny." Yusuf growled. *"Belette muet."*

"Oh, but it is, *gai sauvatge*. Here you are, the world's most rational man, cursed."

"Hush, you'll wake her."

Their whispers tumbled into Arabic.

Taresa pressed Sebastián's shirt to her nose and curled into a tighter ball, pondering the new chaotic world with Pedro dead and perhaps a curse possessing her brother-in-law. With no real idea about how to call magic, she tried again to conjure her absent lover, seeking to see his face, hear his voice. Yet all she had was Sebastián's scent on his shirt.

And her lips throbbed, bruised from that woman's kiss.

9
Wood

"WAKE UP, TARESA! WE HAVE to go. Now."

Ai, Sebastián!

No, Qasim's hand shook her.

"We're in a Crux Lunata house. We're going now." Qasim's voice was lost in a clatter when he pulled chainmail over his head.

"*Silenci!*" Yusuf warned in a loud whisper.

"What? How?" She dressed, which meant pulling boots over stockings still soaked from the previous night. Qasim and Yusuf had already tied up their travel packs.

It's impossible to put on chainmail silently, but Taresa imitated Qasim and muffled the chiming of iron links with her surcoat, all while thinking of Sebastián's elaborate stories of how the Crux Lunata, rogue crusaders, had worked for generations to obliterate the *bonfraires*. Crux Lunata had been crushed at Las Navas de Tolosa. But anyone who'd spent time with Sebastián knew to flee any sign of those rogues.

Soon, *los tres amics*, all in black, moved through the shadows in the great hall. Qasim pointed to that quartet of windows high up along the south wall.

"Up there!"

The dawn light crept through one stained-glass window, a shield with a yellow-gold field and three red crosses, black crescents at each point of each cross.

"And there."

On the rusted lance that the baron claimed drew Saracen blood, near where the shaft entered the iron head, three *crux lunata* signs were slashed in the wood.

Taresa followed where Qasim pointed, felt her jaw drop like a witless fool. "*Jhezu*—" No, she didn't want to swear like a Toulousain street-thug. What did her uncle used to say? *Saltant cabres!*

"Leaping goats!" She stepped closer to the trophy wall. A wooden practice stake on the lower tier had markings too. She took it down, finding three simple Xs hacked on its grip, crescents at the end of each arm of the cross. They'd followed a beautiful, seductive stranger into an enemy's den.

As if reading Taresa's thoughts, Yusuf whispered, "The baron must have crawled home from Constantinople and curled up here like a scorpion under a stone."

He hoisted his travel pack.

It's impossible to move quietly in chainmail.

"*Bon día, mon amics.* Up so early?"

Baron Ricart manifested in the room like an ephemeral spirit, rubbing his hands while greeting them, his watery eyes fixed on the door to Blanca's chamber.

"We have a rendezvous for which we're late." Taresa greeted the baron with the broad smile that women in the baggage train claimed could charm snakes.

"But Blanca, *ma dòmna*—"

"My cousin decided last night that she'd prefer to spend more time with you, senhór. We're on our own."

That broad smile hurt her face, like gritting your teeth when a splinter is being pulled. Behind the baron, Yusuf and Qasim stood at the door to the courtyard, Qasim holding it open with the toe of his boot.

"We don't want the morning to get away from us!" She swept her hand up, indicating the grey dawn leaking through the windows. When the baron turned where she pointed, Taresa clanked to the doorway, straining to seem light-hearted while the baron made a fool of himself over Blanca. "The road calls us, senhór. We thank you for your generosity. In Girona, we say, '*A qui madruga, Déu ajuda.*'"

God did indeed seem to be helping them to help themselves, because the baron lost interest in them and instead took a chair near the door leading up to Blanca's bedchamber, his face comically distorted with longing. Taresa pressed her hand to her mouth to keep from laughing, then sobered at the memory of how she'd been made Blanca's fool the night before.

The great hall was empty of servants or other retainers. *Los tres amics* strode to the stables. Appearing bold. Though Taresa guessed Yusuf and Qasim felt as vulnerable in the empty courtyard as she did. The baron's men who'd shot arrows at them the night before must still be in bed.

Qasim sniffed the air. "Easy to find the stable."

The baron's stable proved to be a low wooden structure of half-rotten timbers with missing roof tiles and limited capability for keeping animals and fodder dry in the coming winter.

Inside, one of Blanca's dipped-in-woad guards—Taresa couldn't tell one from another with certainty—had Qasim's horse out of its stall. He'd put on the bit and harness and, holding the reins to steady the animal, he examined it as if this were horse-market day in Toulouse.

"Senhór, that's my horse." Qasim seemed calm, given the nature of the guard's trespasses.

"My lady suggested we trade one of our palfreys for yours."

"Your lady should first ask me," Qasim said.

"We do her bidding." The guard smirked. "Haven't you already learned to do as she asks?" He pulled at the reins in his hands.

Qasim's horse didn't like it and stepped sidewise, intending to harass the man, but he had tight hold of the reins, which he jerked, pulling hard at the bit, hurting the horse's mouth. Flecks of blood splashed when the horse tried to lurch away.

No longer calm, Qasim shouted what must be invectives, but not in any local tongue. He charged the guard, hitting him in the chest with his shoulder, dropping him to the filthy stable floor. One punch to the face echoed in the stable.

"Enough!" Taresa shouted, sickened by that echoing *thwack* of crushed nose bone.

"Not even close to enough." Qasim punctuated each word by kicking the horse-molester twice in the ribs before the brute could curl into a ball to protect himself.

"Peace, brother." While calling to Qasim for peace, Yusuf had his sword out.

Qasim stomped on the man's hand, then went to calm his horse.

Hands shaking, worried about consequences, Taresa walked a wide arc around the man moaning in the muck of the stable floor. She hefted Qasim's saddle over to him and then began saddling her own horse, which trembled under her hand, disturbed by the commotion.

"Come on, Yusuf. Saddle your horse."

Qasim said, "I'll take care of it," his voice a deep rumble.

While Yusuf stood over the moaning guard, Qasim harnessed Yusuf's horse, speaking softly to calm it. Or perhaps to calm himself. He'd cinched up the saddle and was convincing the horse it was happy again when Blanca's other three guards appeared.

They drew their weapons and advanced in a line.

"*Ai*, senhórs." Taresa was generous, calling them gentlemen. "It's a small personal disagreement. Nothing to make more of than…"

Qasim drew his sword, pausing to slam his boot into the man in the straw, who'd tried to rise. Qasim kicked the man's sword hand, which sent his weapon spinning out of reach.

"Our Castor is the soul of kindness." Taresa talked to distract Blanca's venomous guards. "But your friend injured his horse. A man must stand."

¤

Yusuf advanced on the other three, he and Qasim both checking their position. Taresa's heart beat hard, but the rush of blood didn't fog her thinking; they had to fight, three-on-three. She drew her sword and stepped into line with them, drawing her sword.

Except she held that wooden stake from the baron's weapon rack, not Sebastián's sword. When had she slammed that stake into her empty scabbard? She snatched her dagger from its baldric and took the steady, balanced stance that Sebastián taught her.

Qasim waited for the attackers, a figure of muscled menace, furious over grievous wrong-doing. Yusuf presented a perfect fighter's stance, sword in one hand, dagger in the other. The pair had spent a year studying with Pedro's best warriors, while all she'd learned was French and close-hand dagger work to thwart an attacker.

However, it was Taresa's duty on this journey to avoid danger, and she needed to stop this quarrel with words, so she continued to chatter about personal tiffs and no need to break the peace of God.

"*Vivètz Valerós!*" Yusuf shouted Sebastián's battle cry, which might as well be Arabic, but his voice rang out deeper, more commanding than she'd ever heard him.

Qasim yelled the same in *valencià* dialect.

Negotiations over, she too shouted. "*Valerós victoriós!*"

The guards shouted Toulousain curses, raising their swords.

Look for weakness. Taresa was listening again to admonitions from Sebastián in the training yard. For one, Blanca's guards hadn't seemed to notice that the Valerós allies wore chainmail until Qasim stripped off his surcoat. The angry guards were without armor, dressed in woad-dyed fustian.

Taresa bashed that wood stake against her arm. Her chainmail chimed, even under her surcoat. The sound surprised the guard approaching her, enough that he lost the tension of his stance for a single heartbeat, leaving an opening. He was shorter than Taresa, had less of a reach, but was eager for her to raise her sword. Instead, she launched a kick for the man's middle, intending to follow with an elbow to his nose when he folded, the way she'd been taught.

But she didn't have her footing right and instead jammed her boot in his groin, which put her off balance, so she pitched forward, knocking the man over after he fell to his knees.

"Don't let him rise!"

Whether Qasim or Sebastián shouted at her didn't matter. She bashed the side of the man's head with her dagger's pummel.

He wasn't getting up yet, but she kicked his dropped sword the way she'd seen Qasim do. It tumbled as far as a muck-filled puddle.

"*Merde!*" A crash.

Yusuf had backed his attacker into a manure cart, which collapsed with the man's weight.

That left only Qasim still fighting one man, both men shouting.

"*Estòp! Arrèsta!*" Blanca shouted from the stable door, her voice piercing for such a small woman. "You ill-licked cubs. I should let these men toss your gizzards to wild cats to feed on."

"Your ill-mannered guard cruelly hurt Qa—Castor's horse." Taresa jabbed a finger at Blanca, accusing. "Apparently, at your command."

But Blanca chided her own guards, not *los tres amics*. She flew to Qasim's side. "Dear boy, I'd never mean for harm to come to your horse. It's valiant to fight for justice."

Hands on her hips, Blanca continued to hector her guards, who were rising from stable-filth and infamous bruising. Taresa felt magnificent; *los tres amics* would have won the fight anyway, but having a tiny, imperious woman dressed in scarlet-dyed leathers further humiliate their attackers? It awakened an excited child within, Taresa wishing she'd seen her worst bully in Girona scolded by a small woman.

That childish joy lay smashed in the muck in one heartbeat. Ricart appeared at Blanca's side, his motley henchmen straggling behind, remaining in the courtyard. Ricart blinked repeatedly, as if his watery fish eyes needed extra practice to be able to see.

"*Ma dòmna*, may I assist you?"

"No, my beloved Ricart. It's just a squabble."

"Men always quail under a woman's rule. Permit me to—"

"Don't tease, baron. No man ever quailed under my rule."

"In my day, we used the rod. Most men need scars to learn true respect."

"Under me," Blanca spoke lightly, her hand on the baron's forearm, as if they were trading jests, "no man has to be asked twice to keep the peace. Am I right, *mon amics?*"

Her men were upright, one needing to lean on another. They nodded, not looking at each other, or Blanca, or *los tres amics*.

Blanca clapped her hands, once. "We have work to do in Cahors. Let's be on the road."

Ricart squeezed Blanca's upper arm. Taresa, standing so near, noticed her flinch. "*Ma dòmna*, I hoped to entertain you until Michaelmas."

"I'll stop on the way home, dear heart. I made a promise to another friend. To keep my honor, I must complete my friend's business before indulging my own pleasure."

One of Ricart's men called to him and he turned, as if creaking with regret, to step away from Blanca and find who called for him in the courtyard.

"Nice sword work for scholars and pedants. Your tutors must be proud," Blanca murmured, so close to Taresa that it tickled the tiny hairs on her neck. Blanca crossed her arms, that same bemused expression as just before she'd kissed Taresa, spreading her pall of seduction over everyone. "Ready to go to Cahors?"

"*Òc, ma dòmna.*" Qasim had been made into her obedient servant.

"Let me be clear, *ma dòmna.* We do not need your help to travel." Taresa once more asserted her role as the leader among *los tres amics.*

However, the heretic hunters arrived just then.

10
Steel

"BON DÍA!" A VOICE BOOMED in the local tongue, French accented. "This is the glorious day that the Lord has made."

The king-killer.

Milon in his dancing-lion surcoat stood by two of the chainmail-priests from the Templars' great hall, each holding swords. Along with those priests, three French soldiers with crossbows formed a line across the stable door. Milon licked his lips, launching his slow, pouting snake's smile. He idly swung his sword with one hand, and with the other, he tapped the priest beside him, the one with a face too big for his head.

"Didn't I tell you this would be a good day? That we'd find a bushel of heretics today?"

"Heretics?" Ricart seemed confused.

Los tres amics furtively checked where they stood in the suddenly crowded, stinking stable. The five hunters stood behind Milon, blocking the doorway. Ricart faced Milon, with Blanca's guards in a line behind him, blocking Blanca from the hunters. *Los tres amics* stood at the side, Taresa closest to Milon.

Milon waved to his soldiers, who stepped closer to Ricart. His tongue snaked out, to begin a smile.

"Your neighbors say a band of heretics camped in your barley field last week. And you let them glean your grain." Milon had a heretics' coin out and fingered it in his hand. "And here you are, sheltering three heretics we chased yesterday."

He pointed to Taresa, then past her at Yusuf and Qasim.

"No!" She yelled, but her voice was drowned by Ricart shouting his own denial.

Milon held his coin high for a moment, then raised his voice, his eyes heavenward. "We declare this domus seized for sheltering heretics. All here will answer to the Church court for—"

"But I pray to the Blessed Virgin." Ricart stiffened. He babbled in French, his hands folded in prayer, pleading. "Monsieur Milon, it is so many years. Perhaps you don't remember your good friend Ricart de Marais, from those days in Acre—"

"In Acre? Where you lied about saving Philippe in battle?" Milon looked down his long nose at Ricart, all the while fingering that gold coin, knuckle over knuckle. "And then you lied to Count Raymond when you came home, and won this beautiful castle as your reward. When it was I who saved Philippe."

"It wasn't that way." Ricart whined, but with good reason, since one of the French soldiers had his cocked crossbow pointed at the old baron.

Taresa listened closely, once the pounding pulse of fear and hatred faded in her ears so she could grasp what these two men argued. Her French lessons seemed invaluable.

"What did they say?" Qasim whispered. "Why do the hunters want us?"

"Milon and Ricart have an old quarrel." She needed to concentrate to understand what they said.

"Are they looking for us?" Qasim persisted.

"Òc," Blanca whispered. She fluttered a finger, motioning for silence. And she glared at her guards, who moved into a tighter line to protect their mistress.

Ricart's voice squeaked. "I swear by the heavenly crown of Sancta Maria that I never—"

"Do not foul your mouth with any saint's name." Milon raised the sword that he'd swung casually at his side throughout the conversation. "I have suffered for your lies, Ricart. They call you baron, don't they? For what you stole from me?"

"I never—" Ricart raised his sword. It quivered in his hand, the same way words quivered in his voice.

Milon ran him through, then jerked his sword up, intending a death cut. He pushed the groaning baron away, not looking down where Ricart fell.

Blanca's guard stepped even more tightly in front of their mistress. Taresa wanted to step away from the horror, but she was stuck between Milon and a stall wall. Qasim and Yusuf stepped up, and she recognized that they intended to form a defensive line in front of her, which caused Taresa to join their line instead, which meant remaining too close to Milon and the dying baron.

While twitching that appalling smile, Milon made a sign over the baron, like children do when playing Church, shouting a portion of the benediction, in Latin the way a priest would.

> *Novo cedat ritui:*
> *Præstet fides supplementum*
> *Sensuum defectui.*

A true benediction falls on a penitent like a cloak of comfort from God. But not when it's said by a murdering knight, repeating words made foul in his mouth. *Give way to the new rite; let faith provide a supplement for the failure of the senses.*

You couldn't say the stable was silent. Yusuf twitched as if crawling out of his skin, his eyes rolled back, listening to the wretched Latin. Blanca's guards breathed so hard, Taresa could see their woad jerkins rise and fall, whispering their panic. Horses nickered. The priest with the bulbous, overgrown face muttered more in Latin, his hand extended over the baron. Ricart moaned, gurgled blood.

"Does anyone else want to argue about how we perform our sacred duty?" Milon looked from one man to the next, his eyebrows waggling in query, examining Blanca's guards and *los tres amics* as if for the first time, and still ignoring the man dying at his feet.

Blood pounded again in Taresa's ears, so hard that others must have heard it. Perhaps her loathing drew Milon's attention, like a lodestone draws iron. He stepped close enough that he grabbed her arm, his hands big enough to snag hold through chainmail, the links chafing in spite of her quilted undercoat.

"The pretty boys who say they're not from Aragón, eh? Heretic lovers like your dead king?"

Smothering the fear and loathing in her heart, Taresa asked in French, "Are you the knight who claims he killed Pedro at Muret?"

Whatever else happened in the morning light, perhaps others would hear his confession.

Milon's tongue snaked out, his lips convulsing, as if half of his mouth tried not to smile, while the other half couldn't help it. At last, his wet lips unfolded in a prideful grin. "You heard my story about Muret at the Templars' new farm last night."

"Òc, senhór." She returned her own broad smile, for the man she wished dead and rotting in a black abyss. "I also heard you brag that you murdered Pedro."

Milon, neither agreeing nor disagreeing, said, "We are all called to act for the sake of heaven."

Behind the murderer, Yusuf seemed ready to flee or fight. His lips begged Taresa for silence, but she badly wanted others to hear Milon's confession.

"When God speaks in my ear, it sets my heart on fire." Milon's smile twisted into a smirk. "And I must act."

"More men should hear of your actions on God's behalf."

Taresa flattered Milon, which turned her stomach as much as the groans from the dying baron. Milon's head wagged, taking in the glory of praise, but then he turned cautious and pulled her closer. She had to endure the stink of him, pain shooting through her arms from his grip.

Then he had a hand in her surcoat, and she held her breath in fear that her chainmail might not prevent his hand from discovering more about her. He groped too long, since warriors have few places to hide things in their surcoats. He muttered in her ear, "What a pretty boy you are. I see why Pedro kept all three of you to himself."

She sneezed.

> He pressed deep into the embrace he'd longed for, that he'd die for, though he'd been forbidden to beg. Lips against his, tongue exploring his mouth, tasting of resinous honeyed wine. His fingers twisting long blond locks, he pressed his own tongue back into the man's mouth, tasting the salty sweat of a hot day by the Great Sea. The setting sun ignited

the darkening sea, while he burned, his groin and member calling out for love, for the touch of…

She jerked away from his probing just as Milon found the letter roughly stitched inside her surcoat. He tore at the lining to remove the packet, which sent pinpricks of fear through her arms and legs, but he had to release her to open the packet and read the letter. Taresa shook pins-and-needles from her arms and wiggled away, not wanting Milon to touch her again.

"*Qu'est-ce que c'est?*" Milon frowned, not able to read it, and passed it to the big-face priest.

"It says these ambassadors of Aragón are guaranteed free passage by Pedro *le Roi*." Just like his face, the priest's voice was outsized for his body. "Though the only safety Pedro can guarantee is on the road to eternal damnation."

"Pedro *le roi défunt?*" Milon sneered. "There was a fire and a murder at the Templars' barn. But you left us. Is that because—"

"They were attending me." Blanca's voice floated warm and sweet over the fear and death in the stable. She stepped from behind Taresa, surprising Milon. "Doing what I asked, like all of these men."

"*Ma dòmna!*"

"*Bon jorn*, Senhór Milon. Hunting heretics now? You, a hero of so many battles?" She spoke in the local tongue, not French. "You didn't recognize me last night?"

As if Blanca's imperious being cast a spell on men, that entire crowd stood transfixed while she held out her hand, intending that Milon show devotion. That is, she transfixed every man except Yusuf and Qasim who, like Taresa, were looking for a way out of the stable, past both Blanca's guards and the heretic hunters. The grey morning beckoned. The sky wouldn't grow lighter than the steely grey that allowed no sun. But the phalanx of heretic hunters allowed no exit.

"Serving my Church and my God." Milon's tongue wormed out of his mouth as he smiled, then he bent to touch his thick, wet lips to Blanca's hand. "I have unusual talents for this age."

Taresa had claimed the same when bragging to Blanca, yet the king-killer's words hardened her spine. She shuffled for firmer footing, which caused her to notice that Blanca's guards were creeping toward the line of soldiers and priests. A thin quivering grey spirit-mist hung for a moment over what had been the baron of Marais. It faded faster than the spirit-mist over the poor boy in the Templars' barn.

Blanca held Milon's hand. "I remember you, Milon, from my husband's camp. Surely you belong with a grand lord again. Not—"

"*Ma dòmna,* Church business isn't for women. That's when it gets confusing, determining who's a heretic. Even for a lady who no longer has a noble husband to protect her."

Milon reversed the grip, closing his hand over hers and pulling her close. Milon's tongue snaked out to launch a new smile, and he nodded to his line of heretic hunters.

"Kill them all. Except this lady. As they say throughout the land where men say *òc,* God can sort them."

¤

As if a crashing wave flooded the stable, men moved on each other. One of Blanca's guards rammed his sword into the neck of the broad, dark young priest who'd laughed with Milon in the Templars' great hall. At the other end of the line of heretic hunters, a woad-clad guard ripped the crossbow from a French soldier's hands, which released the trigger and sent its bolt into the shoulder of the other French soldier close by. The guard jammed the crossbow into the face of the man who'd lost it, then rammed him again, the sound of cracking facial bones rising above the other action.

Yusuf stood too near to the king-killer, and Milon raised his sword to strike him next. Yusuf parried with his short sword, and then swung back up with his dagger, the one that never kept an edge. When Milon swung again, Taresa jumped, hoping for his middle, hoping his sword missed her legs. She missed his middle but struck his knees. He fell, and Taresa knocked Milon on the temple with her dagger handle, then kicked him in the head after he crumpled.

"*Mercé,* Master Tarek!" Yusuf called a thank-you for saving his life, but he'd already leaped down to fight beside Qasim.

Free of Milon, Blanca stepped away from the fallen knight. Taresa passed the knife from her boot to Blanca and pushed her further into the stable.

"Back to back!" Taresa commanded. She stepped into a fighter's stance, her dagger out, though they were too far away to be pulled into the melee.

Qasim scrambled across the stable to defend the guard he'd kicked to the floor earlier, but he got there too late. The big-face priest stabbed the unarmored guard, who fell at the priest's feet, as if in supplication. The priest stepped over the fallen guard to fight Qasim, who kicked the ugly priest in the groin and then jammed the pommel of his sword up under the priest's chin, so that heretic hunter fell, sprawling over the other priest.

Taresa couldn't see past Yusuf to know what happened with Blanca's remaining guards and the French soldier. Yusuf stepped aside just as the stable became deadly quiet, except for the strained breathing of those left standing.

Qasim and Yusuf.

Taresa and Blanca.

Yusuf towered over the unconscious Milon, dagger in one hand, sword in the other. Dressed in black, Yusuf hovered like God's avenging angel, his face as dark as the day's thunderclouds.

"King-killer." Taresa repeated it again in every language she knew.

Qasim still gulped air, waiting for Yusuf to decide. Then Qasim went to Yusuf's side, took the dagger away, and wiped it on Milon's surcoat, though Yusuf hadn't drawn any man's blood in the fight.

"King-killer? Truly?" Blanca repeated the words, questioning whether she understood.

"Òc. Milon murdered Pedro." That fact had set Taresa's brain on fire from the first moment Milon entered the stable.

"We can't just butcher him." Yusuf clutched the pummel of his sword with both hands, gripping so hard that the sword shook. "He can't defend himself."

"No reason not to," Blanca said. "Milon has been a cheat, a liar, and a bully as long as I've known him. I doubt he'd have the courage to kill Pedro, but if he did—"

"Killing an unarmed or unconscious man goes against any notion of honor, even if the man has no honor." Yusuf thrust his sword into its scabbard.

"Well, then." Blanca clapped her hands. A single smack, like she used to get her guards' attention. "We need to go to Cahors."

Taresa knitted her wits back together. Not all these men were dead. "Where are Ricart's men? Why didn't they—"

"Ran away, I assume." Blanca returned Taresa's knife. "It's likely that Ricart didn't pay well."

"What about—" Taresa had the same questions as in the Templars' barn. "If we run away, we'll be accused."

"We didn't kill anyone here," Yusuf said. "Qasim stopped a man from hurting his horse, and your guards attacked us. Then the heretic hunters appeared and—"

"Yes, yes." Blanca had grown impatient. "I promise you that we shall find sanctuary in Cahors."

"Leaping goats!" Taresa exclaimed. "You once more promise safety? And we should believe you?"

"This castle would have been a perfectly safe place if you *children* hadn't started a brawl."

"We didn't. One of your guards hurt Qasim's horse, and the heretic hunters came—"

"*Ai.* I have no time to quarrel. It's a sad accident. I need to go to Cahors. Now."

Taresa went to retrieve the letter of passage from the big-face priest. He'd fallen on his hand, so the letter was buried beneath his massive body. She nudged him with her toe, to turn him over, and he groaned. She leaped back, then examined Milon's other soldiers. They weren't all dead, though none moved. Blanca said, "We should take all the horses, so Milon can't follow us."

Yusuf said, "Stealing horses is wrong."

"Such a moral philosopher." Blanca grasped her travel pack and, by way of a signal Taresa missed, she had Qasim saddling her horse for her.

"What's this?" His chainmail jangling, Qasim bent to pick up the gold coin Milon had dropped. He handed it to Yusuf. At least *los tres amics* recognized it as the heretics' gold Milon had shown men at the Templars' farm.

"Since you're such noble philosophers," Blanca said, "just let their horses run free. But we'll take my guards' horses, since I paid for them. Can you care for the extra horses, Master Castor?"

Blanca offered Qasim that warm, seductive smile, the one that rained personal blessings upon whoever had the good fortune to receive it. While not once looking to see how her guards fared.

No smiles reserved for Taresa, who calculated that she'd learned more that morning than in most all of her journey into Andalusia. It was as the oldest women in the baggage train insisted: *Trust no one but your true friends.*

With everyone ready to ride, Qasim paused at the castle gate to drive off the hunters' horses. The guards' horses were on leads, palfreys now serving as packhorses. Qasim had tied the crossbows, swords, and other weapons from the hunters and guards onto the palfreys' packs. "To sell or barter," he said.

When Taresa prepared to mount, her boot skidded on something hard. She bent to pick up a crossbow bolt, either from the cuckoo-bird's excuse of an attack that Ricart had made on them the night before or from the heretic hunters. She threaded the bolt through the lacing of her scabbard.

"What are you stealing?" Yusuf pointed to her scabbard.

"A spent iron arrow."

"Useful. If we knew how to fire a crossbow."

Qasim said, "It'll hurt more the next time *el cavaller de cabres* bashes someone with her scabbard."

Yusuf adopted a maddening sage expression. "All good things come to our jackdaw. We should call you *Corvus,* the crow."

"Can we go now?" Blanca called to them.

Qasim, with a touch of his knee to his horse, rode at Blanca's side, having appointed himself her new personal guard. Blanca pointed to the northern horizon. "Cahors is that way. Two days' ride."

"We need to ride there today," Taresa said. "We have our own need to be there as soon as possible. And, *ma dòmna,* we are now your protection."

"God is great. God is good," Blanca said, but Taresa was certain she didn't mean it.

Taresa longed to retrieve her lost letter of passage, even if—as the priest claimed—Pedro couldn't protect them from the chaos unleashed in this new world. But she wasn't about to touch the body of the huge, big-face priest to get it.

It began to rain again, mildly for two heartbeats, then a deluge.

11
Knights Errant

THEY PELTED DOWN THE ROAD that led to Cahors. Three leagues from Ricart's *crux lunata* castle of lunacy, Qasim insisted they rest the horses. Blessedly, the rain had let up, at least for a few moments. With the rain stopped, the odors of rosemary and lavender rose from the underbrush of the forest.

"Now, if only we had food," Qasim's breath hung steaming white in front of him in the cold, "my stomach wouldn't be trying to eat my liver and kidneys."

Taresa produced the packet of provisions she'd gotten from the ancient priest at the Templars' farm the night before. Which served to reassert her role as caretaker for their journey.

When Blanca went off into the undergrowth of the forest, for what she called personal business, it was the first time *los tres amics* had been alone since dawn.

"Crux Lunata isn't after us now," Qasim said.

Taresa offered him more bread and cheese. "No, only Simon de Montfort's heretic-hunting army. They'll say we killed a priest."

"No one knows we were at Ricart's castle," Qasim said.

"Except for the men left alive. Who will speak evil about us to Simon and the Church."

Too fastidious to attempt to speak while finishing a bite, Yusuf held up a hand for silence until he could talk.

"They weren't priests." Yusuf swallowed again. "Perhaps they were once, but not now."

"What?"

"They're merely bandits."

"How do you know?" Qasim asked.

Yusuf took another bite, which meant they again had to wait for him to be free to speak. Behind him, a jay settled on the lower branch of a holm oak and began begging for food. Or mocking them. "At the Templars' great hall, while Taresa was putting up the horses, those so-called priests were laughing and cursing in Latin." He took another bite of cheese and bread.

"Saying what?" Taresa, impatient, wanted to hear the story and fought the desire to snatch the food from Yusuf's hands so he'd finish telling what he knew.

"You want to learn Latin curse words? That would be superior to your favorite—"

"I want to know what they said."

"Me, too." Qasim shoved Yusuf in that peculiar way men do.

"They cursed that the Templars enjoy far better food and more comfortable quarters than they'd ever known."

"That doesn't mean they aren't still priests." Taresa wanted it to be true, what Yusuf claimed, that they hadn't witnessed the murder of a priest. A murdered priest is what led to the invasion of the south and brought Simon de Montfort to power.

"The older man with the odd face, too big for his head?" Yusuf wrinkled his nose, waiting for Taresa and Qasim to acknowledge they knew which man he meant. "He said to his friends, 'Now that we're free of the Church, we'll do far better for ourselves. The bishop's punishment is our gift from a bountiful God.'"

Taresa remained unconvinced. "That doesn't mean they didn't sign up to be heretic-hunters."

"Their form of heretic hunting is itself heresy. No courts. No justice." Yusuf lifted a chunk of bread and cheese to bite into, but Taresa stopped him.

"How can we be sure?"

"You heard them, Master Tarek. Tell us what they said to Ricart. When they were speaking French."

"Milon seized the baron's castle for sheltering heretics."

"We got that," Yusuf said. "What did he say about Acre?"

"From what I gathered, Ricart won the castle from the count of Toulouse as a reward for saving Philippe Augustus in the battle at

Acre. Which was when the Angevine and French kings were on crusade in the Outremer." She calculated. "Twenty years ago? Milon claimed that Ricart lied, and the castle should belong to him."

"Then you see, don't you? They came to attack Ricart," Yusuf concluded, "and take his land. It had nothing to do with us."

Blanca appeared then, seeming to have heard Yusuf's words. With praying hands, she silently pleaded for Taresa to share food. "Josep de Morella is correct. Both Milon and Ricart were liars from eons past. That little scene had nothing to do with any of us."

When Taresa didn't pass the food packet quickly, Qasim offered to share his with Blanca.

"Only the tiniest portion." Blanca blessed Qasim with her soul-warming smile.

"Take what you need."

Five heartbeats' of patience was all that Taresa cared to sacrifice to this woman, who seemed to be done with Taresa once she'd realized "Tarek" wasn't a man. Now Taresa posed an obstacle to whatever Blanca wanted, which seemed to be that every man worship her. There'd been a similar Blanca in the baggage train who stole another woman's soldier-lover and, after the man died in riots in Toledo, the Blanca-from-camp stole yet another woman's lover. Not that Taresa was jealous of the attention Blanca of Avignon lavished on Qasim, since the worldly lady had noticed that neither Yusuf nor Qasim had any interest in women. And Taresa wasn't jealous after that bruising kiss in Blanca's bedchamber. Taresa had Sebastián and therefore, except for the sole woman who was a *bonfraire* knight, she had no reason to be jealous of any woman on earth.

But the previous night, Blanca and Taresa had spoken intimately, traded secrets, one woman trusting another. Acted like friends. Maybe Taresa was ignored now, not because she had breasts and no *punxor*. Maybe it was worse. Maybe after they'd shared intimacies, Blanca decided that she didn't like Taresa.

"That's how they do it in the Count of Provence's court." Blanca ran one elegant finger down Qasim's arm. Tiny chainmail chimes answered her touch. Taresa's meditations caused her to miss the context. "You'll see that kind of grace in my friend Giles's house. He's a good man. The best of the new seigneurs."

At that moment, Taresa lost all patience with Blanca's habitual bewitchery. "We followed you for safety last night, *ma dòmna,* and woke up in tragedy this morning."

"I had no idea Milon knew Ricart or that Milon was coming for revenge." Blanca said, her hands busy tracing the story with strokes in the air. "I met Milon when he was a trumped up lordling in my husband's army. He left for crusade a decade ago under Simon de Montfort, said Simon was his cousin."

"That probably means that Simon gave him a warrant to ride around the country killing people." Yusuf's eyes darkened, flitted left to right, as he considered that gloomy idea.

Taresa asked what she most needed to know. "Do you have other friends in Simon's court, *ma dòmna?* Other friends among king-killers?"

"No. I...my..." Blanca stumbled for words, her gestures pausing mid-air. "My entire life is antithetical to what Simon believes. He wants the south as his kingdom. To force us all into his barren world of prayers and penance. I'm a creature of the noble courts of the south."

"The poets' courts of love?" Yusuf asked.

"*Òc,* however much you scholars might consider it silly. The courts of the south are filled with beauty and music and civilized discourse." Blanca's elegant fingers traced her vision of those courts. "We don't pile weapons in alcoves or leave people to die in the street."

Taresa bit back a retort: *You left your guards to die in that barn.* Instead, she asked, "Why shouldn't we leave you at the first travelers' inn? Or a cottager's hut?"

"Please ride with me as far as my friend Giles's house." Blanca didn't beg, but she didn't answer the question.

"Is he another knight of Simon's?" Taresa asked. "Another decrepit crusader?"

"He was a crusader in the Outremer and at Constantinople, but he's different from Ricart. He shines in every Court of Love he's visited since he came home. Now he's retired to the country. He's...we've...discussed marriage for more than a year. If he'll help me with my friend's task, I'll offer my vows."

"You're selling yourself for the sake of your dead friend?" Taresa should cease being amazed at what Blanca said or did.

"No. Giles is a brilliant man, from a family equal to mine. He has ideals. He has…honor."

Blanca's hands swept aside the notion of selling herself, while Taresa caught the idea: Blanca believed herself a station above Taresa, though she'd cited no proof. Inside, Taresa cradled her own sense of worth: she was the senhóra of Valerós, whose master was Pedro's favored commander. This false comtessa could ride goats in the Court of Love, for all Taresa cared.

Then Blanca's hands spread effusively, her voice warmed. "Giles incarnates all that the troubadours say a knight should be. It's hardly a sacrifice to find shelter in his arms."

"And not aligned with Simon?" Yusuf asked the key question, while Taresa silently applauded her own worth, tallying all the land Sebastián held from Pedro or had inherited from his father and grandfather, and the land she'd inherited in Girona. Blanca could ride two goats as far as—

Blanca rested her hand on Yusuf's. "Of course not. You have nothing to lose, staying at my friend's house tonight. He's just south of Cahors. You can ride on to Cahors in the morning."

"Madam, a word, *per favor*." Taresa stepped between Yusuf and the scarlet-clad Blanca, walking her away from the two men.

"Yes, Master Tarek?" Blanca was smaller, had to look up when speaking at close range, the way she'd had to look up when she kissed Taresa.

"Leave Castor and Josep alone. Don't practice on them what you did with Ricart. It demeans you and my friends."

"Are you jealous?"

"I'm dismayed, watching a woman use her sex to get men to do what she wants."

Blanca offered on a friendly smile. "I don't use it for men alone."

"Stop. We come from different worlds. We may both be traveling to Cahors, but since you travel under *our* protection now, please leave my friends alone."

"We are the same, you and I. We both want what we want, and will do anything to get it."

We're not the same. I use my wits. You use people to—"

"You'll change your mind when it's time to ponder your regrets, the first time you spend a dark night of the soul."

"I have no regrets," Taresa said. "I've done nothing that would lead to regret."

"O child!" Blanca kissed her again, then stepped back. "If we go to my friend Giles's house—"

"We need to be in Cahors as fast as our horses can carry us." Taresa refused to let Blanca commandeer their travel plans again. "We'll take shelter only if God pours out more buckets of rain than the horses can endure."

¤

For a noble mission such as theirs, helping to rescue the child-king of Aragón from Simon de Montfort, the day's ride proved boring.

Trees.

Rocks.

Stream to ford.

More trees and rocks.

Hills to climb.

Two days earlier, each view from a new hilltop brought joy, each September meadow still sunlit with golden flax, each blossoming of honeysuckle in the hedges where birds trilled and squabbled.

Then the rain came, and Pedro died. The journey became bum-numbing endurance. That, and the effort it took Taresa to avoid remembering the butchery and the smell the offal in Ricart's stable. Or that poor boy in the Templars' barn.

Qasim was insistent about how often the horses needed to rest and when they needed to swap saddles and ride different palfreys. Like the water clock she'd seen in Barcelona, Qasim had an internal clock that told him, *It's time!* Sebastián had taught her to take the same care, though Taresa didn't have sufficient practice, because on the baggage train, the captains had that job.

"It's time," Qasim called. "We need to rest the horses again."

Then they'd practice mind-numbing chores, unpacking animals, wiping them down, hobbling them amid the best grass they could find. Piling their gear under waxed canvas. Pitching a temporary pavilion to wait out of the rain if they couldn't find sufficient shelter under the oaks, beeches, and sweet chestnut trees.

Taresa shared out the food among the riders. By mid-afternoon, one portion for each of them remained, since the food had been divided among four people instead of three.

After taking a personal break in the undergrowth—one hundred heartbeats of solitude—Taresa emerged to find Blanca busy persuading Qasim and Yusuf to travel to her friend Giles's house, to spend the night there before riding on to Cahors.

Leaping goats! Qasim was on his knee before Blanca, listening earnestly. Blanca had a hand on Yusuf's shoulder, speaking with intimacy and warmth. Like she had with Taresa the night before. Taresa looked away, embarrassed about how she'd been seduced by Blanca's courtly ways. And los dos amics were just as easily persuaded.

"Are we ready to ride?"

Taresa didn't wait for an answer, saddling her horse, mounting, doing her best to wrap her rain cloak in a way that might fend off the next flood from the skies.

The others dallied before mounting. Then Taresa let Qasim and Yusuf ride ahead before she cantered up alongside Blanca, who wasn't burdened by having to lead the extra packhorses. Qasim had taken charge of Blanca's share.

"*Ma dòmna*, you travel as our guest." Taresa again made this assertion. "We are not your charges or paid retainers. We have our own business in Cahors and sufficient resources to make our own way there."

"*Ai*, are you leaving me at the side of the road, Tarek of Girona?" Blanca asked in her warm, teasing way, not at all worried about being deserted.

"No, I'm asking you to agree upon how we travel. I negotiate all business with strangers. And I make the decision about how far we ride today and where we stop."

Blanca coughed so vociferously, it startled her horse. "Fine. If I can't persuade you to stop at my friend Giles's house, can you get us out of the rain soon and into safe beds for the night?"

"We need to ride farther. The horses don't mind the rain as much as you do."

Blanca kicked her horse and rode on ahead, catching up with Qasim and launching into banter with him. Yusuf fell back, riding beside Taresa.

"*Cherchez la femme?*" Yusuf sought to tease an outburst from her.

"Your French is improving rapidly," Taresa said. Indeed, his accent was remarkable. "Practicing with your new friend while you ride?"

"You're not happy with our lovely companion?"

"I don't trust her." Taresa spoke absolute truth. "I don't think she's our friend. Maybe not anyone's friend anywhere."

"Does this insight come from your woman's natural magic? Reading that lady's mind?"

"Watch how she acts." Taresa masked a scowl that sought to break free. She didn't want to betray emotion for Yusuf's inspection. This was all rational, not emotional. "She's tried to seduce each of us, as well as that decrepit baron."

"It's her nature to be friendly."

"She left her dead guards without looking back once." Taresa hadn't been able to get that bloody scene out of her mind all day. It had merged with the scene from the Templars' barn. And each memory reminded her that Pedro's murderer still lived—and likely would pursue them.

"I'm not sure they were all dead." Yusuf held out his hand, rocking it, weighing truth. "And I believe Blanca cares about the mission for her friend as passionately as we do about our work. She sees everything else as either helpful or in her way."

"Then we agree." Taresa nodded, indicating that Yusuf should look ahead, where Blanca gestured with her hands, telling a story that made Qasim laugh. "If we arrive at her friend's house before dark, we leave her there and go on our way. I don't want any more second-hand hospitality."

"I'm not eager to spend a night in the wilds, wet and cold," Yusuf said. "It's unlikely that we can make Cahors, even if we ride far into the dark night."

"Then we should find a safe camp with whatever travelers we meet next on the road."

"And still make Cahors by tomorrow?" Yusuf's face didn't show it, of course, but he sounded concerned.

"It's what's most important to right now, isn't it? Getting to Cahors?" She wanted to reassure him that she was doing everything she could to be in Cahors. "We'll find your Perseus and go on to Paris the next day."

They traveled on companionably for some ways. About the time that it began to rain again, as gently at first as a sweet spring shower, Yusuf said, "You aren't going to Paris."

"Of course I am. I'm taking you and Qasim to Paris. And for my reward, the *bonfraires* will make me a knight."

"My Perseus will bring his knights to Paris, taking Qasim and me with him," Yusuf said. "He'll find passage back to Toulouse for you that's safe as any laundry women's train."

She glanced to see if he was serious.

"*Désolé. Je pensais…*" Yusuf paused, seeking the right words in French, getting the accent close to perfect. He was his most sober and stern scholarly self. "I believed it was best to delay your disappointment. But now I think—"

Taresa kicked her horse to speed onward, but she had two pack-horses to lead and so couldn't do it as gracefully as Blanca had done. At last she came between Qasim and Blanca, leaving the pretend-comtessa of Avignon to ride with Yusuf, who at least wasn't seduced by her.

And Qasim was happy enough to ride in silence when the rain began again.

¤

Pedro intended that she'd go home from Cahors. Not onward to Paris. Yusuf had agreed to that plan.

Her brother-in-law had listened to every claim she'd made—boasted—about becoming a knight of the *bonfraires*. And what had occurred on this soon-to-be-aborted trip to make her eligible? Perhaps saving Yusuf's life in Ricart's stable. What else?

Running from the debacle at the Templars' farm?

Allowing Pedro's murderer to remain alive after that tragedy in Ricart's stable?

Letting starving children get the best of her and steal her sword?

Sebastián's sword.

She'd borrowed Sebastián's third-best sword. He wasn't there to ask, but she wasn't about to ride across all of the Languedoc and into the French wilderness with only a dagger as long as her forearm. When Sebastián came home, she'd have to confess that she'd lost his sword to a feral child.

Her chainmail was rusting on the outside from the blasted weather and on the inside from her own sweat. Who knew when there'd be occasion to oil it? Her boots couldn't be more sodden if she'd swam across the River Ter.

And now, it seems, no one ever intended for Taresa of Girona to ride into the French wilderness under Pedro's plan. The plan that Yusuf intended to honor.

Her cold toes burned. Her shin bones. Her knees. Like a wildfire, passion raced up her body. Anger.

No, fine ladies might be angry. Taresa was mad. Mad enough to catch fire right there in her saddle, in the rain, and burn. Not like a heretic. Like the angel of righteousness holding the burning sword at the gates of paradise.

Pedro knew her dreams, her desire. And he'd betrayed her.

She wasn't going to Paris, because Pedro—Pedro *El Católico*, king by Grace of God of Aragón, son of Sanchia Castile, Count of Barcelona and Roussillon, vassal to Innocent the Third of the Holy Roman Church—decreed that she be sent home before the adventure had barely begun.

But Pedro was dead, so Taresa couldn't argue with him about how he'd betrayed her. She'd have to wait. She'd have to believe in heaven, so when she found Pedro there, she'd explain that he'd over-reached his power, meddling in her life and her desires. Angels would stand at her side, the side of righteousness.

While her toes and shins and knees burned, intent on what must be done on her first days in heaven, a jay nagged at the travelers from the undergrowth. Its spirit brother, Yusuf, didn't turn his head to look. Taresa sought the creature in the rockrose and broom scrub. The jay whistled *quee-oo* and chuckled, rustled in the leaves, but never appeared.

Haunted by that chuckle, it came to Taresa that Sebastián—her own Sebastián—had most likely agreed to Pedro's plan *because* she'd be sent home at Cahors. *Because* she wouldn't be free to travel to Rome with him. *Because* she'd refused to leave Toulouse with his family when they fled the siege that Simon threatened as punishment.

She'd argue heatedly about that personal betrayal, once Sebastián came home. She didn't have to wait for Heaven.

She'd shepherded two Saracen-looking *fadrins* out of Toulouse and into the Languedoc wilderness. She hadn't seen a battlefield since Andalusia, but she'd stood witness to brutality and murder. Now she was saddled with a rich, spoiled widow who had seduced her charges into playing knights errant for her. And bruised Taresa's lips for who knows what purpose?

Taresa knew who murdered Pedro d'Aragón, but it seemed no one in Christendom wanted to hear the news from her. She wanted justice for Pedro and the abandoned boy who'd died in the Templars' barn.

All anyone wanted from Taresa was to find sufficient food and a bed before Cahors. Did the *bonfraires* offer knighthood to their chandlers? Their laundry women?

She stoked the fire in her heart again, letting the flames rise, lest the banked anger turn into cold ashes of humiliation. If she didn't hum loud enough to distract her horse, Yusuf's song thrummed in her ears.

> I'm a *cavaller* in chainmail,
> Be a knight! That's all I prayed.

12
Under the Willows

UNDER WILLOWS AND BEECHES THAT lined the river in a narrow valley, a merchant train had made camp, lining up four wagons, with the oldest first and the newest, nicest third in line. Waxed canvas covers stretched over bent willow staves to shelter trade goods from the September deluge. A fifth wagon, outside the circle, had a scarlet-dyed cover, like it belonged to market-place mummers.

The swale where they camped smelled of river and rosemary, and the local underbrush was crowded with rockrose. The layout and manner of the camp—with a pavilion pitched for kitchen work and another for general shelter, and a small crew of women busy at chores, hanging clothes to dry, oiling harnesses—elicited an unfamiliar deluge of emotion that Taresa sought to name.

Nostalgia. For life in a traveling camp of women.

Safe. Laughing. New adventures every day. Friends.

"Hey, Freckle-face!" It was the red-nosed drover from the Templars' farm. His friend remained back, at hailing distance. The other two drovers further down the way weren't familiar, none of them close enough to be chatting with each other. Sentries. "You left like your breeches were on fire last night. And this is as far as you got? Looks like you found all your palfreys, but where's all the men that rode out with you?"

"We've parted company." Blanca spoke, though Taresa had earlier demanded to manage all negotiations.

"It's wet enough to drown fishes." Taresa drew the men's attention back, commenting on the weather, and then introducing her companions. But Taresa's broad friendly smile was not gaining a welcome from these men. Likely, *los tres amics* should have climbed out of their chainmail shells before approaching the merchant train. Taresa tried a new tactic.

"We've found it unsafe for travelers, with all the rumors flying. Yesterday at the Templars' farm, we had to leave our arms outside. We can do the same if you make us welcome for a night."

"Unsafe world, eh?" The drover looked up the road in the direction from which Taresa and her companions had arrived. "What are you afraid of?"

"Bandits and unscrupulous heretic hunters. Will you allow us to share shelter with you for the night?"

The two drovers traded emotion-free glances, trying to decide. Their answer might have been yes, no, or perhaps, except Blanca coughed violently. Her horse reared up and threw her to the ground. She cried out in pain.

Qasim rode in pursuit of Blanca's horse, leaving Yusuf to manage the rest of their animals. Taresa jumped down to go to Blanca's aid.

"I think it's broken." Blanca bit her lip. Tears trickled along her cheeks. Taresa had to admire the woman's bravery in the face of pain, especially since she'd become disenchanted with Blanca that day.

The drovers stood over them.

"We have a healer visiting. Can you walk, *ma dòmna?* Or should we make a litter?"

"I can walk." Blanca's voice broke. Taresa made awkward efforts to help her up. Qasim returned and came to assist Blanca to her feet.

The dog beside the drover, a monster half the size of their horses, as big as a wolf, left his master to beg Qasim's attention. It looked large enough to eat you, but from the way it begged for attention, it'd most likely lick you to death or bash you to pieces with its wagging tail. "*Que és un bon noi?*" Qasim asked. The dog barked a short, sharp answer and was rewarded with more ear scratching.

Its friends stood up or stopped what they were doing, looking to what their friend was getting that they might be missing. Four dogs loped to Qasim's side, mobbing him with demands for his friendship, ignoring their masters' calling of dogs' names, crazy for Qasim's friendship.

Once the men got their dogs back under command, one of the drovers instructed Yusuf and Qasim where to hobble their horses, and then got busy helping them. Two remaining drovers continued to watch the road while the red-nosed drover led Blanca and Taresa into the camp.

The larger pavilion had been created out of stitched-together waxed canvas that must have been rescued from an abandoned army camp, but the patched-together shelter kept the rain out. Two women cleared off a camp chest they'd been using as a bench and begged Blanca to be seated while they fetched the healer.

Her broadest smile in place, Taresa tried to make friends. "I'm Tarek of Girona. This is Blanca of Avignon. We are traveling to meet friends in Cahors."

You'd think these people's mothers had never blessed them with a name. Taresa felt like a blacksmith pulling teeth in the Toulouse market square, trying to coax names from this crew of skittish women.

A couple of women, as if under duress, admitted they were both called Joaneta.

"Is this a congregation of Joanetas?" Taresa joked, hoping she sounded hearty.

No one laughed.

An infant cried. One woman wrestled within her shawl, putting the baby to her breast. Other women stepped closer as if by instinct, surrounding the new mother, murmuring in the local tongue. *Precious lamb. Sweet, sweet thing. Angel kisses on her neck. Promises of the Good God's guidance at every step.*

Angel kisses. Pale birthmarks on a new baby's neck or head. Taresa wanted to see, but the women surrounded the mother like a shield line in battle.

In this small crowd of women, Taresa couldn't now take off her men's travel clothes and say *I'm just like you*. She kept her broad smile in place, feeling Blanca wilting beside her, pain robbing her color and spirit. All the while, it was taking forever for the healer to appear. Half the women in the camp hovered, not returning to their tasks, like spirits caught between life and death. Taresa took a risk, seeking another way into being welcomed among them.

"The sky is weeping for the loss at Muret, don't you think? Tears from heaven, crying for—"

Two women burst into tears. Arms around each other, they fled the shelter of the pavilion, darting through the rain to clamber up into one of the wagons, out of sight.

"You have a way with words, Master Tarek," Blanca said.

As if a haze lifted from her vision, Taresa saw the women, and the men too, as mourners at the height of grief. Yet these people didn't know Pedro. They hadn't lost him as a friend and rescuer.

One of the Joanetas touched Taresa's shoulder. "Let me make a tisane for the lady, to warm her."

> Men in a water-marsh, as if spied by a watcher hiding in the river rushes, were searching bodies, shouting victory cries. Others lay in the field, dead or begging to die. Crows settled. The watcher wept soundlessly, gagging on salt tears.

Grief choked Taresa, grabbed her belly, turned her heart to a fist, like when she'd first heard about Muret. Of course. Hundreds, perhaps thousands of men had died, from Toulouse, Aragón, the local countryside. It must be that every soul in these parts had lost someone to Simon's onslaught. Humbled, that her grief had been so narrow over the past day, Taresa stopped pretending good-humored friendliness.

Instead, Taresa turned to traveler chatter—the condition of the roads, the sudden rarity of food due to Simon's incursions, the hopes that farmers could finish the harvest amid unseasonable rain—all the while Blanca smiled beside her, her lips pressed tight, never complaining.

When one of the camp's Joanetas appeared with a steaming tisane in a tin mug, Blanca accepted it with a pale, shaking hand, speaking in the local tongue. "*Mercé, la miá bona femna.*"

Joaneta looked startled. Taresa prepared to step in, to say that Blanca just meant a compliment, she wasn't calling Joaneta a good-woman, a heretic. Joaneta pinched her lips into a hard line at a glance from women around her.

"Here's the healer now. She came from Cahors to—"

Taresa twitched, sneezed, and the odor of burnt sugar-apple filled her nose. A veil blurred her vision, so she blinked several times, needing to see this already-lived moment. From the trees along the river, a tall older woman appeared. She came up the path serenely, taking care to dodge roots, summer brambles, a stone in her way. She wore a black veil, similar to what foreign women wear in Toulouse and Barcelona. The woman's severe cheek bones and pronounced nose, together with hooded eyes under dark brows, made her seem exotic. A shining blue aura floated around her, the blue of the Great Sea when the sun shines high and bright, the color Taresa saw around the wisest women she'd met, healing women who worked hard to serve others.

The woman had pinned a linen apron over her dark-grey woolen robe. A she approached, she unpinned and folded the apron, tucking it into the satchel over her shoulder. It took all those moments for Taresa to recognize the apron's russet and crimson stains.

"*Bon día.* Is there trouble I can assist you with?"

The woman, on the further side of fifty, spoke the local tongue with an accent. She cast those luminous dark eyes over Taresa and then focused on Blanca. Taresa felt an unreasonable longing to have this woman's attention. To be liked and admired. Taresa shrugged off the feeling, since her emotions had been flooded with the torrent of grief over what these people were suffering.

"I'm called—" The tall woman's attention was pulled away again when Qasim joined them in the pavilion. She blinked, as if assessing his chainmail. "Kalypso."

Taresa took the initiative, because Blanca gritted against pain.

"*Mercé, bona femna.* This is Blanca of Avignon, who fell from her horse. We fear her arm might be broken."

Kalypso, her voice warm and comforting, said, "May I examine you, *ma dòmna?* My hands are clean, but cold from the river."

After feeling the bones and asking precisely how it hurt wherever she touched Blanca, Kalypso took a vial from her satchel, added drops to Blanca's tisane, and gave it to her. "Drink up, *ma dòmna.* It's not a bad break. It might even be a sprain. Let's splint it and make you comfortable."

Blanca let a breath out, as if she'd held all the pain inside. She began to relax, but it couldn't be from the drops. Rather, it seemed to come from Kalypso's magical ability to create calm around her.

At Kalypso's instruction, Taresa held Blanca steady, cradling the smaller woman, while Kalypso splinted the arm. Touching Blanca led Taresa into another flash of comfort, nestled in the strong, scarred arms of a warrior.

"Is she well enough to ride to Cahors?" Taresa asked. "Or should we stay here?" The merchants hadn't offered, but perhaps Kalypso might secure an invitation for them.

"It's too far to Cahors for an injured woman," Kalypso said. "And with this weather, so little remains of the day. But I want to see your friend more comfortable than this camp can offer. May I suggest—"

"Giles de Nully," Blanca said, her words sleepy sounding. "We were on our way to his house. He's an old friend."

"Giles? A good man." Kalypso brightened. "The men with me can take you there before dark, if you can sit a horse."

Blanca insisted she could ride, but her good hand shook, her bad hand was red with cold where fingers poked from the wrapped splints. Insufficient strength showed in Blanca's face for the first time since Taresa met her.

"*La dòmna* can ride with me," Taresa said.

Qasim spoke for the first time. "Or, better, with me."

"Best choice," Yusuf said, just joining them.

"*Ai!*" Kalypso stared at Yusuf, her hand frozen in mid-motion, that vial of pain-potion hovering above her satchel.

Her brother-in-law had once again made an older woman's heart beat too hard. At the next opportunity, Taresa had to explain to Yusuf that he was too pretty for this world. Perhaps Yusuf might perceive that was as one of many reasons why he needed Taresa to travel on to Paris with him.

Still trying to measure Blanca's pain and strength, Taresa introduced Kalypso to Castor and Josep of Morella, their names barely out of her mouth before Kalypso said, "I shall ride with you. I need the rest too."

Kalypso pressed on Taresa's hand when she rose from where she'd knelt to attend Blanca, sending a flash of horror.

> Men screaming in pain, fainting when a hacksaw took a leg, a forearm. The stench of burning flesh from cauterizing open gashes, a rasp of stitching. Repeated murmurs under

the wretched screaming. *All will be well. God holds you now. All will be well.*

Taresa gasped at the images, her ears ringing with screams.

These merchants were sheltering soldiers who'd escaped Simon's butchery at Muret. Or had been hunted when Simon sent his men to crush all defending soldiers. The trail down to the river led to a hospice under the willows.

Meanwhile, Qasim was brushing away the dogs that wanted his love. He mounted his horse, and one of the drovers handed up Blanca into his care.

13
Shelter from the Storm

THE POUNDING RIDE BEAT DOWN Taresa's emotions from the merchants' camp and trampled her resentment that Blanca managed to divert them to her lover's house. The relentless rain, however, did not drown Taresa's bitter feelings about the loss of Paris as her future destination.

Conversation with her two friends wasn't possible on the ride. Qasim sheltered Blanca. The healer Kalypso kept asking friendly questions of Yusuf, who responded with scholarly rather than personal answers. That left Taresa blessedly alone, since the four men traveling with Kalypso weren't talkative. Taresa had that coin inside her glove, the one the dead priest had dropped at the monastery, and kept worrying it across her palm and back again while pondering what to do next.

By the time they neared their destination, Taresa had considered a pocketful of ideas about how to bring Milon the king-killer to justice. If they forced her to return to Toulouse, then she'd ask Raymond, the count of Toulouse, to hear her story. More people would have heard that Milon de Breteuil killed Pedro at Muret, knowing that he was killing a king, because Milon couldn't help bragging. Paratge, the deep honor of people in the south meant everything to Count Raymond. He must care about justice for Pedro. Someone in Sebastián's family could introduce her to the count. She'd consult with the *bonfraires* knights about what to do—if most of them hadn't slinked off to adventures in Rome with Sebastián.

And what if Yusuf was wrong about how to take revenge on a murderer? What if you can remain right with God if there's no other way to punish a murderer? Perhaps the conversation she most needed was with Tomás, Sebastián's father. He knew about revenge, having battled Crux Lunata for years, and he'd been close to Pedro.

The garrigue scrubland, with its wild mix of herbs and low brush, smelled strongly of sage where they were riding. Taresa sneezed. Dreading yet another already-lived moment, she buried her nose in her horse's mane, breathing animal funk to avoid any scent of burnt sugar-apples.

Yusuf rode up, so he was just behind her, close enough to talk again. Taresa slapped her glove against her mouth, to keep from saying what she'd been considering about Yusuf's…betrayal.

"I know you're still worried about Sebastián." Yusuf's voice was as warm as when he sang a sad song. "But I assure you he wasn't at Muret. He didn't die there."

"Though who knows if he's being chased by Simon's hunters like everyone else," Taresa said. "Who knows if Rome is safe for anyone from Aragón?"

"I recommend not worrying until you possess facts."

"Like you didn't worry about being late to Cahors until the whole world was in chaos?"

He ignored the jibe. "You're worried that if you lose both Pedro and Sebastián, you must rely on Sebastián's family, and you hardly know us."

"Rely on his family? What are you talking about?"

"You're worrying about who will take care of you if Sebastián is…lost. You don't need to worry about that because—"

"I don't need someone to take care of me. Sebastián doesn't *take care of me*." Her voice rose. She coughed and then spat out the annoyance that choked her throat. "Leaping goats! How do you think I got this far in the world, *gai sauvatge*? I'm not an infant. I have my own land and house in Girona. I don't need—"

"Why are you worried about returning to Toulouse, then? You weren't worried enough about the siege to leave with Sebastián's family, when you'd be safe with them."

"I'm not *worried* about returning to Toulouse. I'm *furious* that you and Pedro betrayed me. You kept secrets and treated me like a spit-licking yard chicken."

"Then why worry about Sebastián for no reason?"

"Because I can't hear his voice." She finally spoke her secret fear. "Sebastián hasn't spoken to me since the Templars' farm."

"Then you do need him, even in your mind, to take care of you."

"What kind of women did you grow up with that you think that? I don't need a man to take care of me. I just plain need Sebastián. I need to hear his voice. I need to…" She stopped before she said it: *smell him.* She was about to give up on making Yusuf understand until one clear idea occurred to her. "Do you need Qasim to take care of you?"

"No, of course not. I—" Yusuf stopped. "Oh. I see. I'm sorry."

"Pedro asked me to come along to keep you safe."

"And Sebastián commanded that Qasim and I do everything to keep you safe."

"I didn't come on this journey to be safe. I didn't agree to hide in the hills when the siege threatened Toulouse, because I don't feel a need to be safe." Taresa let her anger unwind. He'd said he was sorry. "We are *los tres amics.* Not *dos amics e la siá sòr.*"

"*Ai, cavaller* in chainmail. I won't be mistaken again."

"And don't sing that song again, *renrén.*" She called him a fool, the way her aged uncle used to condemn her errors. "It's much simpler than you tell it. I will get us to Cahors tomorrow. I will seek justice for Pedro. And—last chorus—I want Sebastián and will find him."

"*Oui, soeur.*" He switched to French. "Is this the kind of moment when a man says, 'You're beautiful when you're angry'?"

"Leaping goats! Where did you grow up, *gai sauvatge*? In a brothel?"

"That's not what they call it in Cairo."

¤

That's when they came to the castle of Blanca's friend, Giles de Nully. Like many castles in the Languedoc, it rose from a cragged hilltop. The compound included two towers and a defensive wall along just one side, because the hilltop jutted up from the valley as a steep, rugged slice of land, heaved up by giants. The trail they'd climbed was the sole approach that didn't require ropes and hooks to reach the compound. Laying siege to a hilltop castle like this meant blocking wagons—a year's work to defeat the inhabitants—because siege engines could come nowhere near the defenses.

Unlike the Languedoc castles that had suffered under Simon de Montfort's sieges, these towers stood pristine in the wilderness, their plastered walls white, even on a grim, rainy afternoon.

The travelers paused, out of arrow range, while Qasim and Blanca rode ahead to the gates. Qasim's well-mannered horse didn't prance while waiting, and neither horse nor its riders seemed bothered by the late afternoon mist. Qasim threw aside their rain cover, and Blanca slipped to the ground with his assistance. The gates opened and a single tall, unarmed man appeared, gliding to where Blanca waited, embracing her with demonstrable care.

Waiting back in the mist, Taresa watched the drama between two lovers. She'd been kissed like that twice, swept off her feet into the warm embrace of a strong man. Sebastián, of course. Both times. Which led Taresa to longing for him again, forgetting that what she most wanted was to get out of the rain.

The tall, silver-haired figure swept Blanca up again, this time into his arms to carry her through the gate.

"Maybe that man is your Perseus," Taresa whispered to Yusuf, who seemed defeated by the rain. She prompted once more for a response. "If not, then we just explain we're scholars and ask to be set on the road to Paris."

Yusuf lifted his shoulders, so that rain cascaded from the waxed canvas that enveloped him.

"Are you well, brother? You keep blinking and jerking, as if you're half way to a St-Vitus dance." She peered through veil of rain, trying to assess Yusuf's well-being. "Do you want me to ask this seigneur your Perseus question? How does you secret query go? 'Who did Perseus kill?'"

"No. 'Did Perseus slay Medusa?' Ask if you like." Yusuf seemed to have surrendered his inner fire to fatigue. Or illness. "I don't have a sense of this *domus* as our destination."

"But it is I who possess *Sensus Naturae*," Taresa said, thinking an argument might perk him up. "Your knowledge comes solely from books."

"Yet I've lived in more cities than you have, *cavaller de cabres*. Met more kinds of men than you."

"I've been a woman in a former life, while you've always been a man, even when you were a bird, *gai sauvatge*."

"Hola!" Qasim shouted, waving them forward.

Inside the gate, the castle's seigneur had his arm around Blanca's waist, holding her close in that possessive way Taresa had seen some husbands do, announcing their intimacy to the world. The divine rose-gold haze of joy that spread from the seigneur enveloped the passion-bright carmine aura around Blanca.

"You're a month later than you promised," the seigneur chided Blanca. "Then you arrive battered and broken. You're breaking my heart with fear for you, *ma dòmna*."

"*Ai*, beloved, I'm here now." Blanca, relaxed in his embrace, offering him all the earnest heat that Taresa had received the night before. And that Blanca had spread over Qasim all day. It would be interesting to see what Blanca had reserved for the castle's seigneur. "I'm safe now, here with you. Giles."

The seigneur turned, his arms still around Blanca, to greet the other travelers.

He proved to be the silver-haired gentleman who'd saved them from the wild boar. The man with the lop-sided smile and a desire to embrace the adventures of life.

"We are at the djinni's glass castle," Yusuf muttered.

Qasim whispered too. "He might be your secret Perseus."

The seigneur, however, greeted Kalypso, not yet noticing *los tres amics*. "*Ma dòmna*, was it you who rescued my dear friend? I'm so grateful. What brings you out into the wilderness?"

Kalypso handed her horse to one of the men traveling with her, and then offered her hand to Giles the way men do. Or maybe it was the foreign woman's own peculiar sort of greeting. "By pure accident, I was helping a woman in childbed in a merchants' train. And your friends appeared. Now I'm also asking shelter, since it's too far to Cahors tonight."

Except Taresa—and the four armed men with Kalypso—knew that Kalypso lied, that she'd been nursing injured soldiers. The falsehood seemed to indicate that Kalypso didn't trust this seigneur with the truth. However, it wasn't Kalypso's personal secret, so perhaps she couldn't honorably share it.

"What an unexpected honor!" Giles kissed the healer's hand the way knights honor ladies. "My cooks have been ready for visitors for days now. Come in and—"

That's when Giles took real notice of *los tres amics*, though of course they'd been shrouded in rain capes.

"It's my young friends from the back hills! Are you the heroes in my lady's rescue? Of course you are. Fate playing games with us once more!"

While Blanca repeated their names in a weak introduction, Giles clasped Qasim's hand, braced his shoulder as if they were comrades. Yusuf hung back, but Taresa offered Giles her hand, as boldly as the seigneur's own grip.

> Sunlight bounced blindingly off the blue, blue sea. Raucous laughter rose over the echo of crashing waves. Hands passed cold stone bottles. Wine burned the tongue with resin-heavy bitterness. Falling dizzily in a delirium of joy, then caught by bare-chested men, all slick with sweat from heat and exertion, and sticky from trickles and splashes of sweet, resinous wine.

The seigneur's memory showed Taresa a happy man, joyous with his friends, like the memory she'd seen when he killed the wild boar. He slapped her shoulder, the way he had Qasim. "Come in where it's warm, *jeune homme,* and tell me your stories."

A profound feeling flowed through her, warming her blood, tugging at sinews. Taresa hadn't felt that sensation grip her since she'd been welcomed outside Barcelona by the laundry women from Pedro's army.

Invincible. Profoundly safe. Happy to be in this world.

However, this rose-gold French lord was not the warrior in Blanca's comforting memories of her *bien-aimé.* Nor had Giles de Nully appeared in that woman's heated memories of aroused passion, memories sprung free when Blanca first saw Yusuf.

¤

Unlike the baron's *domus*, the servants at the silvery seigneur's castle were well-dressed and well-fed. Some took charge of the travelers' horses, others carried the travelers' gear out of the rain. One fellow led Kalypso's men to the kitchen and promised beds in the barracks.

"Inside where it's warm" proved to be a great hall much larger and finer than Baron Ricart's modest gallery. A fire burned in the mammoth fireplace, even though it was September.

"Too comfortable," Qasim said. "Makes me want to sleep here instead of riding on to Cahors in the rain."

Their host, also unlike Ricart, was generous with his candles, many of which were real beeswax rather than tallow, so the room smelled warm and welcoming. The fireplace had been newly relined with clean, smooth stones; its face was shaped from white limestone that must have been transported a considerable distance; these weren't limestone hills they'd ridden through.

One alcove to the side had been lined with planks of oak. A bench set between two shelves for books held embroidered cushions. A rug, probably from the docks of Narbonne, newly arrived from the Outremer, covered the alcove's flagstones.

The rest of the room, its freshly whitewashed walls gleaming in the candlelight, had carvings and tapestries hung in all the places that old crusaders would hang their weapons. Half the carvings were hawks—in flight, at rest, seizing prey. The others were gargoyles and woods creatures. Ornately carved chairs held linen-covered cushions. No weapons on the wall. In fact, a stand by the fireplace held the only iron in the room, the tools for poking red-hot oak logs.

More servants appeared, focused on making Blanca comfortable with a blanket and seated near the fire. While Blanca was making introductions, Kalypso accepted a mug of hot wine. Soon, they all held clay mugs of hot wine.

Yusuf and Qasim still hung near the door. Yusuf looked drained. Qasim kept glancing between Blanca and Yusuf, as deciding which most needed his attention, then decided on Yusuf.

"Brother," Taresa murmured, not intending to draw attention. "Did you take ill in the rain? Do you need the healer?"

"No need for herbs from a hedge-witch." Yusuf's voice reported exhaustion, even if he denied being ill. He held out that coin Milon had dropped in Ricart's barn. "Qasim, take this away from me. My bones have felt pulled from their sinews since you picked it up this morning."

"Is this coin magic?" Qasim accepted the heretics' gold coin, the snake shining in the candlelight. Identical to the one in Taresa's glove.

"No, it just reminds me of what's being done to heretics in this part of the world. Not magic. There's no—"

"—such thing as magic," Qasim and Taresa finished for him.

Near the fire, Giles offered an intimate toast to Blanca. "*À votre santé.*" Then, as if having remembered that others were present, he called them over and toasted good health to Taresa and her friends. "*À votre santé.*"

"*Et à la vôtre,*" Taresa said. Qasim's eyes searched between the toasters, not understanding the French. Yusuf seemed to have lost his newly learned French and to need more help for his health than Blanca did. Taresa spoke to Kalypso in a patois of French and the local tongue, "*Et vous, ma dòmna,* for keeping the world well."

"*Pour garder le monde bien.*" Giles repeated the words as if pondering them, then lifted his mug to the healer. "We would be in chaos, but for kind people such as you, senhóra. *À votre santé.*"

Taresa drank a drop of the hot wine, which was as over-sweet and resinous as the wine she'd tasted in Giles's memory. Qasim wrinkled his nose after sipping it, then gulped a second swallow. Yusuf mirrored that reaction, his nostrils flaring, but he didn't gulp after the first sip.

Giles's servants scrambled to assemble trestle tables and dragged benches from the walls to seat everyone. Giles arranged so that Blanca sat as queen of the feast, and he and Kalypso at her right and left hand. Yusuf sat by Kalypso, Qasim alongside Giles, leaving Taresa at the table's end, observing them all—and hoping that Kalypso felt Yusuf's heat and malaise and might know what to do for him.

More hot spiced wine was poured.

"Now you must all sing for your supper, like troubadours," Giles said. "We get little news up here in the wilderness. I'm eager to hear your adventures. *Ma dòmna?* Your tale?"

Every time Giles spoke to Blanca, he touched her hand. Or her arm. Or the gold filigree knit-basket that held her hair. Blanca held her breath in pleasure at each touch and then sighed, flattered, comforted. And expecting his attention.

"We've had a series of adventures." Blanca set aside her wine to tell the story. "I'd intended to stay at the monastery hostel on my way here. But the Templars purchased the monks' farm. Can you believe it? Now women travelers are—"

"Cast into the night?" Giles shook his head, rueful and dismayed for her sake.

"Yes. And so we sought shelter last night with Ricart de Marais."

"Not what I'd advise," Giles said. "He doesn't seem to understand local traditions of paratge and hospitality required of seigneurs."

"I'm sure Ricart tried," Blanca said. "But his *domus* is in ruins. He must not have had a brass bezant to his name."

"Many southern seigneurs have endured hard years." Giles seemed uninterested in Ricart's travails.

"Ricart did not endure," Blanca said. "Your old friend Milon de Breteuil appeared this morning with a small troop of heretic hunters."

"Milon? Haven't seen him since Constantinople." Giles sipped his wine, so Taresa couldn't detect his reaction to mention of Pedro's killer. "Heretic hunter, eh? Simon de Montfort is his cousin, but Milon never seemed a fervent believer."

Blanca stroked the back of Giles's hand where it rested on his cup of wine. "Milon felt fervent enough this morning that he cut Ricart down with his sword, calling him a heretic."

"*Mon Dieu!*" Surprised, Giles struggled against spilling his wine, had to wipe his lips with a finger. Yusuf seemed just as startled, though he'd witnessed that assassination.

"And his henchmen killed my guards." Blanca pouted, the first emotion she'd shown over her dead and injured guards.

"Barbarous! Killed your guards? How did you make it here?"

"Who knows where I'd be if not for my friends." Blanca swept her talkative hands to include *los tres amics*. Qasim twitched a smile in response, Yusuf nodded solemnly. Taresa kept the reins on all the rancor she felt for Blanca, especially for deserting her injured guards.

"*Mon amis,* I salute you as heroes." Giles raised his cup again. "To masters Castor and Tarek and Don Josep."

Qasim said, "It's mere luck that we were the last men standing."

"This morning's business wasn't noble," Taresa said. "No one acted like a hero."

"*Ai,* modest gentlemen of the south. True paratge." Giles still praised them in spite of Taresa's denial.

"We aren't from this part of Christendom," Taresa answered, as she always did.

"I do remember that you told me you hailed from Girona. So please tell me I'm not compromising my immortal soul by entertaining heretics." Giles's mouth tilted into the lop-sided smile he offered everyone except Blanca.

Blanca laughed, giving Giles's hand a playful slap. "I'm not compromising your soul any more than I ever have."

Kalypso fingered a silver cross that hung around her neck, but didn't answer Giles's joking question.

Taresa checked Yusuf and Qasim, where the servant was pouring wine, hoping they had no inclination to answer, since she wasn't sure either of them believed anything at all.

Qasim stroked the side of his wine cup, smiling when attention came his way, but otherwise studying all the wood and stone work in the room while assessing Yusuf's well-being.

Yusuf murmured an answer to whatever Kalypso murmured in his ear, showing her the callous on his left hand. "I make my way as a scribe."

Giles didn't let go of his curiosity, however. "What do they believe where you come from, Master Tarek? Girona is in Aragón?"

"We call our part of the world Catalunya," Taresa said.

Kalypso tilted her head, asking Yusuf, "Where do you come from, Don Josep? Not Girona, from your accent."

"You might say I'm a native of the road," Yusuf said. "I've been traveling as a scholar for so many years, I don't have a single place that I call my own home."

"*Ai, fadrin.*" Kalypso answered warmly. "I lived that way for twenty years. I hope you find succor when you reach your true home, like I have."

This was the most Kalypso had revealed about herself since they'd met. Twenty years living on the road! Taresa longed in every muscle to ask about that life.

"What a tale that must be!" Giles exclaimed. "Indeed, I did ask you to sing for your supper."

Kalypso said, "I must decline tonight. It's been a busy day."

"I shall sing," Yusuf said. "I have noble companions, but Tarek sings like a crow, and Castor is mute as a...swan. Do you want to hear songs I learned last year with the army in Andalusia?"

Ah, brilliant! Taresa wanted to praise Yusuf for diverting Giles's probing interest in their homelands, their destination, their spirituality.

¤

Yusuf first sang about the ancient hero Roland, but from a version that Sebastián's Catalan fighters had concocted to insult *ultra-montana* soldiers on the journey into Andalusia. That choice didn't put Taresa at ease, since all her attention was taken up by guessing whether in fact they'd found safety at Blanca's lover's castle. If Yusuf had consulted her, she'd assert that insulting a French host wasn't a strategic choice.

However, singing seemed to restore Yusuf's energy. The beautiful Blanca was not taken by the song, perhaps didn't even understand it, but her lover Giles seemed entranced from the first chorus, not taking his eyes from Yusuf, though his hand still rested on Blanca's, his arm around her shoulders at times.

Taresa, watching Giles, couldn't detect that the French knight took offense at the song's story, ridiculing Frankish fighters who couldn't pass both ways over the Pyrenees without getting themselves killed. Giles caught Taresa watching and winked, a finger tapping the side of his nose to indicate his amusement. He stroked Blanca's hand when she again demanded his attention.

"In addition to insulting our heroes, can you sing in French, Don Josep?" Giles sounded warm, good-humored. "Did your travels ever take you among the Franks?"

Yusuf bowed the way he did when entertaining high lords. "Everyone east of the Rhône sent fighters to Andalusia last year, monsieur. I learned songs in many tongues."

He sang one men begged for every night on the journey home, a too-sentimental *cançó de cruzado* about the loss of Jerusalem, accentuating the sad tones in the French song as if it were about the pangs of a lost lover.

After the first chorus, Giles silently applauded Yusuf, appreciating the singer and his choices.

Qasim, of course, listened as he always did when Yusuf sang, the way you're supposed to attend when the priest says mass, because the heavens are raining blessings. Although following Pedro's instructions for this journey in most everything, Taresa never considered coaxing Qasim into masking the depth of his friendship with Yusuf—how could she, when she longed to be bonded in a faithful brotherhood? Here at the two towers, she watched Giles assessing Qasim's rapt attention to the singer. His lips twitched into an appreciative smile that brightened his face.

Kalypso listened the way men in the camp did every night, as if Yusuf sang tales of her own heart. Kalypso first wiped a tear at the same place in the song of lost Jerusalem where Yusuf brought grown men to tears—at least, Catalan men, who always weep when they feel strongly about love or loss. This austere lady gave into her feelings, deeply affected by Yusuf's haunting tones.

Blanca, however, still stroked Giles's hand, seeking his attention, offering her cup to beg more wine, tugging his sleeve. Giles ran a finger along her jaw, gently twisted a lock of her hair. But he kept his attention on the singer, as entranced as Kalypso. Giles's face shifted with the emotions in the song; he swiped his hand over his eyes, wiping tears. Seeing him moved by Yusuf's music led Taresa to feel better about her host than she did about his lady-love. She wasn't yet prepared to believe *los tres amics* were safe here, but she no longer feared what Blanca might have dragged them into with her trickery.

When Yusuf sang the final chorus, Kalypso hid her face in her hands.

Over the long final notes of sadness, Yusuf's voice remained steady. But one finger trembled above his wine cup. Yusuf needed to eat. He needed to rest. In all likelihood, he needed medicines from

Kalypso's satchel. How could Yusuf make it all the way to Paris without Taresa alongside to notice that he needed care?

¤

Servants returned from the kitchens with hot food, a true feast after the trail biscuits and burned lentils they'd endured since Toulouse. The food absorbed all of Qasim's attention. He piled his trencher with roast pork basted in sweet wine, adding one more heap of chickpeas stewed with what must be the local style of bacon.

Yusuf accepted the sautéed fennel and mushrooms with leeks and declined both the roast pork and the bacon-and-peas, though Taresa had never seen Yusuf avoid meat. At Kalypso's urging, he took two barley rusks when the servants offered, but ate them dry.

Taresa dipped a barley rusk in a dish of oil, which proved to be melted butter, and found the rusks sweet, yet leaving the burn of cinnamon on her tongue. Between hot wine and food nagging her to consume it, she listened to what Blanca and Giles shared.

Giles seemed to notice that Taresa enjoyed the rusks. "You like the *paximadia*, Master Tarek? My cook learned to make these in Venice, on our way to Constantinople."

"That's a decade ago, beloved." Blanca laid her hand over his. "We were children then."

"You were, my dear. Constantinople was my last brush with heroes. I'm now retired from the wide world."

Though Taresa had few markers for guessing Blanca's age, ten years ago that woman must have been well beyond childhood and already well-practiced at seduction.

"Heroes?" Blanca chided Giles, waving a single elegant finger. "I knew the kind of men who went to Constantinople. Few were heroes. Most were plunderers, no better than pirates."

"Yet I'm a fool for nostalgia, for the days when we valiantly traveled on crusade." Giles seized Blanca's chiding finger and kissed it. "Do they have a word for that in the local tongue? Or is nostalgia a peculiar French notion of romance?"

"It's the same word," Taresa said. "Differently inflected. Perhaps not an emotion that people in the Languedoc entertain in their current peril."

Giles lent Taresa a tight smile, but plunged on, dipping into his own memories. "I cherish a romantic memory of the years I traveled with real warriors. At my table, we eat barley rusks to honor what soldiers have endured for the sake of Christendom."

Still wanting to know where Giles's loyalties lay, and how safe *los tres amics* were in this house, Taresa raised her wine cup. "We all honor what soldiers endure for the sake of Christendom."

Everyone raised their cup, though Yusuf seemed to barely have strength to lift his.

"The question everyone in the countryside must be asking," Taresa ventured, "is which soldiers are now serving Christendom. Aren't both Aragón and French armies made up of good Catholics?"

Kalypso laid aside her barley-and-cinnamon rusk after a single bite. "Monsieur Giles, may I beg your mercy to conclude the night? It's been a wearying day, and I need to seek the bed you offered."

"Of course, *ma dòmna*." Giles came around the table to offer Kalypso his hand, then motioned for a servant to guide her to a bedchamber. "It's wearying for women to listen to crusaders' stories."

"Not at all. And I must say, you've made this into a lovely hall, senhór. I hope all of your *domus* is faring as well." Kalypso's voice trailed off when she followed a servant out of the room.

Taresa wondered, not knowing Kalypso at all, if perhaps the healer preferred not to listen to glorification of crusaders after spending the day sawing limbs and stitching up men. When Giles sat at the table again, Taresa's question remained unanswered. Blanca rushed to change the subject, as if she and Kalypso both declined to hear the answer.

"Indeed, my love," Blanca said. "Your house is as beautiful as you insisted last winter in Avignon. The tapestries alone must have cost half your fortune."

"Its beauty is your punishment." Giles kissed Blanca's fingers again. "Because you waited so long to come to me."

"You've newly taken this castle, senhór?" Taresa asked in the local tongue, seeking a departure from the excessive love-making she'd been forced to witness, though *los tres amics* were intruders, uninvited guests. "Did you lose family and therefore inherited? Or did you conquer the former seigneur in armed combat?"

"*Ai*, no, Master Tarek." Giles turned that ten-candle smile on her. "I bought an abandoned holding from the count. The former seigneur died without heirs. It's a sad story that a husband and wife ended their days with no children or even cousins to claim the land."

"And therefore," Taresa persisted, "not a reward for participating in Simon's crusade?"

"No, all I've offered Simon is help in understanding the ways of the south, its customs and traditions." Giles glanced up, thoughtful, pondering an idea that must include her unanswered question. "I've long thought that if Simon could grasp the ideals of paratge, of honor and fidelity, then peace would quickly return to this land."

"The sole combat Giles endures now is with the law, helping to defend seigneurs when adversaries try to seize their land." Blanca traced the back of Giles's hand with her little finger. The seigneur's hands looked twenty years younger than what must be his age, except for large, raw knuckles. "His weapons are parchment scrolls and vellum bound into volumes. Do you even keep an armory in this house, *mon ami*?"

"I preserved the weapons of the previous owner," Giles said. "To show respect for true warriors."

"And I'm hoping you'll be a warrior of the law, to fight for me." Blanca leaned close to Giles again. A total stranger might think she was helpless.

Taresa tried another blunt question. "You have this castle from the count of Toulouse, but you serve Simon in the courts? Is that awkward?"

Giles turned his full-of-light smile upon Taresa, letting go of Blanca's hand to tap the table top. "God gave Raymond of Toulouse the job of protecting the people here. And He gave Simon the job of enforcing Church law. If the two diverge, then it's a matter for debate in the courts, not for taking up arms. As I learned in Constantinople, I'm much better at arguing than I am at armed combat."

"Would you surrender people from your land to the heretic hunters?" Even while Taresa asked the question, it was as she heard Sebastián, Yusuf, and Qasim calling for her to shut up in several languages.

"I've been successful here," Giles said, again with the full-sun smile, "at convincing false believers to return to the Church. I remain convinced that kind and truthful argument is better than the sword for changing people's minds."

"So, never?" she persisted.

"I shall never face the dilemma." Giles became solemn, touched his heart as if he'd made a vow. Then he returned his attention to Blanca, who'd begun to pout at his abandonment.

Taresa let a bite of chickpeas and bacon dissolve on her tongue, soft, savory. A crumb caught in her throat, forcing a cough, which she attributed to being unable to swallow how Blanca sought to ensorcel Giles, having unknotted the ropes she'd used to pull Taresa and Yusuf and Qasim to her, no longer needing them. Further, Blanca's "broken" arm didn't seem to trouble her at all once she'd provoked everyone to ride to Giles's house. Which meant that Blanca had needlessly interrupted the important work Kalypso performed by the river, behind the merchants' wagons, and led Taresa and her friends away from their quest.

Taresa squeezed her nose to repress a sneeze.

Rather than a magical, already-lived moment, Taresa had to endure yet more kissing hands and soft touches between the handsome seigneur and a simpering woman who hadn't bothered to look over her shoulder with regret when her guards died. Giles held all the correct values for a seigneur, praising paratge and offering openhanded hospitality. But Taresa felt disappointed that he'd wandered into Blanca's trap; it called his judgment into question.

Blanca dragged her little finger along the side of Giles's hand. Trying not to roll her eyes, Taresa looked up to the rafters. A gargoyle peeked at them where the walls met the upper-floor timbers. Carved from a sweet chestnut tree, a wide-eyed wooden man in a foreign-looking hood leaned over the room, a bag of coins in one hands, a wine chalice in the other. The gargoyle's mischievous expression convinced Taresa to yield to compulsion and interrupt the *canço d'amor* Blanca and Giles played together.

"Do you prefer *cançós de guèrra* above other songs?"

"I shall always offer praise and gratitude for the true heroes and crusaders of old." Giles shook out more drops of nostalgia.

"Like Roland? Or like the Cid of Valencia?" Taresa asked, stewing in antipathy for Blanca, the heartless seductress. "Or Achilles? Was it Perseus who killed Medusa?"

A flicker of confusion crossed Giles's handsome face. "I believe Perseus slayed the minotaur. But Roland and the Cid were true heroes of Christendom. However, it's a long time since I listened to aged sergeants telling stories around the campfire."

Taresa masked her disappointment. Blanca didn't hide her boredom. She once more tapped Giles's finger for attention. "Like our healer, I too seek to enjoy your hospitality. It has been an exhausting day. Do you have a bedchamber for me?"

Giles leaped up at the request. "Of course, *ma dòmna*. You've come to my house like the heroine in a song. Let's see if you approve of the bedchamber my people prepared for you."

He led Blanca to where stone stairs climbed into the upper reaches of the tower. She leaned against Giles like the distressed lady in a troubadour's song, clutching his elbow for strength.

14
Castle in the Clouds

"THIS SEIGNEUR IS NOT YOUR secret Perseus who'll help us get to Paris." Taresa spoke as soon as *los tres amics* were alone.

"Disappointing." Qasim gnawed a roasted songbird. "Though he seems nice."

"My own *Sensus Naturae* proved true," Yusuf said. "Perhaps I was a woman in a former life."

Taresa let that flow off her like the day's rainfall. "I'm going to check the horses. We may be safe here, but I'm not convinced. We need to ride for Cahors as soon as they're rested."

"I'll come along." Qasim rose, still holding the roasted songbird in his hands.

"No, stay with Yusuf and finish eating."

"I'm sure *le gai sauvatge* is safe here," Qasim said.

"Not if Blanca decides to eat him for dessert." Taresa didn't hide her distrust of Blanca.

"She's devouring your seigneur boyfriend," Qasim said. "She cannot desire more than the sweetness our host heaps on her."

"No, *belette muet.*" Yusuf yawned, shook all over, then rubbed his eyes. "Blanca pushed our host into all those embraces, mostly by feigning injury."

"Feigning?" Qasim chewed on this idea.

"That fabulous stunt with her horse?" Yusuf said. "It forced us to go where she wanted."

"Shall we take our horses and go now?" Taresa asked, gratified that Yusuf saw through Blanca's seductive ways.

"I want to say yes." Yusuf yawned again. Qasim looked wary. "But we all need rest, even though this house makes me uneasy. As if the earth itself is pulling at my bones."

"Do you feel ill?" Taresa asked, though Yusuf typically resented the question.

"I feel that I'm not real." He toyed with his wine cup. "The world is foggy, not because of the rain, but like in a dream where it's snowing. Needles and pins sting my arms and legs. My stomach keeps flipping, and my heart won't beat, until it suddenly races and pounds in my ears so I can't hear."

"Then you are ill."

"No. Most of the time I'm outside my body, watching."

Taresa struggled to piece together what Yusuf reported. "Is it this house that bothers you? Or are you possessed of devils?"

Qasim had that heretics' coin out, studying it. "You'd think I'd be the one prone to devil possession, given how easy it is for either of you to convince me that things aren't what they seem. But this house is warm and pleasant. And this coin from Ricart's stable that you gave me? It isn't pulling me in one way or another." He pocketed the coin and turned his attention back to the food in front of him. "I say we sleep here."

"I wish we didn't have to. We've lost a night and a day already by galloping down false trails," Taresa said. "Let's forget Perseus and go on to Paris tomorrow."

Yusuf yawned a third time. "We need Perseus to help make sure Philippe *le Roi* listens. We need Philippe to hear how important our mission is, to rescue Aragón's baby-king and stop Simon from making himself king." He sipped the resinous wine, frowning at its bitterness. "And you need to return to Toulouse, as Pedro planned."

Taresa snatched three apples from a bowl, so the horses might also take joy from Giles's grand dinner table. "We'll leave before dawn. Since we don't have to wait for the imperial lady to join us."

"That gives us one final day to enjoy Taresa telling us what to do." Qasim dipped a barley-cinnamon rusk in the now-congealing butter.

¤

The sun had set. Lamplight from the castle and from the servants' shaded lanterns cast argumentative spears of light, crossing and then abandoning each other.

Rain no longer fell. Instead, the wet hung in the air, not quite a mist, not quite fog. And the stable lay back down the hill, alongside the lesser tower they'd passed when they entered the compound. The servants here must endure extra toils, trudging between two towers. Taresa set out for the stables, walking toward lantern light that must come from the second tower.

The warm food in her belly could not smother the cold stone of anger that had lodged there since the night before. Yet Taresa wasn't a person who walked around angry all the time. The anger wasn't just from resenting Blanca's manipulation—except that the lady would enjoy sleeping with her lover that night, while Taresa would once more wrap her arms around Sebastián's shirt, trying to rest beside *los dos amics,* who tended to shut her out of their private world.

Her heart clenched into a fist and that cold stone nestled in her belly for one reason.

Pedro was dead. Killed.

The world had changed forever.

She hadn't felt such a perpetual nagging at her heart when her ancient father died. Or when her childhood friend Felip had been killed in Andalusia. Pedro was dead, and this chaotic world had to be built again anew. But grief kept her from starting the work of rebuilding. She could not manage to roll away that cold stone.

Because the king-killer had spread a cloak of grief over all the Languedoc.

Along with the butchery of thousands of soldiers, and hundreds left hiding in the wilderness, hoping not to die.

And along with thousands left orphaned, like those feral children who stole Sebastián's sword, who needed silver to buy food to feed infants who were younger, hungrier, and more miserable than their caretakers.

Perhaps the king-killer robbed that sobbing boy in the Templars' barn of his life too. Heretic hunters had parted that boy from his grandmother, who'd fled into the wilderness because she was a goodwoman, a heretic.

What paratge meant, Sebastián told her, was that they were all connected, each person to another, and each *domus* to its neighbors, each count or marquis or seigneur to the others. And the king-killer had frayed the binding cord of honor by cutting down a king.

A sound she'd never heard before escaped Taresa's throat, more than a sob, the sound of a rift in the ties that joined heaven and earth.

They'd murdered a king.

To steal the Languedoc.

To send people fleeing in terror from their own lands.

However, if she couldn't persuade them otherwise, then Yusuf and Qasim would continue on to Paris and she'd be sent home. She felt her heart like a fist of anger, punching in her chest. There had to be a way to go to Paris and yet also pursue justice for Pedro.

She'd walked around the first tower, unsure if she'd set off in the wrong direction, too consumed with thoughts of how God let evil angels toss dice with the fates of innocent people. Candlelight spilled from a window high up the tower wall, its shutters flung open in spite of the November-in-September weather. Blanca's voice drifted out with the candlelight.

"I'm here, and I'm saying yes."

"I'm thrilled. Should we toast to all the good things that will come to our partnership, *ma dòmna*? Ready to claim your rightful lands?"

"Not yet. I have a duty to Maria. She was a friend to both of us. Will you help me?"

The seigneur's melodious voice vibrated on the night air. "I'm prepared to move mountains for you, *ma dòmna*. Any mountain you might choose."

"And you haven't fallen in love with that fey boy? You never used to appreciate music like you did tonight."

"Don't tease. I'm sorry for him, being sent away by his family. That's how I ended up in the Outremer."

"You were a child in the Outremer," Blanca teased.

"Hardly. I was as old as that young man."

"Prettier," Blanca said.

"You're flattering me, *ma dòmna*." Silence for a moment. "Any decent papa should spend his gold to keep such a pretty boy safe. Unlike my father, who sent me off to sweat and die in the Outremer.

And like most men back then, I never saw Jerusalem. Pray God that his father will do better by that boy than mine did me."

Interesting. The wealthy and elegant seigneur began as an exiled prodigal. What had been his youthful transgression?

"You saw the quality of their clothes. And their horses. That boy doesn't have to pray to God for a better life." Blanca's voice warbled with laughter. "All three boys insist they know just what they're doing, without praying for help."

Pray for help? Taresa didn't believe that prayer would help a world in chaos or help *los tres amics* who'd be pulled away from their journey's goal. She prayed, certainly, the way the Roman priests taught. She knew when to bend her head at mass and when to lift her eyes to heaven. In fact, she liked mass, which was a good thing because the priests were declaring the need for mass every fourth day besides Sunday and feast days on that journey to Andalusia. She liked the priest's words in the mass, which sounded like a language from an imaginary land.

She could recite the prayers as well as anyone in the baggage train, but what she didn't understand were the ones that Yusuf called "prayers of supplication and intercession," when you ask God to do something for you or someone else. From what she saw, there was no telling that such supplications were heard or answered. For example, the ancient crusaders they'd met had prayed for God's help before every battle—but so did the Saracens. And often as not, the soldiers praying in Latin were losing battles in the Outremer. In fact, the battle at Las Navas de la Tolosa was one of the first in years where God granted victory to the soldiers who prayed in Latin.

Whom could she ask for guidance? The women in the baggage train claimed that anyone with a decent mother knew the power of prayer. When Pedro overheard her discussing prayer with Yusuf, he insisted they stop playing with heresy, and if Yusuf didn't have enough to keep busy, he could finish that copy of St-John's gospel the king had commissioned.

The only person who agreed with Taresa—that is, agreed that supplication was a puzzling question—was Sebastián. His mother prayed, but he had a grandfather and a stepfather who maintained that you go along with the Roman priests because any other action is too costly. That was among the first of many things she and Sebastián came to agree on, that they liked standing in the morning sun and hearing voices swelling in prayer across the wild expanses of La Mancha. "We cry 'God save us!' with everyone else," Sebastián said. "But my grandfather said God seems to save the man who moves his ass to save himself."

The Valerós chaplain, Father Anselm, overheard Sebastián repeating what his grandfather claimed, but the chaplain wasn't a censorious kind of religious man like most priests. He said, "It seems confusing because you hear people petitioning God for all sorts of things. But you'll see soon enough in this life, there's only one thing to ask for."

"Don't say 'salvation,'" Sebastián argued. "Because we get that by believing the Creed."

"No. Just ask for peace. Your own private personal peace."

Pray for peace? Pedro—who mostly certainly prayed for victory before the battle at Muret—was dead, and now there would be no peace.

¤

Taresa shivered in the cold damp, lost the sound of Blanca's and Giles's voices, and walked toward distant lantern light through the heavy mist. She ended up at a well near the path.

An old man bent to raise the well's bucket and rested it on the edge of the well. He lifted the lantern, peered inside the bucket, sloshed its contents, and then fished something from within it. When he shook away water, it proved to be a heavy iron cross on a rusting chain.

She hailed him in the local tongue. "*Hola! Bon nuit!* Can you point me to the stables?"

The man turned to answer, his hand raised in greeting. She'd guessed he was old because, even in the thin lantern light, his hair appeared whiter than sea foam. Up close, he proved to be skeletal and pale, the kind of old person who seemed drained of blood, moving solely on sinew and memory.

"You are one of the lord's friends come visiting?" His breath hung as a white veil of mist when he spoke, his voice rheumy. A similar veil hung over the well, as if it breathed out its own mist into the September damp.

"Guests. We've strangers here." Taresa pointed to the bucket and cross. "Purifying the waters from ghosts?"

"Shall you laugh at us, master, for our country ways?" He set down the bucket and began wrestling the well's wooden cover back into place.

"Not at all," Taresa said. "The senhóra who lived next door to me purified her well every feast day. Surely she knew her own ghosts."

"You believe ghosts walk among us?" The old man paused in his labors, the wooden cover a third of the way across the well. His wild brows climbed up his forehead. Taresa shivered again—because of the cold, she hoped, not because of the intensity of the old man's question.

"Not like the tales told to frighten children." She grabbed an edge of the well cover to help him. "But spirits linger after tragedy. I've seen them. It's sad, not frightening."

"*Ai*, then you know a bit about this world." The old man nodded, reassuring himself.

"This *domus* suffered tragedy?"

"*Òc*, seems eons past now, like in a poet's long song about heroes gone before us. A master of this *domus* was tricked by his enemies, killed with his own sword, and then his wife tossed into this very well."

"Leaping goats!" That veil of mist over the open well was more than weather. She and the old man finally slid the cover so that it thudded into place. "It's only natural, that a devoted wife will linger."

"No one who knew her could forget her grief. Let me take you to the stable. Though I promise you, there's no place on earth where your animals will be so well tended."

She followed the ancient figure through the night-mist. At least Qasim would sleep peacefully that night with the news that their horses basked in luxury.

The old man pointed to the stable, but stopped outside where a tile-shingled shed covered a goat yard. When the man reached over the fence, wiggling his fingers, five goats galloped toward him, bashing into each other, colliding with the fence, needing more than anything else in this life for the old man to scratch their heads. Taresa forgot the horses, and just about everything else, to join in petting goats.

For a few moments, the old man addressed the goats in baby-talk. Then, without looking her way, the old man spoke low. "You cried '*Saltant cabres*' in surprise at the well."

Taresa ran a knuckle down the boney part of a brown-and-white speckled goat who'd leaped for her attention. "I try not to utter oaths with the Lord's name."

"We're happy to see any friend of the Good God."

He offered the goodmen's common greeting, in the local tongue. In this new world of chaos, she didn't know how to show acceptance of a person's so-called heresy, while not committing to being one of them. She dodged.

"My uncle used to cry, '*Saltant cabres*.' I'm from Girona. We don't know all the customs in this country."

"*Ai*, master. We are all strangers now, in this new world. You and I—" The old man stepped back from the fence, looking over her shoulder, and then bent his head in a submissive bow.

"Should I let you near my stables, Master Tarek?" Giles startled her, speaking close behind her, his voice like the plucked tenor notes of a fine-built lute. "You burned the Templars' barn and killed men in Ricart's stable. What risk do I take with you?"

¤

"You fed us better than the Templars or Ricart did. So, you can trust us, at least until we see what kind of breakfast we get." Taresa forced a teasing note into her voice; however, she must have betrayed that he'd startled her, because he stroked her shoulder as if to calm her.

"*J'rigole, mon ami.*" Giles, claiming he jested, flicked his silver hair away from his face. "I trust you. I came to ask my captain to ride to Ricart's *domus*, to find anyone who might need help."

While Taresa was busy letting a goat lick the traces of dinner from her hand and yet keeping her fingers intact, Giles gave orders to the old man, to be delivered to his captain. Six men were to ride to Ricart's castle at dawn.

"And I'd hoped for a private word with you, Master Tarek."

"*Moi, monsieur?*" She answered him in French, and that's how the conversation continued.

"As I see it, Don Josep is your company's intellect, and Castor is his *garde du corps*. Are you responsible for common sense?"

"You might say so." She offered the friendly smile that the baggage women said would keep her safe everywhere. "However, Josep can find an argument amid all of his philosophy to persuade you otherwise. And Castor will fight you if you harm his horse."

He shared the smile he usually saved for Blanca. "In all seriousness, Master Tarek. I'm sure Girona did not send a fool into our country. Tell me what happened at Ricart's castle."

"I'm flattered." She liked being flattered; she wasn't going to get it from her friends. "We went there at your lady's insistence, seeking refuge after the monastery fire."

She repeated the basic story, but omitted the details, like the scene in the Templars' barn and the poor dead boy.

"She had her guards with her when you first met?" Giles dropped the friendly banter and became an earnest interrogator. "Were they from Avignon, too? Christians? Or heretics? Or what?"

"I don't know. The four of them spoke the local tongue. They weren't friendly. Didn't even tell us their names. Does it matter?"

"I want to understand, since I shall now be defending my lady. You will ride on to Paris, but I've made promises to the lady of Avignon. I'll be here answering questions about the mishaps that pursue her."

"Of course." The goat who had her attention liked the bridge of his nose scratched. "May I congratulate you? I understand you are to be married. May God and our Holy Mother rain blessings down on you."

"*Merci.* She and I share ambitions, and we shall need all the blessings we can garner." While he spoke, the goat whose nose Giles was rubbing jumped at him, trying for a button on Giles's vest. He shoved its face away, scratching the back of its head. "Now, tell me. Who attacked first? Who died in the fight?"

"Her guards provoked a quarrel with us. We all had weapons in hand when Milon de Breteuil appeared with some French soldiers and a couple of—ow!" A goat nipped her fingers before she'd decided whether to share Yusuf's guess that the priests with Milon were defrocked. She concluded, "With heretic hunters who seemed to be priests." She again described the whole scene, who'd attacked whom, and which men were dead and which were alive when Blanca and *los tres amics* left the scene.

"Do you know Milon?" Giles continued to attend to a nuzzle-demanding goat.

"At the Templars' farm, we heard his tale of the battle at Muret. I guessed, but didn't know him for a heretic hunter then."

"And you three leaped to my lady's defense? You succeeded when her guards failed?"

"She spoke to defend us. But after Milon killed Ricart, he ordered everyone killed except for your lady. We merely defended ourselves."

"She must have been frightened out of her wits." Giles mused on this while scratching a smaller goat who'd been desolate at failing to gain his attention. "It's a blessing you could protect her."

"You know her better than I do," Taresa said. "Me, I suspect nothing has ever frightened the good madam."

This produced a warm chuckle. The goat he petted seemed to think the musical laughter was meant for him and nuzzled for more scratching. "Fair enough, Master Tarek. More evidence of your common sense."

"Your lady has a way of commanding every situation. That's how we ended up here instead of continuing our own journey."

Giles shoved one nibbling goat aside to let a younger white-and-grey goat have a head rub.

"Excuse my bold question, Master Tarek, but I am woefully familiar with how troublesome sons are shipped away from home. I enjoyed a sunbaked tour of the Outremer and returned to the Pays de France with the sweating disease, all for the sake of my family's pride. That's why I want to know about the pretty scholar you're shepherding. Did he choose to go to Paris? Or did his family force the choice?"

"It is Don Josep's desire to further his studies in Paris."

"Oh? I just felt... that young man seems hag-ridden. The way he looks to you or his *bon amic* before speaking."

"The pair of them complain that I'm too..." hag ridden? "...overbearing. But a lord...from Girona promised that I'd be made a knight if I got Don Josep to Paris without calamity." That seemed approximately true. "We've galloped in the general vicinity of calamity since meeting your lady. Yet here we are, back on the road to Paris."

"I am happy for him. Not everyone is so fortunate."

This was her chance to satisfy her curiosity about Giles's prodigal past. She touched his hand, the way one soldier might touch another. His silk sleeve brushed her wrist and plunged her into a memory of an afternoon when Sebastián had entertained her while wearing nothing but a silk shirt he'd bought, intending to look like a lord at a court dinner with Pedro.

She sneezed, smelling Sebastián this time instead of burnt sugar-apples.

"*Oh, arrêtez, mon frere!*"

Giles gave up on the goats, staring at Taresa, amazed. After crying *stop*, he braced her shoulders.

"Do you feel it, too? The sensation that you and I said these very words before? Perhaps lived this moment in another life?"

15
Visions of Brotherhood

THE GOAT COULD HAVE EATEN all of Taresa's buttons in the time it took to sputter her way to a calm answer.

"Are you still probing my faith, monsieur? Because I'm not a heretic. I believe God grants us each but one life."

She got the words out, which seemed important to say, then sneezed again, the smell of burnt sugar-apples overwhelming the odor of goat. Giles's fingers dug into her shoulders, down to the bone, and whatever past or future life he saw flooded her senses.

> Sleeping rough in a burning desert, two men lay with hands close to their weapons, dozing yet hearing every noise in the night. Each reached an arm overhead, until they linked fingers, rubbed thumbs on each other's palms.
>
> Two men, so drenched in sweat that it smelled like piss, wrestling naked while a throng of other men shouted, ear-shattering screams:
>
> *Win, you lazy snake!*
> *I have all my money on you, you fetid swine!*
> *You must win or die!*
>
> Laughing, drunk, falling on each other in a dark alley where the people who cried from the windows above for silence spoke an unknown language. So drunk, needing to vomit, needing to...

Giles stared at her, frozen in surprise. "Did you see that?" He still had his hand on her shoulder.

"Òc, that brown-and-white one," she pointed to a small goat, "tends to be even more of a clown than the others." She closed her thoughts, like putting the lid on the well. His vision reminded her of life in the baggage train. Except Giles's memories of male brotherhood smelled worse. Yes, she'd seen it, but she wasn't going to share details of her lifelong affliction, reading people's memories.

"Do you believe that we've lived many lives?" Giles persisted. "That perhaps we might have been brothers once?"

"Like a heretic? No, I don't, monsieur."

The goats, having lost the humans' attention, took to running at each other, bashing heads and falling down. Except one, who leaped atop a manger, balanced there, and waited for the others to challenge him. She directed her thoughts and her expression to the goats, hoping to keep Giles at a distance.

"Master Tarek, I'm telling you too much about myself. You see, at times I'm sure I've lived a particular moment before. And just now, I saw us together like brothers, you and I, on the hot, miserable road to Acre."

"I wasn't born then, so it must have been some other man from Girona that you recognize. We never lose our Catalan accent. Castor says it sounds like I roll my tongue to the back of my mouth and try to swallow it."

"Remarkable." Giles released her and stepped back. He straightened his vest, then the sleeves of his silk shirt. "Did you come to check your horses? Please let me help."

She walked into the horse stable with Giles. While he chatted, she tried to make sense of his vision—they could not have shared a past, though it was pleasant to see memories of his close friendships. She intended to keep Giles out of her own memories.

From a covered bucket, Giles retrieved three lumps of date-sugar, holding them out to indicate treats for the horses. But then he pulled back when Taresa reached for them. He performed a bit of market-mummer's magic, making them disappear, then reappear, then disappear again. Though it was probably meant to be playful, she felt toyed with rather than entertained.

Taresa found the three horses that belonged to *los tres amics* and reached inside her jerkin for one of the stolen apples.

"Why do you want to be a knight?" Giles asked. "You long to be a hero?"

"No, it's simpler than that," Taresa said. "I have no sisters or brothers. My mother died when I was born, and I lost my father long before I came of age. What I long for is to be accepted among a principled body of fighters, who welcome me in as a…brother."

"I'm jealous of your journey to Paris." Giles gave the horse a lump of sugar before she had a chance to share the apple. "You might call it nostalgia. But that's not the right word. I bet you feel it, too, Master Tarek. It's why you signed on for this journey to Paris."

"I'm on this journey in hopes of becoming a knight."

"O noble youth!" He had his hand on her shoulder again. She steeled herself, not to shrug away while closing the lid on her thoughts. He said, "But it's because of your time with an army, long hot days of suffering and bad food, the thrill of the battlefield. The journey into Andalusia last year was the most exciting time in your life, wasn't it?"

"Perhaps."

"It's why you took this job, isn't it? To reclaim that thrill."

"I want to be a knight. I'm working to achieve that."

"But what if the future holds no similar thrills?" Giles seemed charged with emotion. "There's comes a twilight, when crows drop onto the battlefield. And all joy is lost."

"You didn't like life as a warrior?" She reined in any note of judgment, having married into a warrior's way of life. And she didn't want him reading her judgments.

"It wasn't my destiny. And bodies piled high in the stinking heat of summer never solve anything."

"Yet you miss that world," Taresa said. "Or you wouldn't be asking about my life."

She offered the other two horses the stolen apples from inside her jerkin and then prepared to work. Giles shadowed her—truly, since his shadow cut through the light of the lantern he'd hung by the stall.

"Tell me about being a soldier in Andalusia, Master Tarek. When did you first kill a man?"

¤

People didn't ask that question. At least, no one had ever asked Taresa. But it was easy to answer. "In Toledo. In the Easter riots last year."

"A sword then, hand to hand?" Giles sounded eager for details. "A brutal way to start a fighter's life."

"No. After dark we were sent around to dispatch the injured who had no hope to live another day."

"Cutting throats, then?" His voice trilled up.

She began to check the horses' hooves, though Qasim had taken time with them at the merchants' camp.

"I'm strong enough," Taresa answered without bragging, "I prefer breaking a man's neck. He's surprised, but not frightened. And he doesn't vomit blood on you."

Giles gripped her shoulder again, but she dodged away before he could dig in his fingers or send his memories to her. "You're the quiet kind, aren't you, Master Tarek? Do your friends know the deep river flowing within?"

"Don Josep and Castor don't know about my chores in Toledo. But they saw similar work at Las Navas de Tolosa." She finished scraping one hoof and then bent to attend another. Deep river? Was he indeed reading her memories? She shoved the imaginary lid more firmly in place, like the wooden cover on the well. "I was on death detail for that battle, too."

"Easing injured Christians' way into heaven."

"No, Saracens. With so many bodies, the kings commanded they be burned as quickly as possible. To keep the Christian camp from infection."

"But that means you're one of the heroes come home from crusade in Iberia, eh?"

"Òc." She couldn't judge Giles's tone. Her muscles screamed *Caution!* She shouldn't tell a stranger anything more. "I was lucky to come home alive after my...master died. Then I found new a new master."

"How did you like battling the Saracen? Did you enjoy the opportunity to take a good Christian blade to infidel flesh?" This question disturbed her to the core, but then Giles offered that lop-sided smile, which seemed to mean he was jesting.

"Are you teasing again, monsieur? I'm not yet a knight. If you traveled with an army, you know what my work was—clean and repair and bear burdens from one camp to the next. And on battle day, I pushed dead Saracens into pyres. And the Saracens who didn't die, they all ran away."

Another hoof done. The first horse was ready to ride in the morning. She skirted past Giles to check the next horse's hooves.

"Not like the Saracens we fought in the Outremer, then." Giles seemed to be musing on his own memories. But she didn't want to touch him to share.

"O monsieur! Your time in the Outremer makes my days in Iberia look like...the training yard," she said. Soldiers always defer to any crusader who'd fought in the Outremer. "Did you know Ricart de Marais there?"

Giles brushed the idea away with a wave of his hand. "I met Ricart here, as a neighbor. We were worlds apart in those days. I served an uncle who wouldn't let me ride as a full knight. I am sympathetic to how you were held back in Andalusia."

Giles continued asking about her travels, nostalgic about army life. She answered. They seemed to be friendly comrades.

Except: Giles kept touching her. Hands on her shoulders, seductive smiles, flattering words. He believed he spoke with Tarek of Girona, not Taresa. That heightened her wariness when he bent his head to hers in intimacy. Both Giles and Blanca were masters at deploying seduction as a siege engine, a weapon for conquest armed with deadly smiles.

He put his hand on Taresa's back, running his fingers up her spine. She could no longer tolerate the confusion about what he wanted from her. Therefore, she asked.

"Monsieur, do you want to sleep with me?"

¤

That didn't come across properly, judging from how wide Giles opened his eyes, how deeply he tilted that infernal smile.

"I don't mean that as an invitation, monsieur. I want to understand you."

"I'm French. We're friendly. But I don't want to sleep with you. I will soon have a wife who's more to my taste."

"Do you touch me to read my thoughts? My memories?"

"You are an extraordinary young man." This time he punched her arm, the way comrades do. "I've never heard of such a thing."

"In Iberia, one of the laundry women read men's memories by touching them. Your friendly ways remind me of her."

"Weren't baggage-train women touching you for more than to read your memories?"

"My master was strict, declared me too young." How had she let this tête-à-tête stray so far into the weeds?

"We're very much alike, you and I. Like how we care more and take better care of our friends than they care for us." When he smiled, she felt as wary as she had after Blanca kissed her. "But reading thoughts—like magic?—that's hedge-witch heresy, isn't it? Don't ever let a woman deceive you that way. Take advice from an old man like me."

"*Oui*, monsieur. Though you are far from an old man."

They'd reached a stall that held a horse so tall its head and haunches appeared above the sides of the stall. "Come take a look at Bucephalus."

Taresa felt she should recognize that name, so nodded, pretending. She let Giles drag her over there, though she wanted to be back with Yusuf and Qasim, wanted to share her uneasiness, to ask Yusuf how you could tell if a man possessed *Sensus Naturae*. Giles chatted on about his massive horse.

"I bought this great big beautiful beast off Odo, the Duke of Burgundy. His cousins are breeding up bigger destriers in the north, mating good stallions with farm horses. This big boy has served his time of the battlefield."

"Biting and kicking?" She hadn't seen it herself, but Sebastián complained about the stallions the *ultramontanos*—Frankish fighters—brought to Iberia.

"I haven't seen him do it, but I've heard his sons are battlefield fighters. Bucephalus is as retired as any general in Saladin's army. Now, his sole job is to work as a stud on my farm."

It was the largest horse she'd seen that wasn't pulling a load on a farm. "A lovely burnt-sugar color," she said.

"Caramel. Come see the blaze on his beautiful face."

He led the way into the stall, and she followed cautiously.

The hay in the loft tickled her nose. She sneezed.

The horse kicked.

Its hooves hit the stone side of the stall, not her.

But a wooden saddle fell from the top of the stall, banging the horse's hind quarters. It stepped sideways, shaking off either the pain or the weight, pinning Taresa to the side of the stall.

She hadn't taken a breath after sneezing, and now couldn't catch her breath. She bucked, pushing at the horse with her body, since her hands were trapped, gasping the whole time, not getting air. The horse resisted her push, crushing her further against the stall's stone wall.

Giles picked up the horse's hind quarters and moved the huge animal away from her.

Taresa sucked for air again. Two tries before she could breathe. Then she had to break away and vomit. She bent, hands on her knees, spitting to clear her mouth and throat.

When she stood, Giles was calming his horse, saying sweet things, offering a lump of sugar.

"You saved my life." She spit again.

"I'm sorry. Bucephalus didn't mean harm."

"Òc. I startled him." She sneezed again, sending a trail of vomit up her nose. She spit and blew her nose with her fingers.

"But you're fine?"

"You picked up that horse and moved it. Like magic."

"No, just gave him a shove. Not even Hercules could pick up that horse."

"But I saw you."

"While you were choking?" Giles tipped his lop-sided grin. "People can do amazing things in dire straits. But I just gave him a good hard shove. Bucephalus and I have an understanding. He does what I command. Like every animal I keep."

¤

On their way out of the stable, Giles asked if she wanted to see the mews for his falcons.

"Òc." That was about as much as she could say. She needed a moment to recover. She'd almost died. Not like being threatened in

E . A . S T E W A R T

Ricart's stable. But truly two heartbeats away from dying. Giles had his hand on her shoulder again. She moved away, because she didn't want to share his memories.

"I'm the sort of man who takes his falcons everywhere. If it's not my famous gyrfalcon, it's one of my dear merlins." Giles chatted, politely ignoring that she still had to calm herself. "My cadger is getting on in years. He's that fellow you met earlier at the well. He's no longer so keen on beating through the countryside."

"What's a cadger?"

"The fellow who keeps the traveling cage when we range away from home to hunt. You don't know?"

"Neither my old master nor my new one hunt with hawks."

"Alas for your poor fortune. If you pass this way again, when you are a knight, I'd be honored to teach you."

"Does your lady hunt?"

"Not yet. She's not enamored of birds, so I shall have to take time to teach her about their fine beauty and noble ways."

Around the other side of the tower, away from the goats and horses and dogs, a square shed stood up against the tower wall. Two of its sides were stone also, the front a woven wicket with a door. Perches stood in front of the shed. The shed's roof, like the goat pen, was tiled.

Giles lifted the punched-tin lantern he carried so she could better see his hawks' house. Gloves and other equipment hung under the shed's eaves.

"Peek in." He held the lantern near the wicket screen. His huge gyrfalcon sat on a perch in the center of the shed, its head hooded in black leather. "This bird is worth more than twice its weight in gold."

"He's a noble creature." What else could she say? Her impulse to return to Yusuf and Qasim was growing by the moment.

"I'm writing a book on falconry. Do you think your scholar friend, Don Josep, would help me with it?"

"You'd have to ask him. I can't speak for him."

"Now tell me, Master Tarek." Giles stepped away from the falcon's house. She followed him along the path to the other tower.

"*Oui*, monsieur?"

"I'd think that moment of jeopardy we shared—" Giles pointed back to the stable that held his caramel-colored, monster of a horse "—means we can trust each other. I like you. And I promise I don't want to sleep with you."

"Trust?"

"Yes. Don't we value the same things? Paratge. Strictly honoring our *domus* and our comrades in arms."

"It seems we do."

"I honor the way you guard your friends. You show more loyalty than one can purchase from a mercenary. When you pass this way on your journey home, please visit again. I'd like lure you into my employ, because you are a man I can trust. I can make you a knight if your master fails you. You'd live with my knights, who have their own confraternity, like brothers who trust each other to the gates of hell and back again."

"*Merci,* monsieur." Her chest still hurt when she gasped for air, but this time because Giles had touched the core of her secret wishes. Trust and brotherhood. She wanted only one thing more: Sebastián. "It's flattering to be considered trustworthy."

"*Et moi?* Can you return my trust? Because I swear on the honor of my forefathers, on paratge itself, that you can trust me with your greatest secrets. The way you trusted me with your life in my stable."

Taresa had many secrets, but she chose to share only one with Giles. Pain in her chest or not, she recognized the flattery as a kind of seduction and didn't understand what she possessed that the silvery seigneur wanted. She followed him down the trail. The mist had settled into fog, hanging on the hillside just below the towers, thin ribbons twirling across the pathway that led to the other tower.

"Monsieur, if you mean it, that I can trust you, I want to ask you a question."

"It will delight me to answer." In the dark, with the lantern light reflected by the fog, he did sound pleased. "Upon my honor."

"You know Milon de Breteuil?"

"That's your question?" His musical chuckle echoed in the courtyard. "I met Milon at the Siege of Acre and again when the Normans took Constantinople. We're distant cousins. He's never amounted to much. No lands won. No rise in the ranks under any general."

She took a leap, hoping to learn more, if not find an ally.

"Milon de Breteuil killed Pedro d'Aragón."

"Impossible." Giles rubbed a knuckle at her temple, perhaps to be intimate, but Taresa compared it to the way he'd rubbed the goats. "Where's your fabled common sense, Master Tarek?"

"I overheard Milon say so at the Templars' farm." She'd heard the boast through the memory of a soon-to-be-dead stable lad, but that didn't matter.

"How many cups of wine had Milon drunk? With what gold laid to wager? Whatever you heard, he is not a credible man."

"I swear it, on my own honor and all of paratge." She let too much emotion seep through her words and felt a fire burning in her heart and belly again.

"I can't argue what you might have heard, Master Tarek. I believe you heard him say so."

"Then please do whatever you can to bring justice."

"*Moi?* How can I do that?"

"You're a respected seigneur in the Languedoc. Tell Raymond, the Count of Toulouse. He'll know what to do."

Over Giles's head, the shutters remained open in Blanca's bed-chamber. Candlelight illuminated a carving set amid the stones below the window. Like the gargoyle in the great hall, a hooded working man peered down on them, wide eyed, hands clasping something obscured in the shadows. The gargoyle's hood was painted a brilliant scarlet, like the leathers that Blanca wore, his face the warm brown of the original sweet chestnut from which he was carved, but the wooden man's eyes bulged, bright white and piercing blue.

The sounds of crunching gravel and leather-on-stone echoed from the tower wall. One of Giles's servants appeared, leading a pair of horses. A man behind him led two more. "You have more guests, monsieur."

"*Merci.*" Giles opened the door to his great hall, waiting for Taresa. Half in shadow, half illuminated by the falling light, he seemed pensive. "I wish I could make promises for you, like brothers would. But who'd ever believe it? I wonder what got into the man. Milon de Breteuil?"

"You called my name? Here I am, *mon ami.*"

"Leaping goats!" Taresa grabbed Giles's sleeve in surprise.

Yusuf's bones had indeed been chased.

Milon sat by Qasim in the great hall, picking through the food left on the table. The big-face priest sprawled beside Yusuf, pouring wine from a pitcher into a cup.

16
Confession

LIKE THE RAIN AND FOG that wouldn't go away.

Like the chorus in a troubadour's song of misery.

Milon de Breteuil appeared again.

First his tongue poked out, and then that smile snaked across his putty-soft face. Milon rose from the bench beside Qasim and came to Giles to embrace him the way soldiers do.

Milon and the big-face priest wore the same torn, bloodied clothes as in Ricart's stable, Milon in French silks and his dancing-lion crimson surcoat, the priest in what had once been a white Cistercian robe. The spidery threads in Milon's aura had become broad, snaking ropes of burnt umber. The priest's angry cloud was now the same mud-brown as the puddle he'd fallen into in the stable. Two of Blanca's guards sat at the farther end of the table, seeming not too much worse for wear, except for bruised faces and rips in their woad fustian tunics.

Qasim sat back from the table, his arms folded. Because of his size, whenever he hunched up like that, he manifested menace—even if he adopted the posture out of trepidation. At every slight movement in the room, Qasim seemed ready to leap across the table and insert himself between Yusuf and the world.

Yusuf, however, seemed to have recaptured his usual spirit, as comfortable as when he sat in the scribes' refectory of Pedro's standing camp.

"Tell me you're happy to see me, cousin," Milon said, his arms still around Giles. "Have you missed me?"

"*Mon ami!*" Giles embraced Milon again, then held him at arm's length before releasing him. "What are you doing out in this wilderness? You're a man of the town."

"I'm working for our cousin Simon, bringing heretics to the Church to judge." Milon affably patted Giles's shoulder. But Giles moved away. "And I see you're holding heretics captive for me."

"You expect to find heretics hiding under my tapestries, Milon? In my granaries?"

"Simon will be interested in knowing whether you've cleaned up your lands." Milon spoke close to Giles's ear, but dramatically let the others hear. "I've been searching for these murderous young rebels all day."

"You are mistaken, cousin." The threat in Giles's voice, dark and thunderous as the day's storm, was not anything Taresa had heard from him in their brief acquaintance.

Further, Milon shrank from the threat. That is, he seemed to grow smaller. Then he reached into his surcoat while that smile began snaking across his face again. He dangled a familiar parchment packet from his fingers. Pedro's letter of safe passage.

"Read this, *mon ami*. Your innocent guests are agents of Aragón."

Giles took it from Milon and slit the waxed seal with his dinner knife. He studied it—there weren't enough words that even a child would take only a moment to read it. "This letter proves they have friends who can buy a letter of passage. It doesn't name them as agents. No court would see it as proving heresy. Have your gold-bug adventures damaged your mind, like too much wine in the hot sun?"

He handed it to Taresa. "Let's give Master Tarek back his letter. It's you who was holding it for safekeeping, am I right?"

"*Merci*, monsieur." Taresa tucked it inside her jerkin.

Distracted by servants appearing, Giles motioned for them to serve, becoming his gracious seigneurial self again. "Ah, I see my people knew what to do. Our new guests need good food. And wine, too."

He pointed where he wanted Milon to sit at his right hand and motioned to where Master Tarek should sit at his left.

Milon nodded to Qasim beside him on the bench. His eyebrows climbed up to the grey-blond fringe of hair when he saw his snake-coin of heretics' gold on the table. He shook an admonishing finger at Qasim, tongued a smile that pretended to be mischievous, and then pocketed his gold.

Tasting apprehension like bile in her throat, Taresa sat with the people who'd tried to kill them that morning, while regretting that *los tres amics* hadn't ridden to Cahors as soon as they'd eaten.

"How did you come here, cousin?" Giles brightened, speaking to Milon while indicating to his servants to pour wine.

"On a horse, like I suspect all your guests do. Like your sorceress ladylove did, to guess from the friends at your table." He pointed to Yusuf and Qasim. "Due to your clever friends, we had a bit of a time finding our horses. But Brother Petrus here is past master at rattling a feed bag to get a horse to come to him."

With a faint gesture, Giles indicated the two silent guards in tattered fustian at the end of the table, who seem to have made peace with the two heretic hunters. "I'm willing to bet that their mistress caused all problems—that is, any you didn't bring upon yourself."

"It's never clear with that woman," Milon was shaking his head, that ridiculous smile contorting his face, "whether you're being gullible or noble, mon ami."

"She and I are united now," Giles said, "as partners. We're building a life together in the Languedoc. So, if you seek to disparage her—"

"Never!" Milon banged the table to punctuate his denial. "I wish you the best of luck in your mutual endeavors."

"It's hard work in the south, right now." Giles seemed pensive. "There's a pall settling, like when Jerusalem was lost."

Milon still shook his head. "We're winning here, cousin. Simon leaves good men free to act, which is why heresy is on the run."

"*Ai, renrén.*" Giles called Milon a fool in the local tongue, breaking from the French they'd been speaking. Milon didn't appear to understand the insult. "Your heretic hunting has no future. The pope stopped it last summer. He'll step in soon and declare that Simon has usurped too much power, that Simon must to yield to the Church."

Milon said, "Until the pope interferes, there's good heretics gold to be found. It's easy work, since they're too simple-minded to arm themselves and fight."

"They also take a vow of poverty, like Jesus." Taresa didn't see a reason to be silent. "Which makes me wonder how you manage to take gold from them, since they're all virtuous paupers."

"Ah, rarely true!" Milon waved a finger her way. "It's wretches like Ricart who are without a bezant to his name. And the cottagers in the wilderness. The aunties and grannies of local seigneurs pretend poverty, but leave a son or nephew holding their fat purses. Perhaps like renegade Aragón messengers."

"Why call us renegades, Monsieur Milon?" Qasim had retained his hostile pose, ignoring the food that servants placed in front of him. "It's you who attacked us for no reason."

"That's the story you intend to tell?" Milon's hands were greasy with roasted songbird. "You're the heretic beggars who burned the Templars' barn. You killed a priest there, and killed another priest at Ricart's castle. Though now that castle is mine, as booty for disrupting heresy."

"Ah, we're neighbors now?" Giles interceded, asking a question about something Taresa had already explained to him.

Before Milon could answer, Taresa began a crusade, to ensure that *los tres amics* were never associated with the past days' tragedies.

"*Excusez moi, monsieur, mais non.* We have never begged, but always paid our way. We did not set that fire or murder a priest. And you accused every man at the castle you stole of being heretics with no proof and no Church court."

She kept her voice as friendly as Giles's and didn't fold her arms in challenge like Qasim, but instead took one of the infamous barley rusks from the bowl and casually munched on it.

"My new friends are paragons of noble virtue," Giles said, seemingly in earnest. "I believe them."

Milon shrugged at the criticism. "In times of chaos, mistakes might be made."

"Ricart slashed to death might have been an accident?" Taresa dunked her rusk in a newly refreshed dish of hot butter. "Then you'll agree it was an accident when I tripped and knocked you on the head to keep myself from falling."

Giles laughed, slapping Milon's shoulder. "You see why we're friends? Master Tarek reminds me of our early days."

Yusuf stared at the cup of wine in front of him, as if he were alone in the room with nothing but his thoughts.

Qasim nodded, then lifted his chin, as if trying to tell her something, and her best guess was his relief that Milon didn't recognize Qasim from Pedro's camp.

At the far end of the table, the two mercenaries (whoever they worked for now) cared about nothing but the food in front of them. And the big-face priest seemed to be practicing what Taresa did: keeping his expression free from all emotion. He might as well have been one of the figures carved in sweet chestnut, decorating Giles's timbered ceiling and pillars.

"As innocent as we were when we sailed from Narbonne? Milon asked. "Or less so, like later, after Acre?"

Ignoring Milon's comments, Giles wagged a scolding finger. "My young friend Tarek just told a story about you killing the king of Aragón. I told him that couldn't be true, because I know you."

That cold stone twisted in Taresa's belly. So much for trust and deepest secrets. How had she let herself believe in this silvery seigneur, an utter stranger?

Yusuf folded his arms just then, mirroring Qasim, his face stern. But he didn't look her way.

Milon shuffled, tongue poking the inside of his cheek like a mischievous child. "*Ai,* Giles! You do know me. Every other man in the south claims he killed the king. I'll tell the same lies as any man to gain a free supper."

Giles's smile tilted. Taresa's heart beat hard enough to break her ribs. Seizing her wrist, Giles placed Taresa's hand over Milon's, holding both of them between his palms. "Surely my friends can be agreeable with each other."

Her hands stung, as if stabbed by a thousand bone needles. Speak of paratge and take a risk? She must now jump off a cliff, without looking to Yusuf and Qasim for help.

"*Oui, mon ami.*" She hoped for her best French accent. "Plead with your friends to leave mine alone, Monsieur Giles. And Monsieur Milon? This is what people in the south see as rudeness from you Frankish men. You cry heresy, heresy, everywhere heresy. We aren't heretics."

Giles increased the weight of his hold, pressing Milon's hand into a trinity with hers. She put a lid over the well that held her thoughts, watching, not judging.

> The three of them were in a souk in the Outremer, touching rough sheep's-wool rugs while vendors promised a low, low price, almost free, and since these special visitors came from Christian lands beyond the Great Sea, he'd share the secret everyone knows in the Outremer, speaking in the broken French that was the *lingua franca*.
>
> *I shall tell you how to command the magic woven into this carpet.*
>
> And they laughed together while eating fiery food at street stands, their hands sticky and greasy when they linked fingers, then bashed wrists, and hooked elbows in a secret handshake that meant they were brothers.
>
> Then, in a burning city, taking a gold coin from a dead man, one slapping the other's sweaty hand away.
>
> *God meant this for me.*
>
> *But all booty goes to the Church.*
>
> And then, not wrestling joyously. Instead, one kicked the other into a mute, pain-wracked pile on the street.

She blinked, trying to see if one man was Milon, the other Giles, but the memory wafted away, like mist over a swamp.

"We can all be friends," Giles said, releasing both their hands. "There's a short, straight path through this misunderstanding."

Taresa stretched her stinging fingers, hot blood flooding her hands as she understood what she'd seen. In the present world, Giles did not like or trust or respect Milon any more than she did. Qasim watched them, probably guessing she'd seen a memory. Yusuf, too, peered at her, as if wondering what she might have seen. He also watched Giles. Did Yusuf guess that Giles might be able to read memories?

Giles hooked Milon by the elbow. "Let me invite my cousin Milon into my chapel, to confess to this good priest that he lied about killing a king. It will settle this entire misunderstanding."

Announcing this in French, Giles clasped Milon's neck with his hand, tipping him close as if they were boys jesting.

Taresa sought Yusuf's reaction, since he'd insisted on the falsity of the defrocked priest. But Yusuf still watched Giles, not responding when Qasim laid a brotherly hand on his shoulder. When Taresa came closer, the heat of a fever wafted from Yusuf, who definitely was ill. But the healer had already taken to her bed for the night.

"*Oui*, monsieur." Milon answered in French. "I shall confess to having jested, the same as most good men in the south. But I'm whole-hearted about helping my cousin Simon pursue heretics."

"What did he say, Tarek?" Yusuf asked in the local tongue, though he'd proved quite adept with French lately.

Before Taresa could answer, Giles repeated Milon's words in the local tongue. Then he added more. "And let's all say our creed. People need to get over the hysteria about heresy sweeping the countryside. Don't you agree, Master Tarek?"

"I'm unfamiliar with that hysteria, as I'm not from this part of Christendom." Taresa replied with the least emotion possible, feeling pestered to answer.

One hand once more on Milon's neck and the other grasping Taresa's elbow, Giles steered them to a door at the end of the great hall. He released both Milon and Taresa to unbolt the door.

Which opened into a palace of wonders.

¤

Servants rushed to light candles. So many candles. The room soon smelled of beeswax and incense. Taresa had been in the cathedrals of Barcelona, Urgell, and Toulouse. This tiny chapel cradled an equally magnificent collection of brightly painted wooden saints and angels, each illuminated with branches of candles. A single window high over the altar also reflected candlelight.

The barrel-vaulted ceiling, a rich azure as deep as a summer's sky, heightened the sense that they'd entered another world. Every pillar was carved with birds and roses, with chiseled ivy winding up pillars, all in brilliant vermillion, vivid green, and gold.

"A spiritual paradise." Yusuf spoke from the doorway, where he tarried with Qasim.

"Don't praise me as a holy man," Giles said, his attention on Yusuf. "It's generations since an old seigneur returned from the first crusade and built this shrine. I imagine that he longed to share his spiritual revelations, having been to Jerusalem. I merely do my duty to preserve his vision."

To the right, above the altar, was a lifelike carving of Joseph the carpenter, the first man called upon to believe the astonishing news. To the right, St-Peter held the keys to the Kingdom of God. Below were smaller carved panels, heavily gilded, showing the travails of the Savior on the way to the Cross. Above the altar stood the Virgin, half-again larger than life, her gilt gown and corona reflecting candlelight, her face beaming with love for the world. The night's weather had crept into the chapel, so a ghostly mist hung in the air above the three figures, as if they breathed, as if lost and grieving spirits had been stuck on a shelf.

"You approve?" Giles prodded Taresa with an elbow, rousing her from amazement, her mouth hanging open from staring upward, like a child new to the city.

"It's astonishing." She remembered to close her mind to him. "You are a fortunate man to have this under your care."

Giles addressed Milon, though he kept glancing at Yusuf. "Now, *mon ami*. Confess before God and Man. You never killed a king."

Giles pointed to the step before the altar. Without arguing, Milon knelt. That big-face priest stood beside him, his hand out in blessing, the same way he'd stood over Ricart dying in the stable.

Milon confessed in French, first calling on the names of the Trinity. "I swear that I did not kill Pedro d'Aragón. My sole sin is telling false tales."

Yusuf, who'd claimed that priest had been defrocked, still loitered near the door. He hadn't said anything to protest this mummers' pretense of holy confession. He stood in the same posture as St-Josep above the altar, except he quivered with illness.

The priest, apparently shameless, repeated a benediction in Latin and began reciting the creed. Taresa felt Qasim alongside her, heard his voice saying the words in Latin. She glanced over her shoulder at Yusuf, who instead of saying the creed gazed up as if in awe at a second Madonna and Child in an alcove. This Holy Mother sat on a gilt-and-ebony throne, dressed in a robe of deep sapphire with gold stars, her head veiled in the same manner as Kalypso's black veil. The child in her lap, dressed in pure gold, held up his hand to bless those who adored him. The Madonna figure held out her hand, welcoming the burden that anyone needed her to carry. Immensely beautiful.

Yet what must have caught Yusuf's attention was the difference between this carving and the others in the chapel, which all resembled people you might see in Toulouse or Barcelona. This Madonna and Child looked like Yusuf. Or perhaps Yusuf's darker ancestor from Ifriqiya or Morocco.

While the priest—whether false or not—repeated the creed in Latin, Yusuf jerked, as if he were being punched in rhythm with the Latin. Giles came to Yusuf's side and seemed to notice that Yusuf was near fainting, because he had a hand on Yusuf's shoulder, bracing him.

> *Credo in Spiritum Sanctum, sanctam Ecclesiam catholicam, sanctorum communionem, remissionem peccatorum, carnis resurrectionem, vitam aeternam. Amen.*

Taresa, worried for Yusuf, wasn't thinking about the meaning of the creed while the big-face priest recited and everyone else mumbled along.

"Remarkable, isn't it?" Giles said to Yusuf after the amens, both of them gazing at the alcove's unique Madonna and Child.

"Stolen from a Coptic church?" Yusuf stepped away from Giles, but Taresa couldn't tell if Giles's intimacy made Yusuf uncomfortable or if Yusuf just wanted to see more.

"Likely an ancient crusader dragged it here from the Outremer." Giles touched Yusuf's shoulder, the way he'd touched Taresa in the stable.

"Or straight from heaven," Yusuf said, who mostly didn't believe in heaven. He took a step closer, reaching out to touch the Madonna's foot.

Milon coughed, sounding like a man in death throes. Startled, Qasim and Taresa both looked his way. Her muscles jerked, as if waking from a dream. She sneezed, her senses flooded with the familiar burnt odor. She blinked, since it looked like St-Josep reached down from the altar for her, like the giant puppet that grabbed her years ago at a feast-day parade.

"*Et beneeixi!*" Qasim blessed her.

A crash echoed behind them.

The Dark Madonna had fallen on Yusuf.

The priest screamed, high and shrill for such a big man. Taresa ran to help. Qasim thrust Giles aside. She and Qasim struggled to lift the carving off Yusuf. He'd been knocked cold. The sainted Mother was too heavy for them, so it took cooperation for everyone in the room to move the carving, Giles called terse commands to get them working together.

"Wake the healer!" Giles pointed to the servant by the door. "Let's move him to—"

"No." Qasim, his face white as stone, blocked anyone from touching Yusuf. "Give him room to breathe. Let's see what harm he suffered before moving him." Qasim began feeling Yusuf's long bones for breaks. Taresa knelt on Yusuf's other side, remembering everything she'd learned while checking injured men left on the field after battle. Fire ran through her veins. The first thing: give up your own terror and horror.

Yusuf breathed, though every tenth breath was ragged, as if he struggled. His lips, ghastly pale, remained dry. Then at least he wasn't bleeding inside. She hoped.

Taresa rested her hand where Yusuf's pulse beat just above his collarbone. His heartbeat was weak, but regular. She needed the reassurance that he lived. Nothing else came through that touch; no memory, no dream, no pages from his studies.

17
Kalypso's Touch

THE HEALER APPEARED, BAREFOOT, her grey robe tied in haste, no veil over long white-and-grey locks that fell down her back. She took Qasim's place, feeling for injury while asking where the crushing burden had fallen on him. In the middle of overwhelming worry, Taresa focused on a single detail, a streak of dried blood on Kalypso's sleeve, a relic of her day's work.

Kalypso straightened at last. "Can you make a litter to carry him to bed?"

The flurry of movement, the flickering of the chapel candles, the noise of busy servants, Qasim's unearthly silence, twisted around all the appalling fear that seized Taresa's heart.

The healer insisted, arguing with Giles, that her borrowed bed-chamber was the best place from which she could nurse Yusuf. After servants brought a litter and carried Yusuf to the healer's room, Qasim refused to leave when she sought to get everyone out. Taresa insisted also, though the chamber was tiny and crowded with a narrow cot, a bench, and a carved wooden chair. Kalypso pointed to the bench, directing them out of her way.

Kalypso knelt by the cot and began gently undoing Yusuf's tunic and breeches.

"I'll help." Qasim was up and in Kalypso's way again, but she yielded and took a seat on the bench beside Taresa.

"Don't worry until you hear from me that it's time to worry." Kalypso spoke in the local tongue. She wrapped her warm, dry hand over Taresa's clenched fist. "Pray, if that stops you from worrying. Or tell yourself stories of a better time, past or future."

"*Mercé, ma dòmna.*"

"He's blessed to have friends who care."

Qasim rose from his task, Yusuf's linen undershirt in his hand. "He's a gravel-brain leper filled with dog's tripe who drives his friends mad."

Kalypso blinked, as if stunned for a moment by Qasim's vehemence. "Did he bring that accident upon himself?"

Taresa laughed, heard all the nervous fear in her laughter. "The one thing he couldn't control."

Qasim laughed, with just as much strung-out fear, then hid his face in his hands. Taresa rested her hand on his broad, shaking shoulders. He wasn't a Catalunya-born man and so hadn't learned from the cradle to cry when it's necessary.

Then they both sobered and watched Kalypso inspect Yusuf's body for contusions. The silence tore at the agony in Taresa's bones. Qasim crossed his arms, rocked himself for comfort on the bench. Then Kalypso left Yusuf's side and opened the chamber door. She looked out, closed the door, and jammed a rug against the threshold.

"I don't believe the Madonna laid one finger on your friend. He's only hit his head and bruised his shin."

Qasim, in a loud whisper, said, "Let all be as it pleases God!" In his *valencià* tongue. Taresa let go of the painful breath she'd been holding.

Kalypso poured an ointment from a vial. She warmed it in her hands and then rubbed where a dark bruise crossed Yusuf's shin. The ointment's aroma evoked misty memories that Taresa's mind leapt to identify. Pruning season in a vineyard or pear orchard, like the green smell under willows along a river. The odor awakened Taresa. She could breathe again. The warmed oil shimmered in the candle light. Though pale and motionless, Yusuf seemed to warm under Kalypso's touch, as if she'd got his blood to course through his veins again.

While corking the vial and replacing it in her satchel, Kalypso said, "Now, will you children please tell me what you're doing in this part of the country?"

"We're on our way to Paris where..." Taresa began as usual, but the disbelieving expression on the healer's face stopped her.

Kalypso brushed Yusuf's hair back, rested her hand on his forehead. He might as well have been one of the chapel carvings, he lay so still, without expression. "Has he been ill? He has a fever, and he's more like a man in a dream than one who's bumped his head."

Neither Taresa nor Qasim volunteered an answer.

The healer's penetrating dark eyes asked the question again. She waited, then spoke. "Master Tarek? Castor?"

Qasim said, "He's been distracted."

"He calls it a curse." Taresa blurted what she'd overhead, unclear whether she was telling a secret.

"Where did this curse come from?" Kalypso folded her arms, standing over them like a stern master. "Constantinople? I think not. Cyprus?"

Qasim nodded, though perhaps he didn't mean to. "How did you guess?"

"He has never seen Morella in his life, has he?" Kalypso again touched Yusuf's forehead with obvious tenderness. "Is he Miquel's grandson?"

Blood rushed so hard and fast to Taresa's head, it swelled her tongue with confusion and relief, so she couldn't get words out.

"Òc." Qasim's voice, low in his throat, sounded thick with fear and misery. "Miquel's son, Don Tomás of Morella and Cyprus, is my master. I'm sworn to guard Yusuf with my life."

"Yusuf? Not Josep?" Kalypso pointed to each of them. "What are your real names?"

Instead of answering, Taresa asked Yusuf's coded question, as best she remembered it.

"Was it Perseus who slayed Medusa?"

"Ai, me! A secret question! Does the answer involve Danaë or Andromeda or an adamantine sword?" When neither answered, Kalypso said, "I'm not Perseus. But I know him. What are you doing in this part of the country? Fleeing Simon's army?"

"No," Taresa dared the truth. "We're on our way to Paris for…" She fumbled, seeking an obscure answer that wasn't a lie.

"For Pedro? Of course! In these wild times, Pedro must be the cause for any expedition." Kalypso's smile twitched, turned downward to grief. "Was the cause."

"How did you know Miquel of Morella?" Taresa wanted to learn more before she revealed more. She touched Kalypso's hand, and glimpsed an image of Yusuf, transported to a desert world, with palm trees and donkeys and camels.

"I knew him for years in the Outremer. Yusuf looks just like him, as if Miquel's ghost returned to us from heaven." Kalypso rubbed her temples as if she had a headache. "If Miquel made it to heaven."

Qasim had managed to get close to Yusuf again and knelt on the stone floor beside the cot, his hand on Yusuf's shoulder the way he often connected with his friend.

"We've been swept into misadventure," Taresa said. "Can you indeed help us find Perseus?"

"Òc. First, however, Yusuf needs to be at my house to be cared for properly."

"But he's so ill." Qasim glanced up from Yusuf's side.

"Exactly. I can't guess what curse is holding his mind, keeping him from rejoining us. But it isn't from hitting his head on a stone floor. Can you prepare to ride? My men know how to transport injured fighters."

Kalypso didn't wait for an answer, leaving them alone with the cold, silent, deathly pale Yusuf.

¤

"Qasim, did Yusuf's grandmother put a curse on him? I heard you talking at the baron's castle."

"It's not a curse."

"Another kind of magic? Tell me."

"It's Yusuf's secret."

"Is it a demon? Is that what's making Yusuf ill?"

"No. You can't make me tell his secrets. He's like my brother."

"Then what's wrong with him? How can I help?"

The chamber door opened. Giles and Kalypso faced each other at the archway.

"Ai, ma dòmna. Why leave in the middle of the night? I can send men to fetch your medicines. Surely after that battering the boy took in the chapel, a night ride—"

"It's not injuries from that fall in the chapel that needs nursing. Don Josep came here already suffering from a disease. He needs medicines and care I can best give at my home. And I want to make sure this fever won't spread through your *domus*."

"Monsieur Giles." Taresa interrupted. "As I learned on the field in Iberia, do whatever a healer advises you."

"Of course. I'll send men to guide you."

Kalypso grasped Giles's hand. "*Merci*, monsieur. There's no need. My men know the way, but I honor your desire to help."

¤

Qasim wanted to stay with Yusuf, but he voiced unease about strangers saddling their horses. Specifically:

"Those *peccador* mercenaries better not touch our horses."

So Qasim stayed behind while Taresa headed for the stable again, her long list of goals and desires now reduced to fear for Yusuf. In the courtyard, Giles stood silvery under lantern light amid a herd of already-saddled horses, the reins of Taresa's horse in his hands. He pointed to the string of horses.

"My men prepared all your horses."

"Only three belong to us. The rest are Blanca's. She didn't want to leave them at Ricart's castle since she'd paid for them."

"Blanca?" He seemed bewildered.

"Your lady from Avignon."

"You don't know who she is?"

"Since we met, we've shared only a great deal of rain trickling down our necks. I don't probe."

"O master of uncommon sense."

His hand was on her shoulder again, as if she were his friend. Taresa closed the lid on her imaginary well, not sure whether to trust him, sure that she wanted privacy. "Don't tease. Who is she?"

"Upon my honor," Giles tapped Taresa's nose, grinning like a child, "if she didn't trust you with her name, I can't break her trust to share it."

"I—yes, that's true, isn't it?"

"Ask her yourself, Master Tarek."

"It's unlikely I'll ever see her again."

When Tarek whispered hello to each of the three horses, checking their saddles and harnesses, Giles asked a question that stopped her. "Did your Don Josep serve Pedro d'Aragón? Is that how you procured a letter of passage?"

Here were the exact boundaries of her trust. She said, "My master hires his men out as mercenaries. We met because he sold men to Pedro for the adventure in Andalusia."

"Does he hire out men like you to Simon? Would he sell your services to me?"

He embraced her, as if they were comrades in arms. She wiggled away, wanting to keep her judgments private.

"My master is Catholic, believes in only one God. We aren't heretics. If that's what you are once more asking."

"Ah, Tarek, master of common sense. Remember my offer. I'll make you a knight and part of my knights' *confraria* if your master fails his promise to you."

"I—" How could she escape this? "Is Milon a member of your confraternity? Do you have other knights like him?"

"You don't trust me?" Giles tilted her head up, a finger on her chin, even though she was almost as tall as he was.

Lines of white light spun around her and remained when Giles touched her, as if he were tying her in a net, like a spider with a fly. What had that old woman in the baggage train said? That the spider sings while it weaves. Taresa had mastered a guileless innocent face on the road to Andalusia, whenever a man kept asking for more than clean shirts, too close, insinuating. When such a man received back his laundered shirt, he found the ties came off in his hands when he dressed, Taresa having clipped each of those white cords. She imagined clipping each of the strings of white light spun from Giles's touch. The man's bright aura dimmed. She'd been fooled into trusting him.

"Monsieur, is it a sin against heaven to kill a king?"

He rested his hand on her forearm. She clipped that white line. "*Oui.* But why are you obsessed with Pedro dying? Nostalgia for the only army you've marched with?"

"*Jhezu del tron,* the idea of murdering a king makes my blood simmer. Are you not enraged?"

"I didn't know him. And men all over the south have feared Pedro's ambition for years. He wanted all of the Languedoc under the rule of Aragón. He seduced the pope and the counts into doing as he wished."

She wanted to argue, but she'd heard men say that about Pedro more than once. She changed the subject. "Yet I heard Milon de Breteuil declare he killed a king. You said earlier that you believed me. Please believe me now when I say his confession tonight was not honest."

"Men like Milon prevaricate." His hands on her again. "But that man is too lazy and not that clever. Do you still want me to tell Simon de Montfort what you heard?"

"No, not Simon. Tell Raymond, the Count of Toulouse."

Giles ran his hands down her arms. His touch added to the confusion his argument raised. She busily clipped the white threads of light.

"Milon is my cousin," he said. "But if you have proof, the man should be punished."

"I have no proof," Taresa said. "But every respectable man must think it's an insult to paratge to murder a king."

"I agree." That lop-sided smile. "And you've been swept into the resulting pandemonium, your adventures gone awry."

"Òc," she said. "With Milon de Breteuil riding the crest of the first wave of chaos. Why?"

"Why, what?"

"Why choose evil, monsieur? Why would a man choose evil?"

"You're better off asking the angels, not me. But I know that Milon failed at life. All of his bad choices are owed to his continual failures."

Giles said the right things, but it didn't loosen the fist formed of pure anger in her heart. She was shivering, like a half-frozen fool. He put his arms around her, like a lover, and lifted her chin with his finger again. "All will be well, Master Tarek. Oh, *mon ami*, and all your wishes will come true."

He kissed her, with the same expertise as Blanca's kiss, yet it kindled no passion. And not because Taresa kept her arms trapped in front of her, shielding her breasts from discovery; her tunic sleeve caught in a button on his vest. She thought he loved Blanca. He'd

---

denied that he wanted anything from her. Yet his hands touched her ears. Which forced his vision on her, of another kiss.

> The scratch of days' old beard rubbing each other. The taste of bitter, resinous wine traded tongue to tongue. The nose-tickling, acrid smell of a man's sweat. Fingers running through long hair. In the French style.

His fingers ran through Taresa's chopped hair. His day-old beard did scratch her face, would leave a rash. But in that memory, he kissed Milon. And now, judging from experience, Taresa believed that she was better at kissing than either Giles or Blanca—or whatever her name was. Taresa closed the lid on her tired thoughts, so Giles couldn't read her judgment.

Qasim called Taresa's name from across the courtyard.

Giles whispered in her ear. "I promise to do whatever I can to make sure Pedro's killer receives what he deserves. Here on earth at least."

Qasim called again.

"You promise?" Her words sounded like beggary to her own ears. At the same time, another part of her clipped yet another thread of the white light spun to trap her. "The count will listen, even though I don't have proof."

"*Oui,* I promise." He let her go. She headed over to join Qasim. "I shall see Simon next week and tell him."

"Tell Raymond, the count!" she called back. "The Count of Toulouse. What good would it do to tell Simon?"

The count—that's what she'd told Giles, hadn't she? The loss of Pedro must be what Simon had prayed for since he first came to the Languedoc.

18
Perseus and the Gorgon

At Kalypso's mansion
Dawn, Wednesday, September 18

WHEN YOU'RE TOO TIRED AND too worried to form a memory of how you got from one place to another—and only become aware that you've traveled because it's dawn and the horses have stopped—then it's like waking from one dream into another.

In the first dream—while riding in the dark, half-awake—she argued with Sebastián that she could still make it right, but he never answered, while she fought to get *los tres amics* on the right trail. At every turn in the trail, things had gone awry. She gave their food to the bandit-children, so they'd had to stop at the monastery. Then she couldn't ask the Templars for help, because of her king-killer vision. She'd run from the Templars' farm with Blanca, because confusion and fear grabbed her for two heartbeats. She didn't stop the first fight in Ricart's stable, because she wanted to be a knight and fight for her friends' honor. She didn't kill Milon in the stable, because of Yusuf's philosophy. She let Blanca come along instead of insisting she stay and care for her injured men. She'd let Blanca lead them to Giles, because she'd believed Kalypso's advice. She believed Giles's friendliness, because he talked about brotherhood and loyalty. "I tried to do the right thing," she pleaded with Sebastián, but he didn't answer, and she followed him down to the camp of horrors behind the willows by the river, searching among the mangled and dying for faces she knew, hoping Sebastián wasn't there.

She roused from that repetitive waking dream, recounting how she'd been a fool to believe people because they were kind, and therefore she'd spawned catastrophe. Awake, she found she'd entered a new, strange world. Early morning sun shone on a mansion, as if God opened a hole in the clouds, solely for this household.

Kalypso's men led them inside the walled yard of a two-story whitewashed mansion with a tiled roof, the kind of extensive *domus* you'd find outside Narbonne or Toulouse. Cypress trees lined the road leading to the low wall that fenced in the farm's pig and goats, but that wouldn't withstand a siege.

Qasim held his horse's reins, ignoring the servants who offered to attend to their animals. He watched as Kalypso's men, with evident care, transferred Yusuf to a litter. They'd been warned three times by Kalypso, that much Taresa remembered, that her men were experienced in battlefield care, and nothing Qasim or Taresa could do would be helpful.

"I can't believe you let him do that," Qasim muttered. "It's bothered me this entire ride."

"What did I let Yusuf do? And when could I ever stop him? I didn't make that Madonna fall on him."

"No, I mean that blasted seigneur, touching you all over, pretending to offer comfort. 'All will be well, Master Tarek. You'll get all your wishes, *mon ami.*' Did you tell him you're a woman?"

"What are you talking about?"

"After we watched him fondle the lady Blanca, I thought he cared only for women."

"He promised to get justice for Pedro. Even though Milon was once his friend."

"You saw all his snozzling with Blanca. Yet you kissed him to get him to take revenge for you?"

"What? No. He kissed me. I think he was trying to see my memories. The same way I see what people remember."

A trio of riders pounded into the courtyard just then, coming in so fast that it riled the horses the servants were leading away.

"Speak of the devil's widow," Taresa muttered.

Blanca dismounted with the help offered by one of the two woad-clad guards who accompanied her. All of Blanca's pretense of an injured arm had been abandoned.

"You left me in the company of that murderer Milon." Blanca stabbed her finger at first Qasim and then Taresa.

"We aren't in your employ, madam." Qasim said it in broken but stern French, words scrambled. He stalked away, following the men who carried Yusuf into the house.

"You had your lover to protect you." Taresa followed Qasim and Yusuf, her shoulders turtling up to her ears, resisting any words or touch from Blanca, or whatever her name was.

The high ceiling of the long narrow room was supported with by four arches, like in an old-style cathedral, its plastered ceiling painted in brightly colored patterns. Every part of the room, save the four alabaster-white arches, was painted in brilliant colors, each section of wall telling a story (none of which Taresa recognized) filled with heroes and adoring minions. The floor was a mosaic of small stones, similar to what she'd seen in the baths in Barcelona, in a pattern of six-sided blue stones, intersections filled with more gleaming white stones, like the arches.

Each element of the room should have inspired one's soul, like in the great cathedrals, except it was littered with children's toys: a miniature wooden wagon painted shiny crimson, with a rope pull; a side table with clay soldiers scattered over the top; two huge dolls, dressed like real children but carved from sweet chestnut; a pony, tall as a mountain dog, on a rocking platform, painted azure and varnished so it shone in the candlelight.

The room—and exhaustion from the ride and a sleepless night—overwhelmed her for a moment. Taresa turned in a circle, staring, then turned back to chase after Qasim and Kalypso. However, they'd entered another room and closed the door before she could reach them.

Taresa turned all of her turmoil on Blanca, who also inspected the room, but not in awe; her nose wrinkled in scorn.

"Can't you leave us alone, *ma dòmna*? We don't want you or need you near us anywhere under God's good heaven."

"I heard what he promised you." Blanca smiled with no trace of goodwill. "I can't stay in his house while he's planning to betray my trust."

"I have nothing to do with your seigneur. What would I want with your old lover? He merely promised—"

"His promises are worthless. And once I learned you were on your way to this house, I had to come warn you."

"Warn me? The healer is the kindest person I've ever met."

"No, not about her, *renrén*." She called Taresa a fool. "We need to join forces. We both need—"

From deeper within the house a man's voice thundered in French. "*Ce qui dans l'Hadès se passait ici?*" Taresa agreed with the thought: What in Hades was going on here? The uproar continued. "Who made my house into a hostel for vagrants?"

¤

A door banged open, its arch framing an extraordinarily large French knight, taller than anyone Taresa ever met. He bent his head in the archway, for otherwise he'd never clear it.

The man was more handsome, to Taresa's preference in men, than the silvery seigneur with two towers on the distant hilltop. Smooth-shaven, a square jaw, long brown hair, and—what was most appealing—broad shoulders that must carry chainmail as comfortably as linen. His blue eyes flashed with anger, the bright sapphire of steel when the blacksmith heats it. And more blue: the aura around him glowed deep woad-blue with wild threads of bright blue, like his eyes. The women in the baggage train would spend two days' debating the virtues of so much male beauty combined with extreme passion in a giant's body.

However, he was marked as a fighter. The knotted scar on his cheek came from a weapon, perhaps in a battle where no healer appeared to stitch it properly. One hand was corroded with burns.

This angry man was also the *bien-aimé* Taresa had seen in Blanca's comforting memory of her beloved.

"*Vous sorcière!* Why are you here?" He pointed at Blanca, accusing, dangerous in his anger. "I just took my wife and children to Arles for safety. And I find my home invaded by..." he sputtered, seeking words "...perfidious infidels."

"*Paix, mon cher couer.*" Blanca spoke softly, as if to quiet him with her voice. "I came to ask your help. For Maria's sake."

"What did Maria do for me—other than offer you shelter when I claimed my own houses? I owe Maria nothing."

"But you can never resist the chance to serve as rescuing hero, Jean-Luc." Blanca applied the same calm reasoning that had dragged *los tres amics* astray over two days. "And the infant king of Aragón needs to be rescued. You owe that to your lofty sense of honor, don't you? If not to the queen of Aragón."

The queen of Aragón? Instead of hearing a warning from Sebastián, Taresa remembered Blanca saying too often, "We are the same, we want the same things." It seemed they were on the same mission, to protect the infant king of Aragón.

Jean-Luc stood like a foreboding giant, unmoved.

Blanca said, "You and I were once the whole world to each other. But from how this house has changed," her hand circled the glorious circus in the great room, "I see that you are happy now. Do a great kindness and help me, to help Maria's child."

When Jean-Luc still didn't answer her, Blanca looked around the room rather than at her smoldering accuser.

"May I sit down? It *was* my house once upon a time. Surely you can spare a chair."

When Blanca sat down, uninvited, the man—his face still ruby-red with rage—noticed Taresa for the first time.

"*Et toi?* What are you doing in my house?" He advanced on Taresa, ignoring Blanca for a moment. "Who are you, *gojat?*" He said *boy* in the local tongue, as if it were an insult.

Kalypso appeared behind Taresa, her hands clasping Taresa's shoulders, the way a friend does. "Our guest is from Girona and has a question for you. If you can cool your head and listen." She squeezed Taresa's shoulders, encouraging. "Ask him."

With all the unexplained emotion in the room—and Blanca seated in a carved chair, steepling her fingers in impatience, not prayer—Taresa swallowed doubt, took a breath, and hoped she got it right.

"Did Perseus slay Medusa?" She said it; he looked perplexed. Had she gotten it right? "I'm pretty sure it wasn't Theseus."

"Who are you?" He repeated his previous question.

Kalypso squeezed Taresa's shoulders again. The woman's touch smothered Taresa's burning fire, but failed to quench all the flames.

"Did Perseus slay Medusa?" Taresa folded her arms in challenge.

"Better still, he rescued Andromeda." The man folded his arms, returning the challenge. "Who sent you? Who are you?"

Kalypso said, "The name I heard was Tarek of Girona, but I'm fairly certain this is Sebastián's wife."

"Sebastián?" The man's face paled to a more human color, his expression now pure confusion. "He's only a child."

"Time passes," Kalypso said. "Isabella mentioned a marriage in her letter last year."

"Sebastián?" Blanca coughed, tried to speak, coughed again. "Not that wild boy from the Pyrenees who stole the Montcava estates in Toulouse?"

Taresa imitated the way Blanca spoke cooling words in a dire argument. "Sebastián of Valerós, who was the greatest Catalan commander in Andalusia last year. Whom Pedro d'Aragón saluted as a hero. *That* Sebastián."

"*Bon dieu!*" Blanca exclaimed. "Did he rescue you when you ran away from that bad marriage contract?"

"I rescued myself." Taresa found, once more, that Blanca reignited her fury. "I've always rescued myself. Without abandoning the men to whom I owe loyalty. Without seducing men to get my way. Unlike some people I have known."

"Then Pedro sent you?" The man unfolded his arms.

"*Òc.* He wants you—wanted you—to go to Paris with us. To beg Philippe's help to restore Jaime to Aragón."

Blanca spluttered, not in a genteel manner. "Damn the eyes of every dancing angel."

At least, that's what Taresa thought the French meant.

The man returned his attention to Blanca. "Madam? You persist in trespassing in my house."

"As I said before, I'm here to beg the same help as these... children. Except Maria sent me, not Pedro."

The man abruptly turned away from all of them, heading for the door he first came through.

"Jean-Luc," Kalypso pleaded, "these guests deserve our hospitality, if not your help."

He waved a hand over his head, as if halting an army behind him. The door thrust open, he shouted to those on the other side.

"Bring us a breakfast in the eastern sun-room. And hot ale for—" he glanced over his shoulder "—four."

Kalypso said, "Tomás's son and his friend are also here. From Aragón, I think. Or Andalusia."

"Of course they are." Jean-Luc shouted down the hall, "Six!"

When Jean-Luc turned back, he pointed to a chair, commanding with one hand that Taresa be seated. "As *belle-mère* Katelina insists, you are welcome here." Taresa glanced at the woman who'd called herself Kalypso, but who proved to be Perseus's mother-in-law. The man called Jean-Luc said, "Now that I know what in the devil's name you're doing in my house, tell me more."

He folded his tall, fighter's body into a chair, one hand on his exquisite square jaw, waiting for an explanation.

"We need you to come to Paris with us, to beg Philippe's help for Jaime's sake," Taresa said. "And to keep Simon de Montfort from making himself king of all the Languedoc."

Blanca said, "I need you to go with me to Simon de Montfort, to fetch Jaime for Maria's sake."

"First," he pointed to Taresa, "I have other business this year that does not include a journey to Paris, which is the least good place to be in winter."

Taresa was prepared to beg. "But Pedro asked—"

"Not to be rude," he folded his hands, "but Pedro is dead, and he never in life commanded me."

Taresa didn't have an answer ready, having never expected a refusal. But Jean-Luc rudely pointed his finger at Blanca again.

"I shall never journey even as far as Cahors with you, Hélène. What are you called now? *Veusa?*" He called her *dowager* in the local tongue. Indeed, Giles had said her name was not Blanca. "You don't continue to tell people you are of the house of Beaurain, I hope—for my children's sake. I hope you are now just another cousin in the extended House of Montcava."

"You are hard hearted, *mon ami.*" Blanca—Hélène—pouted. "It's not your way. You know I have always loved you."

"Yet you betrayed me when I served your husband. I shall not offer you the chance to betray me now."

Taresa listened, still sorting out who these people were, since no one in the room was who they'd claimed to be. Blanca was Hélène, the former marquesa de Beaurain and friend to the queen of Aragón. Kalypso, as it turned out, was Senhóra Katelina, who had been *duena* to Sebastián's mother and aunts, from the sparse stories he'd told of his childhood. Which meant that Perseus was married to Sebastián's aunt. Therefore, he was Taresa's uncle and, based on family loyalty, she could make a stronger claim for help from Jean-Luc, Marquis de Beaurain, than Yusuf and Pedro could claim. She determined to unclench the fist of anger in her heart and loosen the fear in her muscles, and instead be courageous and ask for what she wanted.

A servant appeared at the door, announcing *sotto voce* that food was served in the eastern sun-room.

"Come, my guests." Jean-Luc unfolded from his chair with far more grace than one might expect of a large man. "We shall have a nice breakfast. And then you can all be on the road as soon as you are rested." He headed for a door on the eastern wall. "Without me."

Kalypso—Katelina—didn't rise from her chair. "You're forgetting one thing, Jean-Luc."

"That's not my way, *belle-mère* Katelina."

"The message came from Pedro, carried by people from Valerós. And from Tomás's son." Katelina held her hand out to him, palm down, which Taresa didn't understand. "One or more *bonfraires* is asking for your help."

"Does that mean he has to help me rescue Jaime?" Hélène asked, all of her commanding selfishness on display again.

Jean-Luc slumped back into his chair, head in his hands.

And Taresa learned far more French invective than her tutors had ever shared.

¤

Taresa believed she had enormous self-control, however much Yusuf teased her about leaping into trouble. She acted with firm purpose, not impulse. When Jean-Luc ceased hiding his face and instead folded his hands in his lap like a grudging penitent, she touched her newfound uncle's wrist.

Naked, dripping sweat, his sword clasped in his hand, Jean-Luc knelt at the feet of a man in chainmail who was seated in a carved throne-like chair. The man was ancient and not much larger than a gnome. Misery gripped Jean-Luc's belly. He could not avoid saying the *bonfraires'* oath.

"*Sodalitas, fidelitas, virtus.* Upon my honor I swear absolute loyalty to my brothers when called to arms. I swear to stand by my lord and king. I swear to serve as a defender of the poor and of the Holy Catholic Church."

The old man growled at him in Catalan. "Swear it on the name of Our Savior and on St-Jordi."

"I swear in the names of Christ Jesus, St-Jordi, and the Blessed Virgin Mary." Jean-Luc's hands trembled on the sword's grip, sliding down to the crosspiece. This oath settled like a yoke on his shoulders, the weight pressing down, shooting pain through every muscle.

The grizzled old man leaned close to Jean-Luc's face. "If you have the courage of our *bonfraires*, swear on the blood of St-Jordi that you won't break your father's heart while seeking your own redemption."

Jean-Luc whispered, "I swear." Yet he had no courage, just a raw, bleeding wound where his heart used to be.

The old man spoke again. Jean-Luc bent his head closer to hear. "As your *bonfraire,* I'd give everything to save you. I'd surrender my chance at heaven. Yet, *mon amic,* you must save yourself."

Taresa recoiled, ashamed to have intruded, befuddled by the man's searing pain, which had shot with a jolt through her own muscles. She'd thought that being a *bonfraire* meant being enfolded in a confraternity of loyal brothers. Instead, the *bonfraires'* oath was an agonizing burden.

19
Companions

SITTING TO BREAKFAST WITH HÉLÈNE and Jean-Luc and Katelina, Taresa felt her mind drifting to the room where Qasim had retreated with Yusuf. Jean-Luc dominated the table conversation, offering food to Hélène, and asking Katelina about her work the day before. Since Hélène and Katelina knew him, they seemed to tolerate his domination of the table conversation and didn't press him to answer to either Hélène's or Taresa's request. Though Hélène tried.

"Whoever holds Jaime can rule for him till he's of age. Right now, that's Simon. You do see the danger?" Hélène daintily accepted a cup of hot milk laced with cinnamon from Katelina. "Simon wants to be seen as the greatest knight, reviving Charlemagne's empire in the south. By taking Aragón and all of the south. Aquitaine will be next. That's why Simon has united with a set of knights who want to put Christendom on the right path."

"Simon and his knights seek to push their way of life on people who simply see the world differently. They seek to pervert God's chosen ruler," Taresa complained with more passion than Hélène. Confusion tumbled inside while she tried to understand how she ended up as Hélène's ally.

"Do you claim that whoever ends up king must be chosen by God?" Jean-Luc reached out to touch the garnet at Hélène's throat. "Is that your new passion, *ma dòmna*? That we need to do God's work for Him?"

Hélène seemed so befuddled by Jean-Luc's finger on that gemstone that she didn't speak. So Taresa answered. "Aragón and the Languedoc need rulers who prefer law and justice, and who respect the customs of the land. Not one like Simon, who claims he enforces God's rules while stealing and murdering the people he wants to rule."

Jean-Luc seemed startled, turning his attention from Hélène to Taresa, and abruptly changing the subject. "Were you there when Tomás fetched his son from Cairo?"

"No, I met him last year in Andalusia. After I met Sebastián."

"How did a *jeune fille* from Girona end up in Andalusia?"

"She did a better job," Hélène said, "of escaping a bad marriage than your friend Isabella of Valerós did. She's her own hero. May I call you Taresa now?"

"Don't mock me, *ma dòmna*."

"I swear by the Blessed Virgin that I am not. You have taught me well." Hélène turned to Jean-Luc, which Taresa felt as a merciful escape from the woman's attention. Yet she still felt Katelina's eyes on her. "*Mon ami,* I was to marry Giles de Nully. Did you know?"

"Marry Giles? Where's my horse? I should ride there now and warn him that Circe the sorceress has come to Cahors." Jean-Luc then flushed, angry again. "*Qu'est-ce que c'est?* You're marrying Giles so he'll help you steal Beaurain lands."

"Still so suspicious, Jean-Luc?" Hélène waved a finger, the way she did when teasing. "Hugues made you marquis when he died, because he felt so bad about what you suffered in Constantinople. You wouldn't feel suspicious if you hadn't taken all his titles and land, leaving me with nothing."

"I gave you a house, two houses. And an income sufficient to make any woman happy." He ticked off on his fingers the points he emphasized, his irritation with Hélène rising at each tick. "Both Philippe and Count Raymond confirmed my right to Beaurain lands and titles. Now you want to snare Giles into helping you in the Church courts and—*Vous sorcière!*"

Hélène was laughing, elegantly, but laughing so hard she had to wipe away tears.

"Madam?"

"It's just…" She held up her hand, having trouble speaking over laughter and tears. "I sought Giles's help for Maria's sake. I came to you for help because—"

She began to laugh and weep again, so they all had to wait while she gathered her emotions. Katelina watched, stalwart. Taresa's stomach clenched, embarrassed to be there, stuck where she didn't belong, but she couldn't gracefully escape to join Qasim and Yusuf.

"You see, *mon cher cœur*, Giles wanted me solely for his plan to take the Beaurain title and land." She sobered. "He promised to help me rescue Jaime, but I understand now that he's Simon's agent here. Which is why every seigneur he 'helps' in court ends up losing land to Simon."

"He served beside me under the Marquis de Beaurain in Constantinople. Giles hailed me as a lost comrade when he came to Cahors. He wouldn't…" Jean-Luc trailed off, lost in thought.

"Every other man betrayed you in Constantinople. If they were part of Crux Lunata. Like Giles was. If he does anything for Jaime, it will be to secure Simon's hold. Simon is the best way to power for Giles."

"*Jhezu del tron!*" Taresa forgot her resolution to stop calling on heaven idly. She needed divine intervention. She closed her eyes and bit down on the dismay that roiled in her belly: she'd told Giles about Milon murdering Pedro, asked for his help, seeking justice for Pedro. "*Renrén.*" Sebastián folded his arms, then repeated it. He hadn't spoken in days, and then at this moment he chose to visit over hundreds of leagues to call her a fool.

Taresa didn't need to be told.

"Are you well, Senhóra Taresa?" Katelina murmured beside her, her voice low, as if not wanting to interrupt the confrontation between Hélène and Jean-Luc. "Or merely exhausted?"

"*Òc.*" Taresa couldn't get more words out. Her heart swelled with dismay, shock, disgust, alarm.

"I should have seen it. You should have seen it, *cheri.*" Hélène wasn't paying attention to anyone but Jean-Luc. "Giles came home broke from Constantinople. His father refused to pay his debts. He had no choice but to come south with Simon, to invade the Languedoc. But he knew he'd never rise as a fighting knight. I just didn't hear Giles's story correctly each time he told it. A destitute French knight doesn't have gold to buy abandoned land in the Languedoc.

He might tell us all that story, but he gained that castle solely by serving Simon."

"Madam, you came here to warn me?" Jean-Luc seized Hélène's hand, where she'd drawn circles in the air while she talked.

"*Oui, cheri.* If Simon makes himself king…"

"He'll seize every title and any land granted by Philippe *le roi* in the Languedoc. And Giles hopes to be the new marquis."

"Therefore, you have every reason to help me—and these children," Hélène gestured toward Taresa, "to recover Jaime from Simon."

"Yes, I shall. Starting today."

"Then you'll go to Paris?" Katelina asked, joining their conversation for the first time. "Like your *bonfraires* asked?"

"Not Paris." Jean-Luc turned to Katelina. "While you were away, *belle-mere*, Nunó Sánchez asked me to ride with him to demand that Simon return the king of Aragón to his people. My men are preparing to leave tomorrow for Narbonne."

"The Count of Roussillon?" Katelina raised her dark brows, curious. Taresa knew Nunó as a cousin of Pedro's, who she'd been introduced to once at a banquet, as Sebastián's wife. The same Sebastián that kept whispering *renrén* in her ear.

"*Oui,*" Jean-Luc said. "By some perfidious misdirection, Nunó was late to Muret. Messengers sent his whole band out chasing geese. Now he's taking his army to Narbonne to demand that the archbishop take charge of Jaime." He then turned to Hélène. "So, madam, quite by accident, I'm serving Maria, as you wished. Dealing with Giles will have to wait until I return."

"And the request that Yusuf carries, to help your *bonfraires?*" Katelina asked mildly, while Taresa waited to see if her own mission would continue its trend toward catastrophe. As Yusuf had worried, their French knight had made other choices, because *los tres amics* came to Cahors too late.

"Surely we can figure a resolution for that. Philippe, however, is too far away to be of use in the current chaos." Jean-Luc spoke to Taresa again. "When Yusuf wakes, he and I need to talk."

¤

No longer able to bear separation from *los dos amics,* Taresa begged to be excused, to carry food to Qasim, who had refused to leave Yusuf's side.

"Of course," Katelina said. "Stay with him. You'll feel better. Fetch me in an instant if you need me. But get some rest. We can't help Yusuf if we're dead on our feet."

Blanca...Hélène said, "My best wishes for your dear friend's recovery."

While Taresa wrestled with confusion, since Hélène sounded sincere, Katelina said, "Senhóra Hélène, you must be exhausted, too. Please let me offer my chamber, so you can rest."

In the room where Yusuf had been put to rest in a real bed, covered with a quilted blanket, Taresa sat beside Qasim on the floor. Yusuf still didn't respond when either of his friends touched him, pushed his hair out of the way, offered a wet cloth to soothe his dry lips.

"I found Perseus," she said. "But he refuses to come with us to Paris. He's joining a viscount's army to force the archbishop in Narbonne to retrieve Jaime from Simon."

Qasim broke bread, offering her half of the small loaf. The cheese on the tray had been sliced and laid out in a fan, unlike the handfuls they'd torn from chunks of cheese they'd bought on the journey.

She couldn't swallow food, staring at Yusuf lying in the bed, as inert as those abandoned wooden dolls in the great hall. You had to look closely to see his chest rise with each breath. This was her fault; she'd foolishly believed people and so led her friends into this catastrophe. She had to fix it.

"Qasim, I'm begging you. Share Yusuf's secret. If you're his brother, I'm his sister. We can't find a way to heal him, if you won't help me understand what's wrong."

Qasim continued to eat, pretending to be as fastidious as Yusuf. He sipped from a mug of ale, no longer hot.

"He has a companion."

"Yes, he has you. And me."

"No, he carries an ancient creature made by God that lives in our world in a different way than we do."

"Then it is a demon?"

"No. This creature only seeks to help its companion."

"Then why is Yusuf ill?"

Qasim sighed, the way a priest does when hearing your very poor confession. "Because it's Yusuf. He argues with his companion every waking moment. Perhaps also in his sleep." Qasim rolled his eyes at the foolish thought. "He argues that a philosopher cannot be guided by a minion of the fire lord."

"Who's the fire lord?"

"I'm not sure."

"But it's not a devil? And not magic?" Taresa thought she understood. She knew two Norman cooks in the baggage train who insisted they were protected by *husnisse*, guardian kitchen imps, though no one else could see them.

"Not a devil. Yusuf insists it's just another creature of God." Qasim picked at the last of the crumbs on the tray. "However, his companion taught Yusuf to speak French."

"What shall we do? Can we talk to it?"

"I've tried," Qasim said. "If it hears me, it doesn't answer."

"Maybe if I touch Yusuf," she pondered, "perhaps my *Sensus Naturae* can find out what it wants. If it's supposed to protect Yusuf, it can't want *this* any more than we do." She pointed to Yusuf's pale, motionless figure.

Qasim yawned, obviously as exhausted as Taresa was. He said, "I'm thinking we should sleep. Tomás, my master, says you can't be any use in the world after too many days without sleep."

They crawled under the quilt that covered Yusuf, one on either side of him, neither wanting to be farther away. Qasim fell asleep instantly. But Taresa lay stiffly beside her brother-in-law, touching his hand, trying with all the force of her mind to see or hear his companion. But second-sight had never been under her control. This time she saw a long, ill-lit corridor where a voice sang in the far distance, in a tongue she'd never heard. Children played in that corridor. Yusuf's young brother, a toddler who'd left Toulouse to hide from the coming siege. The wild, cave-dwelling wretches they'd met in the upper hills. That poor boy in the Templars' stable. Another boy stood to the side watching, though another voice shrieked repeatedly. *Jaime, come play!*

Qasim murmured in his sleep, as if he were calming a horse.

Her muscles twitched, agitated, pulling at the core of her bones. Having failed everything and everyone, she couldn't sleep until she fixed things.

So Taresa rose and went in search of her newfound uncle-by-marriage, to beg that he leave enough men and horses to take *los tres amics* to Paris.

¤

"*Mon oncle*, a word."

With brief directions from a servant, Taresa caught up with Jean-Luc on a trail behind the mansion. He stopped at the top of a rise and glanced down at her.

"I guess that's true. We are related."

"I'm here to beg you, monsieur." She thought a moment. "How do I address a marquis?"

"You, my new niece, may call me Jean-Luc. But however you beg, I'm going to Narbonne, not Paris."

She caught up with Jean-Luc just then, at the top of the rise.

The sight below let loose a dam on her feelings; nostalgia and longing flooded through her veins. An armed band of two hundred people was breaking camp, preparing to travel.

"I know these people," she said, then noticed Jean-Luc's surprise. "Not these people, but others just like them. From the journey across Iberia last year. Knights, sergeants, scribes. Yours aren't from the Church, are they? There's a priest—your family chaplain? And your marshal and seneschal. You're traveling with one smith." She'd pointed below as she described who populated the camp. "Your cooks. Servants."

"That man is Count Nunó." Jean-Luc pointed Taresa's attention to a man on a black stallion, "He likes the costumes and pageants of French lords. Do you want to meet him?"

Nunó's hair wafted in the wind, bleached near-white by the sun. His helmet was tied behind his saddle. Near where he supervised from his horse, a half-dozen laundry women were busy getting everyone organized. She longed to greet them, regretting how awkward it would be.

"He looks like his father," Taresa said.

Jean-Luc cocked his head in that way he did when curious, wanting to learn more.

"I washed Sancho's shirts last year," she said, "on the road to Iberia. Your baggage train—smaller than what I traveled with—is as familiar as the streets of Girona."

Though covered against the weather, the contents of the wagons and packs on mules and horses were well known to her: spare harnesses and horseshoes, weapons and armor, canvas for tents, axes and shovels, cooking kettles and tripods, flour for bread and fodder for horses, bacon in barrels, lentils and white beans.

"You are a woman of many surprises," Jean-Luc said. "Is that how you lured Sebastián into marriage?"

"Lured? I washed his shirts and enjoyed his company," she said. "He married me because Pedro forced him to, to keep my land in Girona from being taken by the Church."

"Romantic."

"It has been, in truth."

"But Sebastián is a mere child." This was the second time Jean-Luc had asserted that false notion.

"He's seventeen next Candlemas Day. He's six feet tall. He led two thousand men in Andalusia."

"And what are you? Twenty?"

"Seventeen," she confessed, because he was her uncle-by-marriage and she had no reason to lie to him. "Your camp is familiar. Yet it's amazing. The battle at Muret was five days ago? Six? Seven? And you have two hundred men ready to march."

What she now wanted to ask: How much had his captains taken from local households to provision the kitchens for this armed band? How much gold was hidden in the wagons, to purchase supplies as they marched to Narbonne?

"You want to ask a question," Jean-Luc said, as if he read her mind. "Who's paying these men? Nuñó pays his men, I pay mine. Three marks per person, given that we're marching out of season. And I'm providing the horses and armor for half these men. As for the others…they brought their own, but to a different battle."

The men near them were speaking in Aragónese dialect, some in the local tongue, with Toulousain accents. That meant some must be survivors of Muret, while others were men who'd set out to defend Toulouse against siege but had been chased into the wilderness by Simon's army.

"Leaping goats! I didn't think…" She'd been so concerned about Yusuf, missing Sebastián, grieving over Pedro, upset by the Katelina's field hospital by the river, it wasn't until that moment she considered the deeper terror of Simon's onslaught. She forgot what she'd come to beg, and instead words burst out, while her heart kept beating, though it was more than half broken. "Who'll repay mortgages for all the men killed at Muret? How many people in Aragón and the south will starve this winter?"

"We shall go onward, one step at a time. I cannot console you, like a man should, because you understand how dire the world has become, through Simon's ambition." Then Jean-Luc asked the same jarring question Taresa did when waking each morning. "Shouldn't you be with Sebastián?"

"He's on the way to Rome with a herd of ambassadors, to ask the pope to force Simon to give Jaime back to Aragón."

"Ah! What we all desire! How did you end up on this adventure with Master Yusuf?"

"Pedro asked me to help Yusuf and Qasim travel across the Languedoc. They are…exotic." She wasn't sharing the other part, that Sebastián wanted her out of Toulouse before the siege and didn't want her going to Rome with him; that Pedro wanted her away from the coming battle.

"Why didn't Yusuf's father come with him?"

"He's…doing another task for Pedro."

"God help us all!" He exclaimed in French. "Pardon me, Senhóra. I shared adventures one year with Yusuf's father. It was a perpetual challenge. Do you live with Sebastián's family? Can I help you return to their care?"

"They retreated to the hills until Simon's threats of siege are over. I've lived on my own for many years." She resolved to ask what she most wanted. "I came to beg your help to bring the man who murdered Pedro to justice."

"He was killed in battle. Because he insisted for years on having another man wear his armor. You must know, from your adventures last year, that there's no justice on the battlefield."

"He was murdered. The man who killed him knew he was murdering a king. And I know who his killer is."

"How could you know that?"

"I heard him confess it. Once at the Templars' farm up in the hills. Again at—well, we had an adventure with some of Simon's heretic hunters. Please help find justice for Pedro."

Jean-Luc touched her, not like Giles had, but first one hand on her shoulder, then hugging her like...an uncle. "You are a wonder. Sebastián is lucky, isn't he?"

He sneezed—not Taresa—and a torrent of memories flowed into her belly, her heart, into her blood, into her tingling fingers.

> Men on the walls of a siege city, a crossbow bolt through one man's neck. Hunger, as if one's belly gnawed itself raw, and children crying in the streets for their dying dogs, their chickens, their mothers.
>
> A beloved man, dying in his arms, murdered.

Hunger wracked her body. His anguish burned in her veins. Taresa struggled out of Jean-Luc's embrace.

"I know the pain of losing a friend to a murderer," Jean-Luc said, since he didn't know she'd just lived through his memory. "We need to help the living right now. We need to restore the new king to Aragón. We must end the chaos by stopping Simon's ambition. There isn't time for revenge. Go to Paris with your friends, and get Philippe's help. Then—"

"No, Yusuf and Qasim can go on to Paris. Please let me travel with you to Narbonne. I want to help finish what Pedro asked us to do, making sure Jaime is returned to Aragón."

Jean-Luc had his hand up to stop her pleading, which she appreciated because her voice sounded in her own ears as though she was begging. Because she was begging.

"An armed camp is not a place for a woman. And I say this knowing you come from a family that allows its women to travel with knights into danger."

He meant Sebastián's mother, but Taresa said, "Like Senhóra Kate-lina? The years she traveled with armies in the Outremer?"

"I can't take responsibility for you, Taresa."

"I can take care of myself. I went to Andalusia on my own. There and back again. I need to finish this work for Pedro. I don't need —"

"To learn to take no for an answer?" Jean-Luc said it gently, but she felt it like the crossbow bolt in his memory.

"Fine. Paris it is, then." She fished that heretics' coin from the pouch inside her shirt. *"S'il vous plaît, mon oncle,* if I'm not to go to Narbonne, let me share the gold I have, for your army's pay and provisioning."

Jean-Luc's sapphire eyes glistened with curiosity when she dropped it in his hand. He frowned at the images on the coin. "I'd think, because of Sebastián, you'd be with the *bonfraires* rather than these renegades."

"I found it in the Templars' barn. The man who killed Pedro had a pocket full of them. Made from heretics' gold, he claimed."

"That makes sense. The Wheel and Serpent fraternity of knights rose during that ill-conceived crusade in Constantinople. It's a rag-tag brotherhood of men whose former confraternities disbanded, like Crux Lunata. And who haven't been accepted by the Templars or other military orders."

"You don't want their coin?"

"Oh, gold is gold." He secured the coin within his own tunic. "Whether it's heretics' gold or not, we'll use it to stop Simon. Now, go see if your friend Yusuf can talk with me."

"Òc." If Yusuf was awake, she'd first insist on going to Paris. Yusuf had no power in her life to deny her desire.

¤

Eager to share news, Taresa slipped into the room where she expected to find Qasim and Yusuf sleeping. However, she found Qasim on his knees beside the bed where Yusuf still lay motionless. He didn't look away when Taresa entered. She closed the door and sat on the floor beside him.

"I know that your lord wants you here." Qasim sounded like a man coaxing a child, or luring a cat from under this bed.

Taresa held Yusuf's hand, listening for an answer.

"I understand that this is where you are supposed to be." Qasim continued pleading. "It's also where I'm supposed to be. You must see that he and I are connected, like twin brothers."

That song she'd heard before, the one she didn't understand, grew louder, a series of notes and scales as unfamiliar as the language of the song. It was a sad song, similar to a mournful *canço de guèrra* Yusuf sang at last night's dinner.

"I'm like you," Qasim said, in the same voice that he magically calmed horses. "Loyal. Looking out for my companion."

One long mournful note, echoing along that dreamlike corridor.

"But you must see," Qasim coaxed, "that he isn't a suitable companion for you. Can you tell your fire lord that?"

Qasim and Taresa both breathed deeply, each lying on opposite sides of the cot, their arms wrapped around Yusuf, who burned under the quilt like a child with a death-fever. Hot as blacksmith's fire.

"Taresa?" Qasim whispered. "Are you awake?"

"Yes."

"I have to try something. Since I don't know what else to do."

"What?"

"Just—trust me. And help if I call for you."

"I'm not leaving," she said.

"Fine. But keep silent."

They were both overheated by Yusuf's fever. Qasim threw the quilt to the floor and knelt beside the cot, his hands folded as if in confession.

"Dear creature, I don't know your name," he said. "But I honor you. Because you and I are alike. We care more for our friends than we care for ourselves."

Those words were near to what Giles said when he tried to coax Taresa into revealing what she saw in a vision. Her muscles twitched again, ripping at her anxious core.

Qasim whispered. "Yusuf says there's free will. God lets us choose our fate. You aren't a slave to your lord, so you can choose another host, a better host. Choose me. You can still do what your lord desires. Just use me to protect him."

Taresa's hand scalded where it lay on Yusuf's.

"What magic words can I say?" Continuing to lure out that creature, Qasim recited a series of pleas. "I won't argue with you, dear spirit, since I don't believe anything. I'll take you wherever you want to go. I'll keep Yusuf safer than anyone under heaven has ever done."

Qasim whistled then, notes from that foolish children's song Yusuf sang to annoy them. Then Qasim sang the words, as tuneless as a starling.

> I'm a *cavaller* in chainmail,
> and here's my steely blade.
>
> Unlace my rusty aventail,
> and see if you're obeyed.

Lightning struck the mansion just then, thunder rattling doors, shaking the bed, booming again. Again. The lightning as blinding and the thunder as frightening as the worst of storms Taresa suffered through as a child. Yusuf's hand moved under hers.

An enormous bird, larger than Giles's silver gyrfalcon, swooped through the room, first whistling at an ear-breaking high pitch, then emitting a hoarse screech, its claws out like a raptor preparing to seize its prey. With the creature's second swoop, Taresa ducked her head, covering it with both arms to protect against those hideous claws.

Silence.

Then Qasim was singing that song from the long, imaginary corridor, no longer sad, and almost as beautiful as Yusuf would sing it. He stood from the bed, crossed his arms so he looked like a fearsome warrior, except he twitched like Yusuf, as if listening for sounds that weren't there and then shrugging off gnats. Then he smiled, the warrior disappearing, dimples deepening in his cheeks, as handsome as Taresa had ever seen him.

"Serena Taresa, because you saved Yusuf's life, I'm permitted to tell you—though you must keep it a secret—that my qareen is named Zirari. It thinks you are nice."

"Nice?"

Qasim frowned, tipping his head to listen to sounds Taresa couldn't hear. He said, "As soon as Yusuf wakes, we have to return to Giles's *domus*. I hid Pedro's letter there and need to retrieve it."

"You left the letter behind?" Of all the surprises in the last few moments, this one seemed less a dream and more like a nightmare.

"We didn't know Kalypso was a friend. I hid it when I undressed Yusuf for her. I didn't have a chance to retrieve it before we left. The silver seigneur hung too close by, watching us, shepherding us out of the room."

"Yusuf will choke you in your sleep if you lost that letter."

Beside Taresa on the bed, Yusuf stirred. He reached for her hand, stroked it for a moment, his own hand now a normal temperature.

> The hot Cairo wind blew his hair astray, whipping it over his eyes, stinging his face, but he couldn't grab it. He was smothered, pressed hard again a man's cotton shirt that smelled of both sweat and soap, and then more arms around him. A boy. A woman.
>
> "*Ai, fadrin. We've found you at last.*" The warm, rich timbre of a voice from every dream. His father. "*We're taking you home. If you want to be with us.*"

"Lost what? What did you lose, *belette muet?*" Yusuf said. He stopped stroking Taresa's hand, which shut her out of his memory of meeting his father in Cairo, but warmth from the vision lingered in her heart, in her blood. "We still need to go to Cahors and find Perseus. And I'm dying from hunger. Taresa, do we have anything to eat?"

Yusuf rose from the bed like a man still dreaming and searched for his clothes. He collided with Qasim and stepped back, surprised.

"What are you doing with my qareen, *belette muet?*"

"*Ai, gai sauvatge.* It isn't yours anymore."

"I've had the strangest dream. Where are my breeches? My shirt? My boots?"

With a short, sharp knock on the chamber's door, Jean-Luc stood in the archway, his shoulders filling most of the opening. He said, "Does anyone want to hear my wishes, after begging me to hear theirs? I wish to talk with Master Yusuf. Is that you?"

"*Oui,* monsieur. Who are you?"

"This is Perseus," Taresa said. "He's Sebastián's uncle by marriage. And Kalypso is the former senhóra of Valerós."

Yusuf still moved like a man who'd roused from a pleasant dream, unsurprised by this news. "That explains her Greek accent. Katelina of Naxos, if I remember the stories Sebastián told. *Bonjour, Perseus.*"

"I don't have much time," Jean-Luc said. "I need to learn what you know from working in Pedro's court."

"Actually," Taresa said, "he was right by Pedro's side for the last year, as his chief scribe."

"Even better. If you're well enough, I want words with you." He beckoned Yusuf, as imperious as he'd been with Hélène earlier.

Yusuf didn't respond to the command. "Shall I dress first?"

"While you put on your linen and breeches, tell me all you know about Jaime." Jean-Luc leaned on the archway, arms crossed. "What were Pedro's plans for Jaime and Simon?"

"I can tell you everything on the road to Paris," Yusuf said.

"I'm on my way to Narbonne," Jean-Luc said, "to demand Jaime be returned to Aragón. I can't go to Paris with you."

"But Pedro wants...wanted..." Yusuf stopped, uncharacteristically uncertain.

Katelina came up behind Jean-Luc, and he stepped into the room, overfilling it, to allow her to join them. Katelina said, "Some of our people can take Yusuf to Paris. We can do more than nothing. But I'd like to check my miraculously healed patient before you take him away for an inquisition."

"I can manage both," Yusuf said. "At the same time." He reached for his shirt, which Qasim had left folded at the foot of his cot. He'd pulled it over his head, held the linen ties in his hand, and then seemed to wake from his nice dream to ask, "Where's Pedro's letter?"

20
Heretics' Gold

THEY LEFT JEAN-LUC TO SPEAK with Yusuf, when the marquis made it clear that others weren't invited into the conversation.

Taresa studied Qasim "Since you took Yusuf's creature—"

"It came to me. You can't take or give a qareen. The creature has free will."

"The soft blue light that glows around you is now streaked with deep red lines, like veins in a leaf. You're even more handsome in this new light. And when you touch your sword, sparks jump from your hand."

"I don't feel different," he said. "Perhaps more sure of what to do next. I'll ride out to fetch Pedro's letter. Yusuf should stay here with you."

"No. I'm going with you." Taresa's twitching muscles demanded action, whatever she could do to recover from total failure. Yusuf was safe here, at Perseus's wildly beautiful house until they returned from Giles's towers, where they had to go. "I'll distract Giles and his people while you fetch the letter."

He agreed. They moved through the deserted great room, Jean-Luc's and Yusuf's voices drifting behind them.

Yusuf: "Pedro named me his diplomat. He trusted me to be his best messenger."

Jean-Luc: "Yet he gave you a task you can't do alone. And what about this king-killer? Are you seeking revenge?"

"We don't murder people for justice." Yusuf repeated what he'd said two days earlier.

"But in the extreme," Jean-Luc said, "a life can be taken to stop a greater crime."

"Right now, rather than revenge, we need to stop Simon's plot to make himself king."

Jean-Luc coughed. "That's not the first choice your father would likely make."

"No, but I am my father's son. And I loved Pedro as much as he did."

Then distinct words couldn't be heard. Qasim and Taresa weren't three lance lengths outside the mansion door before Qasim halted. He shook his head, shrugged his shoulders. Took another step. Turned in a circle.

"Leaping goats! What now?" How did she end up *cavaller de saltant cabres*?

"We have to take Yusuf with us. I can't leave him."

"Because your companion says so?"

"It's best for Yusuf."

"The companion who made Yusuf ill? Who didn't protect him in Giles's chapel?"

"Yusuf did it to himself. He was being as stupid as Pedro wearing plain armor." Qasim headed back to the mansion.

"You're annoyed with Yusuf for being in danger? With Pedro for getting killed?"

"It's stupid to refuse the protection the gods give you." Qasim jerked open the mansion door.

"The gods? Like the goodmen's two Gods?"

"Like many more gods than you can imagine. Thousands."

Qasim stomped into the house, calling Yusuf's name. Jean-Luc passed them, headed in the direction of his armed camp.

"Go with God," Jean-Luc said in French. "I've left a dozen men to ride with you."

Yusuf emerged, now totally dressed. "Perseus will send a letter of introduction and horses." He spread his hands, yielding to fate. "It's not optimal, but the best we can hope for. And he has transport to take you to Toulouse, Taresa."

"I'm coming with you. You aren't my master to tell me no. And no one has to take care of me."

"We shall see." He turned to Qasim. "How will you retrieve Pedro's letter?"

Qasim caught Taresa's eye, though not acknowledging her fury. "Taresa has the plan. We'll do what she says."

"What does Zirari say?" Yusuf wanted to know what the qareen thought before asking for Taresa's plan. She kept her mouth closed against protest. She'd fight for justice later.

"Zirari says to be careful." Qasim tilted his head, talking and listening at the same time. Already annoyed with Yusuf, after having spent the night in rigid fear for his life, Taresa struggled against letting that annoyance spread to Qasim and his companion.

"Because another fire creature lives in Giles's tower?" Yusuf said. "Zirari was guessing who else was present before the carving fell. That means—"

"What?" About to mount her horse, Taresa stopped in surprise. "Did Milon use magic to kill Pedro?"

"There's no such thing as magic," Qasim said, at the same time as Yusuf.

"Yet your thing sniffed him and found another creature?"

"It's not a thing," Yusuf said. "You are respectful of people, Taresa. Please respect my—our companion."

"You're defending the...creature...that almost killed you?"

"It wasn't Zirari's fault," Yusuf said. "It was like a wildfire burning us both. I caused pain by arguing that lower-order creatures belong only in dreams and imagination."

"Then you believe in magic now?"

"It isn't magic. It's a creature God made which our eyes cannot usually see. It comes from the same natural world as your second-sight. *Sensus Naturae*."

"But you said...I never struggled over seeing memories and auras. If it isn't a demon or magic, why did it make you sick?"

"You seem to have understood from the cradle that your second-sight is natural. My experience was different. I believed in my rational mind from the cradle. But I understand it now, since we've stopped struggling with each other."

"Instead of fighting it, we need to listen to what Zirari can tell us," Qasim said.

"What is that, Qasim?" Yusuf was deeply interested.

"Zirari insists that there's a bad man in the castle who's possessed by an afritan."

"I had guessed he possessed an ifrit," Yusuf said. "How else could a man like Milon get close enough to Pedro to kill him?"

"Not an ifrit, like you find in rocks in the desert. Only an ancient and fading afritan." Qasim tipped his head, listening to his companion. "This afritan once served the fire lord, but it's been wandering lost in Greek lands for eons, being sold from one conjurer to the next."

"Zi—my companion didn't tell me this in the castle." Yusuf frowned. "As far as I remember."

"Your...my...companion saw it in the chapel, before the afritan sensed it was being watched. It came here from across the Great Sea. The bad man thinks he controls the afritan, but he doesn't. It's a Middle Kingdom afritan that just can't free itself."

"Milon carried it home from crusading?"

"From Constantinople." Qasim listened again.

"Milon used magic!" Taresa saw the image from Giles's memory again, of a brutal fight in an exotic city, over a gold coin. That must be when Milon got possession of his creature, which thrilled her, knowing now what this meant. "We're returning for Pedro's letter and to trap Pedro's killer."

"Zirari thinks it's most important to free the afritan."

"How?" Yusuf asked, as if he were prepared to turn from their real goal, to carry a message to Paris for the sake of the baby king of Aragón.

"Kill its current host." Qasim reported this, not seeming to have any emotional reaction to it.

Taresa watched Yusuf as he pondered this. Previously, he'd refused to consider any idea of killing Milon, insisting they offer him up to judgment under law. Qasim, meanwhile, had checked his horse's harness and Yusuf's horse, and they both mounted, all of them now ready to ride back to the two towers.

"Your companion seeks to keep you safe, right?" Taresa asked Qasim, unsure whether this creature was leading them into jeopardy to free its fellow magical spirit.

"No, it's tied to Yusuf. It's guarded his bloodline for generations."

"Is this afritan a guardian creature like your qareen?" She wanted to know more, while waiting to learn how Yusuf felt about *kill its host* as the next course of action. "What does the afritan want? Does it serve the same god as the qareen?"

"Long ago, yes." Qasim was listening and talking, like a translator in Pedro's court, explaining what spies reported in Arabic. "But it's eons since this afritan sat at the fire lord's feet. So, it has just a modest bit of infernal magic, the same as you'd find in the sacred springs and rocks. It's not powerless, the way humans are. But it's not a djinni who doesn't know evil from good. Its wings are deformed. It can't fly any more. Can't even say the fire lord's name in the proper way."

"You made me sick whenever prayers were said around me." Yusuf, who apparently still saw his qareen, glared at whatever invisible creature sat on Qasim's shoulder. "How can that bad man enter a church and swear oaths if he carries a creature like you?"

Qasim sniffed. "The qareen didn't make you ill. You did that to yourself." He tipped his head again, listening. "You'd compare a barn cat to a desert lion? That is how the afritan is similar to your… my…our companion."

Taresa insisted again, "Yusuf, what does this mean? You don't believe in magic."

"I assess what I see in the physical world. I experienced the qareen. I don't deny its existence, only its right to intrude on my thoughts." Yusuf considered for a moment. "King Solomon converted some ifrits. Can this creature be put on another path, if we free it from its host?"

"Our companion knew this afritan in Persepolis. Its sole power is to make its host invincible to iron weapons. And it prefers women as its host. Zirari doesn't know how a man coaxed this afritan into service. Though that's what Zirari knew three thousand years ago."

"Can we defeat it? How?"

Qasim said, "We'll free it, not defeat it. We can destroy the talisman that binds it to a host. It's only as evil as the human who carries it."

Since Yusuf hesitated, Taresa said, "We need to retrieve Pedro's letter. Then worry about freeing the creature."

And also destroy Pedro's killer, which was Taresa's personal desire. But they were riding too hard and too fast to continue the conversation.

¤

The fog had crawled down from the mountain and muffled the countryside. They'd ridden this road the night before, led by people who knew the way. They'd had no opportunity to see landmarks in the dark and rain then and had no chance to see now. They were at the mercy of their horses.

And Qasim's invisible qareen. Who had unending advice for how they kept safe.

"There's a turtle in the road." Qasim was off his horse, looking for it. He found it, seemingly lost in the center of the lane. The animal's shell was a sickly green; its fat, scaled legs swam through the fog while Qasim carried it to the side of the road.

"They love to do the sweet thing," Qasim said.

"What thing?"

"What married people do. That turtle has five wives and sixty-four children."

"I don't want to know about turtles' married life," Taresa said. "Why did that turtle have to be moved off the road?"

"The turtle says soldiers are riding this way," Qasim said, reporting news from his companion. "We should take cover. Everyone in the forest is getting out of their way."

"Turtle soup is good, particularly in a cream broth," Yusuf said. "Don't you think, *ma belette muet?*"

Whatever Yusuf was teasing him about, Qasim didn't answer. Instead, he said, "The merlins called out to everyone to flee up into the hills. Then the crows began diving, while rabbits are running for their burrows."

"*Mmm,* roast rabbit on a stick," Yusuf said. "Or a nice stew. Do you prefer red wine or white in a rabbit stew?"

"*No ho sé, boca grande,*" Qasim muttered, more *valencià* than Catalan.

"Why are you annoying him?" Taresa demanded of Yusuf.

"He's learning," Yusuf said. "It's difficult to eat little animals that are friends with your companion."

"Leave him alone," Taresa said. "He saved you."

"We shall see," Yusuf grinned.

"The fox said to run for the hedges." Qasim didn't seem to be paying attention to Yusuf.

"Isn't that a children's game? The Fox Says…hide your eyes. The Fox Says…touch your nose. The Fox Says—"

"The fox says there's a trap in the road ahead," Qasim said. "The crows are going for its carrion."

"We need to keep riding," Taresa said. "Not follow critters in the brush."

Yusuf began to sing.

> I'm a *cavaller* in chainmail,
> better than a knight, though waylaid.
>
> We can forget Cahors. It will always rain.
> Still want my love back from crusade.
>
> I'll keep us safe on this sodden trail.
> But do as I say, since I'm not afraid.

The bone-chilling noise of snarling dogs grated in the air. They slowed while rounding a bend. Where the trail narrowed between huge boulders, a fallen tree blocked the way, a beech hacked down with axes. Three hooded figures stood atop the tree's trunk among leafy branches, pointing crossbows at the travelers.

"We need to travel up this road," Taresa called. "Is there a detour?"

"This road is plagued with bandits. Until the local lord can solve it, we're stopping passage."

Hearing the woman's voice, Taresa called her name. "Joaneta?" One of the pair of Joanetas from the merchants' camp.

"Master Tarek? I thought you were traveling to Cahors and Paris."

"We are. We're retrieving possessions we left behind at the seigneur's castle."

"Is your lady companion well? Or did she remain with the seigneur?"

"She's staying with the Marquis de Beaurain. What made you take to barricades?"

Los tres amics dismounted. They stood below the fallen tree, gazing up at the armed women who stood between them and Pedro's letter. When Qasim approached the fallen tree, the dog at Joaneta's side jumped down beside Qasim, not to attack but once more seeking Qasim's attention in that craven way all the merchants' dogs did. Qasim obliged, rubbing that dog's ear with affection, asking several times, "*Que és un bon noi?*"

Ignoring the craven behavior of her dog, Joaneta said, "A pair of heretic hunters and their henchmen came to our camp, not long after you left. Our men were away, and we weren't prepared to defend with weapons, though the hunters were prepared to attack."

"One of the hunters is a gold bug." The oldest woman among them spoke up. "The kind of snake who pretends he can douse for gold, the way there's some can douse for water. He sniffed around our camp, took all our gold."

Another of the women said, "They held swords to our throats, insisting we say a creed and swear loyalty to the Catholic Church."

"While mauling us," the older woman said.

"We've had it with these bandits. Pretending to be God's soldiers. No one passes until the local lord comes to deal with this…" Joaneta sought words. "Travesty."

"But you know us," Taresa said, hoping to speak in her best, friendliest voice. "Can't you let us past?"

The women consulted, speaking so low that Taresa couldn't hear. Finally Joaneta said, "There's a trail back down below, through the beech grove. It circles around this hill."

"But we wish you'd wait," one of the women said. "Until the lord comes to take our prisoners. We can use three good men."

"Master Tarek can stay with you." Yusuf was mounting his horse. Qasim, too, to the heartbreak of his dog-friend. Then they were off, leaving Taresa with the three distressed women.

"Who's your prisoner?" Taresa asked, saving her ire for her deserting friends for another time. Perhaps for idle moments on the road to Paris.

"The gold bug," Joaneta said. "He came back this way early in the morning, and we—"

"*Jhezu del tron!*" Taresa slipped into her old bad habit. "Milon de Breteuil."

She hobbled her horse where it could browse alongside the road, and then climbed the fallen beech tree to join the women.

"You know him?" Joaneta held out her hand to boost Taresa up beside her.

"He's a murderer and a thief." What occurred to her just as she jumped down the other side of the women's barricade was the loneliness of the road during this day's ride. "We didn't pass your messenger on our way back from Cahors. Is he lost?"

"We sent for the neighboring lord, up at the two towers."

"*Aiieee!*"

"What, Master Tarek?"

"Giles de Nully is a friend of the man you're holding. Your messenger may be inviting destruction, not salvation."

And Qasim and Yusuf were riding into disaster.

Which way to turn? They were most of the way to Giles's towers. It was too far to ride back to Jean-Luc's mansion in search of help. Her heart beat once with the thought that this catastrophe wasn't her fault. Perhaps everything thus far was the malicious game among thousands of unknown gods. One of those gods must hold a grudge against people who are simply trying to do right in the world.

"Take me where you're holding him."

Taresa had her dagger out, the useless scabbard with the wooden training stake banging her thigh as they descended to a glade where five more women guarded a man they'd tied to a tree.

Milon de Breteuil, how she'd most wanted to see him: bruised, battered, and begging, crying for mercy, with four slavering, snarling dogs that wanted to tear into him.

Yusuf's philosophy, about revenge not being the same as justice, nagged at her. Yet the dagger in her hand felt as if it had a different philosophy, that it possessed an alluring desire to plunge into the king-killer's throat.

But Milon was protected by magic. Iron weapons wouldn't kill him. Perhaps unleash one dog? Or two?

¤

"Monsieur King-killer, we meet again."

"Ah, Master Tarek. Just in time to help an old friend."

"Have we ever been friends?" Taresa stood with her hands on her hips, looking down at him, not close enough to spit, which is what she wanted to do first. "We hadn't met when I watched you murder that cottager—for what? Lentils and lettuce?"

"That *was* you hiding in the bushes." He smirked, inappropriate for a man tied to a tree, bleeding from the gash on his forehead.

"I don't believe we'd met yet when you murdered that little boy and your priest-friend in the Templars' barn. What was his sin?"

"Blubbering and whining."

"I mean the priest, not the little boy. Yes, the little boy was crying. But you killed him because he'd heard you brag about killing Pedro."

"Who in Simon's world will care that I claim to have murdered Pedro? Every French man and boy in the territory wanted him dead. The priest? He whined and blubbered about that heretic cottager who refused to say his creed, kept shouting heretic prayers."

"I'm persuaded only by my brother's philosophy," Taresa said, "that it's best to deliver you for justice, instead of killing you."

"Are you a killer, young Master Tarek? I don't believe you've ever wet a blade on this earth. Could you even skin a rabbit?" Milon wiggled in his bonds. "Now, if you will convince these women of their error of their ways, Master Tarek, all will be forgiven."

"Forgiven?"

"By God and Church, you shall be free of your error."

"Error? These women captured a bandit, a roadside thief. And they hold him for judgment. The Marquis de Beaurain has already heard of your many sins. Judgment will be swift and sure."

Milon laughed at her, throwing his head back. She hated being laughed at, not least by a king-killer bound to a tree. If her dagger were free to do as it desired, Milon would be answering to heaven.

"Who—who—" Milon laughed too hard to get his words out. "Who do you think will be the Marquis de Beaurain by—let us say— dawn tomorrow?"

A voice hailed them in French.

"*Bonjour, femmes. Que se passe-t-il ici?*"

Two men descended into the glade, their swords drawn. Taresa didn't recognize them, but they wore Giles's colors.

"It appears there's been a misunderstanding," the taller of the two men said. "This man you're holding works for God."

"Òc," Taresa answered. "The misunderstanding is that this miscreant works for a thousand devils."

Two more men came behind them, holding Qasim and Yusuf captive. Things had changed too fast and needed to be reversed.

"Let us reason together," Taresa said, "as men who know the most important thing in life is justice."

Milon said, "The most important thing in life is to do whatever you must to beat scum. My father caused us to live like peasants because he foolishly insisted on honesty and piety, and beat his sons for lying."

"Not beaten often enough," Taresa persisted.

"Indeed." Qasim joined in. "But your father was wrong, Monsieur Milon. Nothing is more important than protecting those you owe allegiance."

Yusuf said, "You all know nothing of philosophy. Nothing is more important than trust. I trust these two, which makes them my brothers, my family."

"Ah, a family that lives together and, now," Milon's tongue snaked out, licked his lips, preparing for a smile, "will die together."

"Call the dogs!" Taresa shouted in Catalan to Qasim, imitating his *valencià* accent.

"*Hola, gos!*" Qasim shouted. The dogs ran from the women toward him. "*Ajuda, gossos!*"

They seemed to know already what Qasim wanted. At his command, in no language Taresa knew, the dogs leaped at the two captors, teeth clamped on calves or hands, while one lunged for another man's throat. Qasim backed out of the dogs' melee. The rope binding Yusuf and Qasim had been abandoned. They grabbed for their captors' dropped weapons.

Of course, the dogs trapping the two men holding Qasim and Yusuf meant that the other two men were free to threaten the women who surrounded Milon.

Taresa, hanging back with Joaneta, saw that the woman froze, unable to let loose her drawn crossbow bolt. Taresa hugged Joaneta from behind, taking time to ensure none of the women were in the path of the bolt before forcing Joaneta to let the bolt loose. The force of the crossbow's release pushed both Joaneta and Taresa, who stepped back, while the bolt winged the man attempting to untie Milon. He screamed.

The other man threatened three of the women with his sword. They backed away just before one of the women atop the fallen beech tree found her courage and fired her crossbow. That bolt tore through the wrist of the man who threatened with his sword, which fell to the ground while he shrieked in horror, staring at his struck hand. His other hand poised, unsure whether to jerk out the bolt.

In the commotion, Milon had gotten free. His hand snaked around Taresa's middle, his breath hot at her ear. "*Allez, garçon doux.* Call off the dogs. Or die." He had a dagger, from who knows where, up by her ear.

Taresa struck back instinctively, moving in the way she'd learned from her first fight master, an ancient woman in the baggage train, teaching young women to defend against over-earnest men.

Step back, mash your attacker's instep.

Elbow up under ribs, to stop his breathing.

Turn, mash up under his jaw, bashing his throat.

Strike again into his middle.

Except she held her willful dagger, which she thrust up and lodged in the man's innards. Shocked, still catching his breath from her first strike, still clutching his own dagger, Milon opened his mouth to speak.

A moment already lived. Blood poured from the dark cavern of his mouth. Demons danced out of hell. The smell of his destroyed guts filled Taresa's nose, overwhelming the metallic tang of blood.

"Goodbye, king-killer. May God save your soul. Or not." It was a sin not to wish God's grace on a dying man. But rather than worrying whether she risked her soul, her dismay was seeing the man's blood on her boot.

"I never—" Milon pitched forward, and Taresa had to jump to avoid having his gore and carcass touching her.

By now, the other four attackers had been subdued and bound, and Qasim called the dogs away for sugar-talk and petting.

"We'll have to tend their wounds," Joaneta said to her friends.

"Of course," two women said simultaneously. The others were already checking the dead versus the living, and stripping anything of value from the dead. Just like gleaning on a battlefield.

"And send a messenger the other direction," Taresa said. "You need help from the Marquis de Beaurain."

"We wait for help?" Qasim looked up from where one of the massive dogs licked him and demanded love.

"Not if you want the letter back." Taresa said. She wiped her dagger clean, first in the grass, then across Milon's surcoat, still looking for how she felt about the death of the king-killer. No rush of triumph. No sense of victory. Something was wrong. "Though, I wonder why you don't just write another one, Yusuf. You inked the original for Pedro. You know what it says."

"I don't have Pedro's seal."

"For God's sake, Philippe knows by now that Pedro's dead. He doesn't know Simon is planning to use Jamie to make himself king. Just tell him when we get to Paris."

Yusuf ignored that she said *we*, but he persisted about what must be done next. "We need Pedro's signed letter. Therefore, we ride back to the two towers."

"Fine. This time, I'm going with you."

"Your horse is back there." Yusuf pointed beyond the fallen beech tree.

"I'll borrow one of those fellows' horses and leave mine for later."

She snatched up the leather thongs that had bound Milon to the tree, also intending to take the best of the attackers' swords, which seemed to be Milon's. She picked it up, then juggled to get that sword into her sheath and the dagger back into her baldric. A smear of blood near the dagger's handle stopped her, since she must have known from the cradle not to put away an unclean blade.

"How do we approach the silver-haired seigneur?" Yusuf said. "Since your friends here sent a messenger about capturing Milon."

"We just ask." Taresa laid aside the booty sword and cleaned her dagger again, still distracted. "We're innocent of anything and everything, aren't we?"

"Just ask?" Yusuf seemed to hesitate, which created uncertainty among all three of them, since he most wanted the letter. "Fine, but we'll be well armed. Come, *ma belette muet*. We ride."

Qasim kissed his dog-saviors goodbye. He straightened, looking astonished, apparently listening to his companion again. "There's no free spirit here, seeking a new host."

At the same moment, Taresa recognized what was wrong. The afritan protected against iron weapons. Yet Milon was dead from her steel blade.

"Zirari was wrong?" Yusuf, for having argued with his qareen over the past fortnight, seemed unable to believe the creature had made a mistake.

"No matter," Taresa said, thinking about how she'd tell this story to Sebastián, beginning to feel a warming satisfaction flow through her veins. She tied the booty sword from Milon to the gear behind her saddle, not wanting to touch it or put it in her scabbard. "A king-killer is dead."

"Zirari isn't so sure," Qasim said.

21
Deja Vu

AT THEIR FIRST MEETING, AFTER rescuing them from the wild boar, Giles espoused the values of the best of southern seigneurs. He smiled in the sunshine, whispering to his hooded hawk as it perched on his heavy leather glove and gobbled its reward. Taresa felt immense joy when she first touched his hand, the joy of young boys who wanted to fly like a merlin.

When she next touched Giles's hand in greeting, he'd looked at *los tres amics* and remembered a rowdy group of young men, all in love with themselves.

Later, when Giles touched Taresa's hand while they petted goats, they'd shared an already-lived moment, his memories again celebrated the joys of young men traveling.

He appeared as a joyous crusader when he forced Taresa and Milon into a hand-over-hand trinity, a memory that ended with one friend crumpled and bleeding in the street. She'd understood that there'd been a disruption in friendship. And she'd guessed that it was Giles who lay in the street in that memory, and Milon who'd stolen the coin that became the mold for melting heretics' wealth into coins.

Except the goodmen and goodwomen of the Languedoc didn't have any wealth. They abjured oaths, and meat and cheese and wine, and shared what they had, living sparse lives, no greater wealth than any of the heretic cottagers in the wilderness who'd sold them food for a penny and a song—or had their cottages burned by Milon and his heretic hunters.

He'd kissed her and flooded her veins with anguish—so that she should have understood then that Blanca—Hélène—was not his true love.

He'd seduced her into thinking they believed the same, in the confraternity of true comrades, because she'd felt alone for a few moments, shut out by Yusuf and Qasim from Paris, not hearing Sebastián's voice. She hadn't doubted Giles until he'd protected Milon—and then she believed it was because of a long-lost boys' allegiance.

Of course, Giles was never going to carry her tale to the Count of Toulouse, seeking justice for Pedro, wanting prosecution of Milon as Pedro's killer.

Yusuf's protector, Zirari, had been deceived. Hélène, too. And that was Taresa's comforting company: an ancient qareen and a long-time seductress had been fooled, just as she had been.

When they paused, a few moments' ride from the tower, Yusuf came to her side.

"I'm sorry it had to be you back there, that Qasim or I didn't come to save you. A man's death is hard to have on your hands, even when you're stopping evil." He embraced her, which he seldom initiated, and she sneezed.

> He looked down at Sebastián's grandfather and nemesis at his feet, dead and never making his way to heaven, if such a child's fantasy existed. Everyone around crying out prayers, shouting for the safety of kings.

> He looked around the kings' pavilion, there on the hillside of Las Navas del Tolosa, seeing Pedro's surprised expression. Hearing Taresa crying because her childhood friend had just been murdered by another man. Seeing his blade, the one Sebastián gave him, to keep him safe.

> He hated fighting. He hated the high value his brother Sebastián and his father placed on mastery of the steel blade. He believed men could and should live in peace, that war and conspiracy and greed were all evil. Vanities.

> He looked down at the man dead at his feet, who'd caused so much pain and misery and death among his friends and

family. The man who sought to assassinate Pedro just five heartbeats earlier. He should feel—what?

He felt like he'd been working all day and needed a rest.

Taresa stepped away from his embrace. "I was there. That day when you saved Pedro. And I feel the same today. Nothing. Relieved that I didn't die. That you and Qasim are safe." He nodded, accepting it, but she added, "And I saved myself. I don't need you or Qasim to save me. Just accept me as a brother."

"Fine," he said. "Except women are sisters, not brothers. And you're a woman."

Except, also, she had seen the rest of his memory: not being able to close his eyes at night without seeing again the blood, the despair, the pain of a soul, even an evil one, cast into the void. Whenever she closed her eyes, or let her mind wonder, that moment came over her, too. The stench of a bad death, the despair of an evil soul cast into eternity at her hand. How many sleepless nights lay ahead, for having stopped that man from killing her?

She mounted her horse, riding between Yusuf and Qasim, to complete the chore of retrieving Pedro's letter.

"Milon didn't carry the afritan," Taresa called back to Yusuf, who rode at the end of the trio. "Giles does. He killed Pedro."

"And since iron won't kill him," Yusuf said, "we fetch Pedro's letter and leave him for Jean-Luc to settle with later. No heroic acts, Taresa. Please?"

"*Òc.*" She hated agreeing, but there was no way around it. They weren't warriors and didn't have magic (which doesn't exist), much less magic strong enough to defeat a king-killer. "And I'm going to Paris with you."

¤

"I lost the silver cross my mother gave me," Yusuf said.

They left their horses outside the gate and walked casually to meet Giles in his aviary, four of his hunters on stands in the yard, the gyrfalcon on his gloved hand. Yusuf nudged Taresa aside and held out his hand to Giles in greeting.

"I'm not sure if it was at dinner or when my friends were nursing me."

His mother? Yusuf's mother lived in a brothel in Cairo. And he'd never worn a cross around his neck in his life. Did Giles perceive that, touching Yusuf when they shook hands? Her own experience was that you saw in Yusuf's memories only dusty scrolls, fat books, and quill pens in need of mending.

Giles reached to shake Yusuf's hand, looking puzzled. If his afritan had felt Yusuf's qareen before, its absence must be confusing now. "You are well, Don Josep? We feared that our good friend the senhóra carried you away to your death bed."

"A bump on the head," Yusuf said. "My clumsy curiosity got the better of me. I apologize for any damage in your charming chapel."

"No harm," Giles said. "Only fears for your well-being."

"May I see that lovely room again?" Yusuf asked innocently enough. "Not just to see if I dropped my mother's cross. But because it's so beautiful. You must be proud."

Giles started along the path with them, his lop-sided smile in place, as silvery and friendly as ever, chatting with them.

"Did you pass Senhóra Blanca?" he asked.

"No, monsieur." Taresa prevaricated, pretending that he meant the lady was still at his castle. "Is she still in bed? Nursing her injuries?"

"She may be malingering, like you suggested."

When they neared the well, that old man stepped back. He had the cover off, the bucket in his hand again. He seemed surprised to see Giles. Or perhaps to see *los tres amics.*

"*Hola.*" Taresa greeted the man, offering her friendliest smile to calm the shivers running up her spine. Giles stood too close, like he always had. He must intimidate the old man, too, for the man backed away, leaving the trio on the path with Giles.

"We did pass your friend Milon on the road," Yusuf said.

"Milon was once my friend, but he became the worst of bad captains who can't understand why he never wins." Giles seemed to shrug off the old friendship like a coat. "He didn't understand last week when Simon castigated him for cruelty, and I fear he's been rather a terror in the countryside ever since."

"You might call it that," Taresa said. "A boy dead among the Templars, along with one of his renegade priests. An old cottager in these hills—the one you sent us to for food the day we met. A dead Crux Lunata knight, whose castle Milon stole."

"That's right." Giles seemed affable. "I'd forgotten Ricart was Crux Lunata in the old days. Such a sorry outfit, bound up in a revenge plot led by half-crazed true-believers. Not a path to power for any knight, much less the hollowed-out shell that Ricart became, long before he grew to be a wizened old man. Not to speak ill of the dead." He let his gyrfalcon fly, watching it swooping high overhead. "Milon is another example of a man who stuck with that outfit far too long."

"So Milon's not a brother in your own *confraria*?" Taresa didn't mean for that to sound like a challenge. "The one you invited me to join?"

Giles cocked his head, like a bird in his aviary, as if studying whether "Tarek" were hunter or prey. "*Oui,* indeed. I lead the Order of the Wheel and Serpent."

"Like this?" Qasim had the heretics' coin out of his pocket, though it didn't flash in the misty air.

"Ah, more of Milon's jackfoolery. You boys weren't taken in, were you? Don't try to buy even horse fodder with a coin you got from Milon."

"The Wheel and the Serpent?" What did Jean-Luc say? Crux Lunata renegades.

"Are you considering my invitation, Master Tarek?" Giles came too close, his hand on her shoulder again, shedding webs of white light, as if to bind her to him. "Perhaps you've decided to come to work for me, since your friends will desert you long before Paris."

Qasim, likely sensing Taresa's unease, stepped between them and touched Giles's shoulder.

A breach of etiquette in most places. A bodyguard initiating a touch with a seigneur. Completely normal in Sebastián's *domus*, where lifelong soldiers of the household and their captains were near equals. Where Yusuf and Qasim were as close as brothers.

Giles jerked away from the touch, as if burned in a fire.

Qasim spoke, not in Aragónese or Catalan or the local tongue or even Arabic from the Valencia docks. Rather, words that must have come from the dark ages, eons ago, the sounds of that song she'd heard in Yusuf's dreams.

Giles whistled. It must have been a command to attack, because his silvery gyrfalcon came down at them with a shriek, claws out for both Qasim and Yusuf. Yusuf ducked at the last moment, crawling close to the well's stone wall. The bird swerved, winged away, then swept back.

Qasim too whistled, holding out his glove-free hand. The gyrfalcon landed, clutching Qasim's sleeve, digging in its claws. If it hurt, Qasim didn't show it. While Giles persisted in whistling and calling command, Qasim whispered into the huge bird's head—where are a falcon's ears anyway? Qasim listened, then whispered again. The bird mewled, dancing along Qasim's arm, then it spread its wings and rose, swooping once around the tower, and then flew away, becoming a speck in the sky in mere heartbeats.

Yusuf and Taresa, meanwhile, circled around Giles, Yusuf brandishing his sword and the dagger that never keeps an edge. Taresa had her dagger out. Qasim joined them. While Giles was judging the danger in Qasim's approach, Taresa kicked Giles's sword hand, sending his blade spinning across the ground. *Los tres amics* jumped Giles at once, and Qasim's greater strength helped ensure that they could bind the struggling and protesting Giles. Qasim double-wrapped the leather thongs that had held Milon previously. He tested them with a tug, though the leather was already tight enough to cut into Giles's wrists.

"You fetch the letter, Qasim. We'll keep watch here," Yusuf said. Qasim nodded and sprinted down the trail to the other tower, then stopped as if he'd been jerked back on a leash. He spun around, hands up helplessly.

"You have to come with me, Yusuf."

"Leaping goats. Not your infernal—" Taresa seized hold of her anger, which was only for Giles. The qareen had helped them.

Yusuf offered Taresa his sword. She switched her dagger to her left hand and accepted the sword, feeling stronger from holding a longer and better blade. "Just keep him here for five heartbeats."

Moments after the two disappeared through the tower's carved wooden door, Giles had worked free of his fetters. He snatched up his dropped sword and lunged for Taresa. Without a thought, she forced Yusuf's blade up into his middle, under the rib cage, twisting.

The wound that can never heal, Sebastián had said. A move you need to know to stay alive.

Giles glanced down, stumbled a bit when she yanked out the sword. Gore on the blade, on her hand. Mere flecks on his vest.

"Didn't work for Pedro. Won't work for you." His lop-sided smile. "Or anyone else."

He grabbed her blade with his bare hand and ripped it from her grasp. He stepped aside when she rushed him with her dagger, which felt like a stick, not a weapon. She whirled away from him, shouting, but he slashed at her hand with Yusuf's sword, slicing her palm before she could move far enough away and put the well between them.

"Why?" she asked. Her cut hand stung. That pain and the belief that *los dos amics* would appear in a heartbeat—together with her own rage—left her free of fear. And Giles loved to talk. "Why choose evil?"

"Evil? No. I choose order. I promised Simon I'd find a way to destroy your antique local customs. He needs a sharp break from the moral morass of the south. I changed the world, so he can create proper order."

"You killed Pedro. And let Milon brag about it." While Giles talked, she circled first one way around the well and then the other, keeping distance between them.

"I don't care what anyone but my cousin Simon thinks. Simon needed two things: Chaos everywhere and Pedro in perdition." He didn't follow as she circled, just watched, as if he waited for some fate to go to work for him. "Simon relies on luck and calls it the answer to prayer. I am his luck."

"Your afritan helped you walk up to Pedro and kill him."

"And then I walked away while Simon took advantage of the chaos I created. He owes what he promised, to make me marquis."

"You played God."

"No. I have come to be, not a god, but greater than other mortals."

Giles advanced on her as if he'd seen a signal. She edged further around the well and snatched at her scabbard, jerking out that wooden practice sword. Running away wouldn't work, so she ran at him, ripping her throat shouting Sebastián's battle cry.

"Vivètz Valerós!"

She jammed that wooden practice stake at his sternum. Giles stumbled against the well's wall.

She struck again, and the stake pierced his vest and shirt. Bones cracked. One more thrust, though you'd think the wooden stake would break before bones.

He reached for her as he tumbled backward into the well. She had hold of his sleeve and the front of his vest, but his weight was too great for her to hold. He fell, screaming.

She was left grasping a torn piece of his sleeve and a button from his vest.

This was the king-killer. The man killed earlier was a butcher who'd robbed and massacred innocent people, both goodmen and others merely standing in the wrong place, all persecuted for nothing but gold.

The man in the well—she looked at that wooden blade, flecks of blood on its blunted tip—had one week earlier walked through all of Pedro's protectors because an iron blade couldn't harm him.

Protected by magic—no. Yusuf said it was just a creature that can't be seen by the eyes God gave humans. A creature now down in the well with its host.

¤

A red-backed shrike, the butcher bird, landed on the gyrfalcon's abandoned post. It stood upright, twisting its head to gaze at the small hawks on other posts, seeking any challenge to its right to perch there. Giles's hunter birds, unhooded, danced along their perches and cawked at the intruder, which took only a moment to determine that the leashed hunters wouldn't attack. It swooped into the rockrose that hedged the castle wall, and returned with prey, a lark, impaling it on a pike stuck into the ground near the aviary. The shrike returned to its newly claimed perch, waiting for the lark to cease struggling and become dinner.

Even if you capture the forces of angels, they can't be relied upon to help you.

Taresa glanced back, instinctively seeking Sebastián. But it wasn't his voice.

Her cut hand burned where she held the button from Giles's vest, threads and a bit of the cloth waving in the breeze. In spite of the persistent mist, warmth flowed through her as if hot honey replaced her blood. The heat rose up through her skull.

Giles's screams no longer echoed from the well.

Fear and pain fell away as if she'd tumbled into sweet dreams.

She glanced around. The fog had lifted. She could see more clearly than on a bright spring day. The pines appeared sharper, greener. The rich, brown soil glowed, as if it had its own life-giving aura.

If being possessed of a creature from a fire lord will send you to hell, this didn't seem to be what hell might feel like. Only a vague pain came from that button burning in her hand.

Toss his silver dagger in the well, too. It's how he captured me.

"Are you there?" She whispered first, but then spoke as if indeed she had company. "Are we companions? Do you talk to me now?"

Taresa never told Sebastián that he was her first real lover. The laundry women cautioned such revelations gave a man too much power over the woman. This felt similar to the first moment of joining with her lover, but without the build-up of passion and expectation.

"Qasim's qareen says you are an afritan. Do you have a name? Do I talk to you aloud? Or do you read my thoughts?"

She didn't hear an answer.

She found Giles's silver dagger and tossed it in the well. Her motion and the racket startled the shrike, which flew into the rock-rose hedge. Taresa picked up a bucket, the one with the massive iron cross on a chain that the old man had used to purify the well. She dropped it over the side. The splash seemed muffled for how heavy the bucket had been. But then also, picking it up required much less effort than expected. In fact, given the cut on her hand and other injuries, it was amazing she'd been able to pick it up on her own.

"You put him in the well?" The old man approached slowly. She was now standing like he had the night before, purifying the well. "Like he did the lady who ruled here before him?"

"Leaping goats! He killed her?"

"Our own seigneur and his senhóra, who were good to everyone. He came here in Simon's name, called them heretics. Ran his sword through our lord. Tossed our good senhóra in the well."

"He said he bought this castle from the count."

"Bought it from an infernal devil in this world of shade. But the Good God is just. Sometimes." He nodded his head, agreeing with the truth he spoke. "But *aiieee*, we shall have to haul water from the spring again. Are you well, young master?"

"*Òc*. Will you find my friends, please?"

Alone, if she was indeed alone, Taresa put the cover back on the well and then sat on its stone edge to count her cuts, which she hadn't felt while fighting Giles. Perhaps some were from the glade where she'd battled Milon. Was this what knights found after battle? Their bodies marked and damaged, cuts from sources unknown, while all it was possible to think was one thing.

I'm alive.

¤

"Taresa? *Nostra noia fina,* are you well?"

Katelina, dressed to travel and leading a horse, called Taresa a fine girl, greeting her as if they met in a garden. A dozen armed men waited behind her in the courtyard.

"Giles de Nully struggled with me and…tumbled in the well. Yusuf and Qasim have gone to retrieve Pedro's letter. Though I suppose all is lost, that Giles already found it."

"But are you well?"

Taresa heard her own voice as if it echoed from the well. "We sent bad men to justice this afternoon." *We*…she'd been the author of both men's destruction, as God already knew. "But if we can't find Pedro's letter for Philippe, then we've struggled to no good end. We will have failed Pedro."

"Qasim found the letter," Katelina said. Rather than an old healer with herbs and ointments, she was dressed as a traveling knight, chainmail chiming under her surcoat. "They were struggling with Giles's men when we arrived. They're cut up but fine. Just worried about you."

She rested a hand on Taresa's shoulder, her touch spreading comfort, further warming her blood. Brilliant sea-blue light surrounded Katelina.

"I guess I'll keep asking. Are you well, Taresa? What happened?"

Taresa pointed to the seat beside her, because she didn't want to get up yet, to start the new work that must be done. "The way I've come to understand it," through fleeting visions when either man touched her, "Milon de Breteuil and Giles de Nully were cousins exiled to the Holy Land when they were youths. They didn't have proper mentors and ran wild there. They took up with Crux Lunata — you know that brotherhood, *ma dòmna?*"

"Too well."

"But that *confraria* didn't help either of them rise as knights. Giles thinks — thought Crux Lunata were too obsessed with revenge rather than seeking power in Christendom. Then Milon and Giles had a falling out in Constantinople."

"Taresa, I was only asking about what happened today."

"But it won't make sense if I don't tell you all of it. You see, Giles stole something in Constantinople, something we'd call magic. It made him invulnerable. He served Simon here to gain the power he'd always wanted. To be — "

"The Marquis de Beaurain?"

"He'd have accepted any similar title. *Mon oncle* Jean-Luc's title and lands were closest at hand, and Hélène was easy prey. Or so he thought."

"Giles was a Crux Lunata knight?"

"Not any more. He'd started his own brotherhood, the Order of the Wheel and Serpent. And Milon, merely by coincidence, came to this part of the Languedoc to serve Simon by spreading terror through the countryside."

"And by killing Pedro d'Aragón?"

"No, Milon lied about that. Or counterfeited, like how he counterfeited the symbol of Giles's order for those heretics' coins he flashed at the Templars' farm. Giles killed Pedro."

Katelina seemed skeptical. "Giles didn't leave here with an army for Muret like other lords did. He told everyone in the area that he was going hunting with his gyrfalcon, not fighting useless wars."

"Giles was at Muret, but not with any army. He used magic to get close enough to Pedro to kill him and then just walked away. Likely got on his great horse Bucephalus and rode home."

"And then you defeated both men with *magic*?" The way Katelina spoke the word, she clearly didn't believe it.

"No. Milon had a dagger at my throat. I fought to get away and—well, what Sebastián taught seemed to be in my muscles and sinews, and so Milon is dead."

"And Giles ran away after he attacked you?"

"He fell in the well." Taresa threw her hands up, gesturing like any Catalan would about the mysterious ways of heaven. "I tried to catch him, but wasn't strong enough. So he's gone. Neither he nor Milon answered my biggest question."

Katelina studied the well, didn't comment on the wooden cover now back in place. But then, Taresa didn't know how she'd put it in place without help. "What question?"

"Why choose evil? Neither Milon nor Giles answered. I still don't understand why they chose to murder and harass innocent people. And now I'm stuck carrying nightmares about them dying, and they only died because I wouldn't let them kill me."

The healer touched her again, which had to account for the rising tide of warmth and the sense of returning strength. It was then Taresa noticed that the clouds had lifted. From the castle's courtyard, it was not possible to see forests creeping down the slopes of *montanha negra* peaks, with patches of golden pasture breaking up the dark fingers of oak and pine and slashes of granite wherever the mountains' edges were too steep for trees to grab hold. A silver sea of clouds still sloshed like waves in the valleys, but in the distance the Pyrenees loomed, sparkling in the day's late sun. Though it was only September, they'd already been dusted with snow. If the world would only tilt, she could see Valerós in the upper hills, right where the Pyrenees became rocky crags. Someday she'd go there. With Sebastián.

"I believed I knew how to judge people," Taresa said. Giles's rose-gold aura, the sign of sensitive, trustworthy people. How had he counterfeited that?

"We were all deceived by Giles. It's not a mistake that you alone made." Katelina still watched her, assessing Taresa's health. "Master Tarek, you've done far more than any hero Pedro might have chosen."

"What a nice thing to say." Taresa found herself shaking when she stood, not out of fear, but more like one of Qasim's dog-friends, needing to shake off whatever brambles and gnats plagued her.

"It's what Sebastián would say if he found you here."

"No." Taresa kicked at that wooden stake, then replaced it in her empty scabbard. "He'd want to know what I did with his third-best sword."

22
Sodalitas, Fidelitas, Virtus

At Kalypso's mansion
After midnight, Thursday, September 19

NIGHT FELL LONG BEFORE THEY reached Jean-Luc's mansion. All along the way, Katelina and *los dos amics* kept asking after Taresa's well-being, never accepting her reassurances.

Inside the mansion, Yusuf and Qasim wanted food. All Taresa wanted was a bed. Katelina led her to a chamber. "When did you last sleep, Taresa? And I must insist on using my talents. You don't want those cuts to go bad."

While waiting for servants to bring a basin of hot water and soap, Katelina offered Taresa a wooden spoonful of a draught that she promised was both healing and restful. When the hot water was delivered, Katelina began washing and examining Taresa, first her arms, pursing her lips but not saying anything, since what had been sword cuts were now tiny slices, already on the way to healing. Katelina washed her thoroughly, chatting as if they were friends.

"How did a young woman like you get here? In a chainmail shell, carrying a sword? Why aren't you—"

"Home with babies?" Taresa said. "I want to be a knight. I want to be a *bonfraire*. To be part of *la Confraria de la Crotz*."

"That's why you did all this?"

"I'd want to protect Yusuf and Qasim anyway. They are like the brothers I never had. But I hoped to prove myself."

"It doesn't take heroics like in a troubadour's song." Katelina said. She wrapped linen around what had been the worst of the cuts on Taresa's forearm, a bandage she didn't need. "You simply promise to support your brothers when they need you. It's not magic."

"I'll have to get Yusuf and Qasim to tell the tale, when Sebastián returns. And beg him to let me join."

"No begging." Katelina had rolled up her sleeves when she began to wash Taresa's cuts. She now turned her wrist, to show the same square scar as Sebastián's. "You've earned this."

"I thought only one woman had ever been made a *bonfraire*."

"No, more than one. My husband and his knights invited me into their brotherhood long ago. I'd say you've done more than any other knight to earn the brand."

"*Mercé*, senhóra."

"Do you pray? Can you say an oath? Because that's also part of this. Or are you—"

"No one would mistake me for a goodwoman. And I can swear an oath."

"Put your hands on this cross and say these words." She placed Taresa's hand on the crosspiece of that wooden stake that looked like a sword. That had saved her from Giles. "'*Sodalitas, fidelitas, virtus*. Upon my honor, I swear absolute loyalty to my brothers when called to arms.'"

Taresa said the words, since she already believed the whole idea. "That's it? That's all?"

"No, there's more."

Taresa repeated what Katelina instructed. "I swear on the name of Our Savior and on St-Jordí to stand by my lord and king. I swear to stand ever ready to serve as a defender of the poor and of all who love God."

"Now, I'm sorry about this part," Katelina said. She held Taresa's hand in hers. Sleepy from that draught, Taresa couldn't see the flash of images as Katelina remembered—something behind a veil of sand, in the desert. She couldn't see, but she smelled burning flesh. It was her own wrist. Katelina held the crossbow bolt from Taresa's scabbard, now hot from the brazier.

"You are a brave girl."

"Doesn't smell as nice as burnt sugar-apples," Taresa said, though the words came out mushy while she struggled to keep awake. Troubling thoughts crawled past, but it took effort to form them into words.

"*Ma dòmna,* how do I know I'm choosing the right action?"

"Because it will be good for at least one person besides you." Katelina said good-night, ready to close the door. "*Cor dolç,* I pray the peace of God for you, and a good rest."

Pray for your own private peace. Taresa hadn't understood what the Valerós chaplain meant about prayers of supplication. Not until the stink and misery of Milon dying rolled over her when she closed her eyes.

She sat up, fully awake, seeing it all again, hearing that dying man moan. Leaving the bed, she searched her travel pack, found Sebastián's shirt, damp from three days of incessant rain. She buried her face in it, seeking any trace of his scent. Back in the bed, burying her face in his shirt, she sought every smell she'd known with him. Baked in armor after a day's ride. Fresh and freezing from a bath in a Pyrenees creek. Over-exerted with her, and sated, in some lord's hayloft in Urgell.

She tossed aside the coverlet and yanked off the night-dress Katelina had given her. Slipping into Sebastián's linen shirt wasn't the same as curling into her husband's arms. But it would have to do. She crept back under the cover, listening for him now, and not just seeking his scent. She rubbed her wrist, the way he did when he'd wrapped himself around her, dipping into sleep.

One idle thought crawled past, that the *bonfraire* burn on her wrist didn't hurt at all. Felt like a hard kiss, the kind that leaves a bruise. Then she tried to remember passionate kisses, but fell asleep listening to music and singing from far down a long hallway, in a rhythm and language she didn't know.

¤

The noise that awakened her wasn't thunder or a clash of steel-on-steel. Only an old woman leaving a tray on the table. The brazier had gone cold. The rush lamp had burned down to a glowing wick in a thimbleful of oil.

"*Bon día, ma dòmna.* Here is your breakfast. Our lady insists that broth and cold meat are best. But I have bread, too, and a baked sugar-apple."

"*Mercé.* And please tell Katelina thank you."

"*Ai,* she's gone, *ma dòmna.* They left for Paris yesterday."

"Yesterday?" She sat up abruptly, then pulled the coverlet tight, since she had nothing on under the bedclothes except Sebastián's linen shirt. She clutched the button in her hand still, so tight that when she glanced down, the wheel was imprinted on her palm.

"It's midmorning, *ma dòmna.* When the farm workers take their second breakfast."

"Can you please tell the marquis I'd like to see him?" Because Taresa wanted a horse, to ride after the friends who had deserted her.

"He left yesterday for Narbonne with Senhór Nunó. Took all his knights, and Senhóra Hélène, and—"

"Leaping goats!" Taresa swore, then apologized, then thanked the woman for the food again. "That's all I need now. *Mercé.*"

"*Ai,* Senhóra Katelina says to tell you that it's best if you go home to Toulouse now. There's spice merchants here, traveling that direction. She asked them to wait for you."

What she'd most wanted—to go to Paris—had been taken from her while she slept. None of her arguments had prevailed. Leaping goats, she'd been left behind, merely so she'd be safe!

Alone, Taresa rose from the bed cursing. *Bonfraires* indeed. Swear to be there for your brothers, who send you home. Where she'd be safe and sheltered, along with other people's children and wives, while her so-called *bonfraires* went off to have adventures and save Aragón.

She threw open the shutters on the room's sheep's-horn window.

September had returned, dragging summer back.

Thunder clouds had wafted away, like a memory.

The sodden, marshy ground was already drying.

In the distance, harvesters swung scythes in the field.

Brilliant late-summer sun shone over her shoulder.

In the light, she examined the sword cuts she'd taken the day before. Two days before? Even the worst was but a thin white line, shimmering in sunlight. That bolt-burn on her wrist—she hadn't dreamed that—had totally healed into a rosy mark, like a tattoo or the angel kisses on a baby's head.

That bolt lay on the table near the window, as if Katelina had left a memento. The wood practice blade lay there also, beside a steel sword, its sharpened edge catching the sunshine, bouncing slices of white light against the stone walls. The grip was newly wrapped in white goatskin, waiting for its owner to mold it into shape. Its pommel was in the old-fashioned style, with letters that must be Greek, worked in silver. Along its blade, near the hilt was an old inscription, almost ground off over the years. Greek on the hilt, but the inscription was in Catalan: To my Andromeda.

Taresa snatched up the wood stake, its dull tan blade now shaded rust-brown. From yesterday's adventure. Without touching any rusty part of that stake, Taresa tried to bend it, the way she had in the great hall of Ricart de Marais's decrepit castle.

It snapped like a thin willow switch. The *crack* echoed in the room as if she'd broken an oak stave.

Beware of splinters!

Taresa whirled around, looking for who spoke.

Then felt stupid, standing in only Sebastián's shirt, holding two pieces of the stake like a pair of weapons, in an empty room where nothing threatened her.

She hurled the pieces out the window, satisfied to hear the *thunk* when they hit the ground far, far away.

She left the sword for you.

This time Taresa didn't flinch or search the room. It settled on her, like a soft, warm cloak on a frosty morning.

"What do I call you? Are you the afritan?"

Amastri. You don't have to speak for me to hear.

"What if I don't want you to hear my thoughts?"

I am your obedient servant. Whenever it's possible.

"Are you a demon from a fire lord?" To have done all that she did and to have sworn the *bonfraires* oaths, only to then end up possessed by a demon—no!

Long before now, I left the fire lord and was baptized by Theodosia. In Constantinople.

"I don't know who Theodosia is."

Sadly, people in this world seem to have lost all memory. Did you meet that clever qareen?

"He—it—Zirari said we needed to free you."

You freed me from that bad man. Now the button links you and me.

Taresa examined the button, tugging away the remaining threads. "What's this? It looks like bone."

It's from the finger of my first companion. It's how the fire lord bound me to that companion.

"Bound you? Like a slave?"

Taresa found the knife that belonged in her boot, the one with a thin steel point. She pricked her own finger three times in the effort, and the scratching hurt her ears, but she finally pried out the bone chip.

"You're free, Amastri. You don't have to stay glued to me. Or however this works."

She wasn't about to struggle with it, like Yusuf had with his qareen, and she wasn't going to take responsibility for more creatures of God than her own friends and family.

Taresa flicked the bone chip into the rush lamp, which held just enough spark to scorch the ancient bone. When the crackle died away, the only sounds came through the window. The distant calls of reapers in the field. A dog barking.

Where would I go?

"Go wherever you fancy."

I fancy staying with you. You're the best host I've endured for many generations.

"I suppose I can't stop you. But stay only if you want to."

Taresa picked up the sword Katelina had left for her. It fit her hand perfectly, the goatskin wrapper warming in her palm, as if coming alive to welcome her. She whipped it through the few moves Sebastián had taught her, liking the sound of it slicing air. She ran her thumb along the edge, which looked recently whetted, but must be dull, since it didn't cut.

"Am I impervious to blades, Amastri?"

Only steel. My power came from the fire lord, the lord of blacksmiths and iron, who gave mastery of the flame to humankind.

Taresa ran the blade through her palm, that same way she'd stabbed Giles with her dagger. The blade passed through, its point outside the back of her hand. She pulled the blade free.

A thin white line snaked down her palm, twinkling when she held it in the sunlight.

By good fortune, you thrust through the webbing between two fingers. It's much harder for me if bone is involved.

"Amazing. It's like magic."

Rather than hoping for magic, it's better if you also apply mother-wit to avoid common harm.

"I had no mother," Taresa said.

Then I have much to share with you.

¤

Taresa's clothes were strewn on the bench, left there to dry, but still damp, not cleaned in any way that a respectable laundry-woman would admit to. Searching her pack, she discovered that the clothes she'd borrowed from Yusuf were gone.

That left the practical clothes Katelina had laid out for her. Taresa dressed in a linen shift and a grey, light woolen robe. These must have been Katelina's own clothes; the sleeves hung over Taresa's finger tips. She rolled up the sleeves and pulled the robe's middle up and over the knotted belt to keep the skirt from trailing on the ground.

Wrapping her chainmail in her last surcoat, she tied it to her travel pack, and thrust her new sword in her old scabbard. She slipped her dagger into the embroidered baldric from Sebastián and slung it over her shoulder.

Then, on second thought, she sat by the table and used the needle and thread—which Katelina hadn't needed for stitching her cuts—to sew that button to her baldric. She untied her robe and slung the baldric and dagger inside, over her shift. Then she tied her robe again, picked up her pack, and went in search of the stables.

More dismay.

"I'll have to steal a horse."

Taresa didn't say it aloud, though she swore aloud when she found that her horse wasn't in the stable. Her horse, apparently, was permitted to go to Paris while she was left behind. And most other horses had gone along or were on the road to Narbonne.

Throughout all the time of human life on this earth, at least since the taming of horses, it has never been wise to steal a horse.

Considering that to be her first lesson in mother-wit, Taresa went in search of the merchants who'd agreed to haul her back to Toulouse.

Ignominy.

You don't know the future. You see only the moment and a dream of the past. I can't tell what will come to you.

This must be what she'd missed by not having a mother to criticize every thought and action.

Is that one of the thoughts you don't want me to hear?

Four wagons. Beside one stood a drover she believed she recognized, at least from the distance. These wagons all had scarlet- and woad-dyed covers with orange and grass-green pennants flying from poles on each wagon, bells on the oxen's harness, as if the journey were its own *bal masque* or a prelude to *mardi-gras* festivities.

As Taresa approached, however, she recognized the iron-straked wheels. These wagons had been camped by the river, where the merchants guarded injured soldiers.

"*Bon día, mon amics.* We meet again." She greeted the drovers, calling out the names of men she recognized. They blinked in surprise and stared at her.

Because of Katelina's robe. The Tarek they met on the road never wore women's clothes. She held her hands high, the Catalan gesture that declared, Who knows the ways of heaven?

"What are we hauling to Toulouse, *mon amics?*"

"Cabbages. Sausages. Turnips."

"What market stall in Toulouse would dare sell sausages from another town?" Every town across the Languedoc insists its sausages are better than any other town's.

"The world is in disarray," one drover said. "Chaos is the only thing that's for certain. Toulouse has been under siege since Muret. They say…"

Taresa couldn't hear what followed. Yusuf had gone to Paris. Sebastián to Rome. She alone among them was riding straight into a war.

"We saved a seat on the second wagon for you, *ma dòmna.* We'll take you all the way to your *domus.*"

Back to that. *Ma dòmna.* No more Master Tarek.

You're a senhóra? With a castle? This is the best that's happened to me in a thousand years.

"I'm a knight." She couldn't say it aloud here, but wasn't it the best that'd happened to her, next to being forced to marry Sebastián? "I'm the third woman ever to be a *bonfraire*, a knight of *la Confraria de la Crotz*."

I haven't been with a woman since Theodosia. Just passed from priest to knight to prince to charlatan. A woman! And not a nun! Do you like men? I mean in that special way where you get to—

"*Ai, ma dòmna!* Here you go!" One drover tossed Taresa's pack into the wagon, interrupting the afritan's excitement. He made a human stirrup out of his hands, offering her a step up onto the drover's platform at the front of the wagon. He took up his willow stick, to walk alongside the oxen, encouraging them on their task. Another frail-looking, white-haired drover climbed up alongside Taresa and took up the reins.

"You'd do better in your own travel clothes," the drover said. "You make a pretty boy, but still less tempting should any rogue hunters stop us."

"My riding clothes are too wet to wear. My chainmail will rust before we get to Toulouse. And—"

The white-haired drover was Isabella of Valerós. Whom Taresa didn't know very well, having traveled with her once over three days in Aragón. And whom Taresa feared a great deal. Sebastián's mother.

"I thought you were in the hills, at Valerós." Taresa blurted. "What are you doing here?"

"My duty. The same as you." Isabella pointed to the square burn on Taresa's wrist. "Best keep that covered when you can."

Taresa hadn't considered before that Isabella's white hair and silver aura formed a corona around her narrow, ageless face. Taresa had been too afraid of her, as Sebastián's mother, the few times they'd met. Intimidated, Taresa had never looked closely enough to *see* Isabella the way she saw others, the way she saw friends in the baggage train. And she'd never met a woman with an aura as metallic silver as new chainmail.

"Welcome, *sòr bona.*" Isabella's thin hand slid down Taresa's arm to grasp her wrist. "It won't make sense to call each other *bonfraire.* They say you have unique talents."

"*Òc*, I suppose I do."

"We've been moving goodmen and goodwomen to safety. Ready to help do what we must?" her mother-in-law asked.

"I believe I am."

Warm blood ran in her veins. That fist released the stone it had clutched for so many days. The oxen jerked into motion. Taresa grabbed the edge of the drover's bench to steady herself, colliding with Isabella's hand.

"Did Sebastián go to Rome?"

"*Òc.* He wasn't at Muret. Have you been worried?"

Yes, every moment. "No, Yusuf told me the plan. But I wish Pedro had told me. I wish Sebastián had. I don't like secrets."

"Yet they also say you see people's memories," Isabella said. "Please don't read mine. I'd prefer to tell you my stories while we travel."

What a kind woman! It felt as if Amastri snuggled down to listen, like a child on a rug before the hearth, waiting for the story.

"Have I ever told you," Isabella's voice rasped, but she spoke with warmth, "that I hate Toulouse with a fire to quench all other fires? I wasn't happy when I lived there, more than a decade ago."

She likes you!

"When I woke this morning," Taresa said, "I was unhappy about returning to Toulouse."

"We'll have to make a plan, won't we? To endure?"

Taresa settled back on the drover's bench. She braced her foot on the box-edge of the wagon, but when it creaked, she drew her feet back, not intending to kick it to pieces with her newfound strength.

"Surely you and I can do better," Taresa said, "than simply enduring."

"*Ai,* a woman after my own heart!"

— END —

From Isabella's Stories

From the stories Isabella told Taresa.
An excerpt: *Trebuchets in the Garden*,
Book 2 in the Accidental Heretics Series

Summer, 1204

AVRAHAM THE TRADER GLANCED up as the morning sun broke over the city walls. White-gold light shimmered on the baubles scattered across his workbench. Across the square, a barefoot farm-boy tapped the rump of a desultory donkey with a stick as they picked their way across cobbles still warm from the previous day's sun.

"*Ai*, Toulouse in summer. Dung, dead dogs, and cabbage-ends, all ready to roast again in the sun." Avraham yawned as he settled his cap in place. His impatient guest had roused him too early in the day. "The air hasn't moved in Toulouse since Shavuot."

"Your people's festival of first fruits?" The visitor, a young donzel dressed in traveler's leathers, attempted to be polite.

Avraham's soft answer was overwhelmed by one of those black-robed street preachers shouting in the market square.

'It was the Dark One, Satan, who shaped Man from clay. That evil God made Man's carnal nature.'

"Sancta Maria, we have to listen to the foolish declarations of heretics all day long," Avraham's young visitor groused. "Souls migrate from beasts to men. A woman who conceives a child brings evil to the world. It can't be called philosophy, much less heresy."

"You and I believe in the same God, *mon amic*." Avraham tapped his bench top as he often did to raise a point in their discussions. The baubles on the bench rattled and scattered. "You and I cannot accept that God is both good and evil."

"*Òc.*"

That hoarse voice agreed with him in the common tongue of Toulouse but sounded tired, as if plagued by sleeplessness for a decade. Copper-colored hair escaped from a felted wool cap. The fine-boned face had no beard. His visitor's page, a mere child, crouched in the doorway, drowsy from rising so early. The donzel's rough clothes failed as a disguise. Nothing could hide that its owner came from among the pampered of Toulouse.

Avraham folded his hands on the work table, falling into the familiar discourse he enjoyed with his young friend. "A clear mind such as yours cannot espouse that this world is evil made manifest."

"If I consider my own life, that goodman teacher might make sense. But then, I would have to forget history, science, and reason." The visitor glanced out the door across the disorder and dust of the marketplace, fidgeting more than usual, hands twitching. "You always say you are a businessman, not a scholar, Master Avraham. Can we conclude this exchange?"

The youth's voice rose to an agitated pitch but did not break. Even nervous and hoarse, it echoed the tones of Narbonne or the southern hills rather than the hawkers or parish priests shouting pieties to drown out the goodmen preaching in the market square.

"You want to trade Greek buttons?" Avraham held up a disc, pleased to tease his visitor. "You want to buy my precious manuscript with buttons and buckles?"

"These are real gold."

The buttons, which trailed threads from the tunic they had once decorated, were indeed gold but of modest value, and Avraham's scroll was worth more. His visitor appeared every fortnight, interested in any ragged manuscript the trader might have recently acquired. Occasionally, a few silver pennies appeared and a purchase was made, but the youth had never sought such a costly text.

Like a father in despair over an errant child, Avraham complained again. "These rubies? You pried them from what, donzel? Your father's dinner knife? Your mama's best goblets?"

"I have no mother or father. If you are trying to shame me, I lost all shame years ago."

Avraham continued his chiding. "These objects defy anything I've seen from you. This little pin," he held up a silver brooch shaped like a cross, "was maybe stolen from your mama's prayer beads?"

"It belonged to my grandfather, who was a true crusader. This is all I have to offer, Master Avraham. Can we strike a bargain?" Empty hands spread, beseeching. Nails bitten to the quick, rimmed black with ink.

"Why so hurried?" The dealer pushed back strands of his greying hair and then lifted another gem with wooden tweezers, peering at the stone for many moments. "You come here every fortnight to read my manuscripts. I always save what you want until you can afford to buy. But today, you think maybe the king of the Angevines will march on Toulouse before you can steal enough from your family? You make me miss my breakfast for buckles and stones?"

"We are leaving Toulouse today. It's my last chance to see you."

"This is sad news, donzel." After teasing all morning, Avraham felt true sorrow. "I don't know where I'll find such entertainment with you gone from the city."

"I'm sorry to say farewell to you. But I long to leave this stinking city more than I long for heaven." The youth pushed the pile of gems, buttons, and brooches into a mound. "Is this enough?"

Avraham shook his head as he always did at this point in a trade. "My scroll is a mere fragment, but it's said to be written by your St-John's own hand."

"Sancta Maria, it's in Latin. And only a fool would think it's a thousand years old," the youth said. "Just tell me yes or no."

"Avraham ben Yitzchak is not the one to argue over your saint's Gospel." Avraham was ready to cede the bargain. "At your last visit, I guessed that you'd want it soon. It's sealed in waxed parchment. Shall I break the seal so you can inspect it again?"

"I trust you."

"And I'll take your buttons and the stones you chipped from your family drinking cups. But you might as well keep this ring." He laid the bauble before the youth.

"You don't want it?"

"It's not worth the brass and glass it's made of. It's as false as you are, donzel." He almost dared to touch the youth's hand. "I shall miss you, *ma dòmna* of Montcava."

For the first time in their friendship, he called her "my lady."

.

"How did you learn my name?" Senhóra Isabella frowned at the ring, a present from her now-dead husband at the birth of her son; of course, her sole gift from Nicolau proved to be dross.

"Last week I saw you come from your church on the arm of a man, with liveried servants behind you," Avraham said. "Was that your husband? He's a handsome man."

"No, my brother-in-law," she said. "It was a memorial for my husband who died on crusade. My father departed this world, too, on the road to Constantinople."

"I'm sorry for your loss, *ma dòmna*."

"It's sad about my father." Isabella grimaced. "But not about Nicolau. The indulgences he earned on crusade might buy him a place in heaven, which is the only way he could get there."

"Five years I've known you. You never say such things."

"You also know me now for a thief and a liar."

"Your minor deceptions are a fair price for the pleasure of your company," Avraham said. "And now you and your family are leaving Toulouse?"

"I'm going alone, with my son." She glanced toward the boy who slumped in the doorway. "We'll join my grandfather and sisters at home. I've stayed in Toulouse too long."

"*Way, way!*" Avraham cried words in Hebrew that he'd told her meant woe. He studied at the boy. "Your son? *Ma dòmna*, why, you can't be more than twenty."

"Eighteen," she said. "If I were older, I'd call on the Count of Toulouse to help me. But instead, I must do this myself. After today, I'm no longer of the House of Montcava. So, please call me Isabella of Valerós."

"May the Almighty go with you, *ma dòmna*." He said it with unusual passion as he handed her the parchment package.

"Thank you," Isabella said. "Though I have long wished the Lord cared more for me than He seems to."

Excited to own anything so precious, she received the scroll with nervous hands. She tucked it into her satchel and hung the leather pouch around her neck once more, now containing just that worthless ring and the most beautiful calligraphy she had ever seen. Her son Sebastián lagged, groggy after being called from bed before dawn. She'd brought him to Avraham's only because she couldn't leave him alone with her dead husband's family.

"Come faster, Sebastián. If you were a crusader, you'd have marched a league already today."

"Òc, el meu capità!" He saluted her as his captain. "I am ready for duty."

As they hurried through the maze of alleys, she repeated the plan to Sebastián. "First we pack the silver we hid in the floor. Then at migdiada, when everyone is napping, we head for home."

"And take back Jerusalem from the infidels!" Sebastián crowed. He'd heard stories each night about his crusader grandfather Pèire, who had served the kings of Jerusalem. He gloried in the blunted knife she let him wear on his belt, playing Crusaders-and-Saracens.

"Not Jerusalem. What do the crusaders in our family call home?" Isabella prompted him.

"Castell-de-Valerós, the domus of the best knights in Christendom," he said. "And then I shall have a dog at last. And my own pony and a real bow. I shall have the best swordmaster."

It broke her heart that Sebastián had never seen their home in the Pyrenees foothills. Her grandfather Pèire hadn't answered her message when she begged to come home now that she was a widow. And so, she had to get away on her own.

Steal food and blankets for traveling.

Cut the buttons from Nicolau's clothes to sell.

Hoard every silver penny she could find.

Trade her dead husband's armor for a horse.

All because a six-year-old boy can't walk all the way to Valerós, though she could, if she were alone. Soon, Senhóra Isabella of Montcava would once more be just Isabella of Valerós.

The early-morning air, thick with humidity and dirtied by smoky kitchen fires, reeked of offal and sewage. Oxen yoked to overloaded carts dropped their own loads of filth while the farmers unpacked garlic and artichokes. Hawkers displayed sausages and honey under makeshift awnings. The more prosperous vendors had tiled roofs over their booths, backed up against the old city walls. Smoke from their open fires burned Isabella's eyes. That young man who hawked near St-Sernin, more handsome than God made most men, called out to everyone who passed him. "Fresh cabbages. For your table or healing your wounds. Cool your belly pain with these fine cabbages."

"Seljuk Turks. Turcopole archers." Sebastián identified strangers around them as enemies. An aged donkey passed, hauling a bundle of kindling. "The Kurdish cavalry of Saladin."

They skirted the market, ignoring the hawkers and dodging the black-frocked goodman who preached near the bakers' ovens, where women lined up for morning bread. As they approached the St-Sernin abbey, Isabella saw the burly frame of her confessor, Father Clémence, lumbering through the abbey's kitchen gate with a pair of chickens. He'd no doubt wring their necks with his own massive hands for the priests' midday meal. She wanted to escape the ugly, censorious Father Clémence along with her Montcava in-laws. Because she had grown up with trustworthy priests, she'd mistakenly told Clémence what the Montcava brothers did to her. Father Clémence declared it her sin and ordered hard penances. Once, for only a single happy week, she had a young lover named Jaume. When he died in an accident, she confessed that timid affair, and Father Clémence demanded tortuous penances for two years.

Please God, may he not see us.

Although her prayers had never before been answered, a passel of mercenaries staggered by just then, laughing and smelling of wine and blocking the priest's view of her.

"Mercenaries!" Sebastián shouted, excited to see soldiers.

Those men wore the cross of the new crusade, like others just returning from that debacle in Constantinople.

"Now we fight for Burgundy," cried one amid a quartet of fair-haired Normans. "I'm happy to spank the Angevine King John, for Burgundy or any other lord."

"*Oui.*" Another Norman agreed, saying "yes" in the Frankish way, rather than "*òc*" as people did in the south. "Let's hope they pay better than the Venetians. May the dark angels take their souls."

"We can hope the Duke of Burgundy provisions better wine," the first man said. "We could pour that swill we had in Zara over the walls of a city and burn it during a siege."

Among those men, a suavely handsome but drunken mestitz man hung on the shoulder of a tall Celt, both a disgrace to the crusader cross stitched on their quilted tunics. Isabella's grandfather had such half-Saracen men among his knights, but all were abstemious and immaculate about their person, as were the Moorish merchants in Toulouse. That extremely drunken man collided with her in the way pickpockets do. Isabella drew her dagger as she shoved him away.

"*Ai Dèu*, put up your blade, man." He knocked aside her dagger with his gloved hand. "We're Christians. We don't fight our brothers." He spoke the common tongue of the south, but with the strangest accent she'd ever heard.

Laughing and hiccoughing, the tall Celt clutched at his companion's sleeve. "Sancta Maria, we never fight Christians," he said in the same accent. "Unless there's a war."

The Celt, who had a rebec slung over his shoulder, ruffled her son's copper-bright hair, which people seemed unable to resist doing. Sebastián offered his dazzling smile, appreciating the attention.

"This donzel must be the same age as your son," the Celt said, nudging his umber-brown companion.

"*Jhezu del tron*, could this one be mine, too?" The man called on Jesus in heaven. His words caused his comrades to fall on each other's shoulders, laughing.

Isabella sheathed her dagger and tugged at Sebastián. As those mercenaries rounded a corner, he sang a counting chant that began, "A mercenary I will be. *Una, doas, tres, quatre*."

"Not like those men," Isabella said. "You are a donzel of the great House of Valerós. You shall be a real knight one day. A man of honor. A guardian of our paratge."

The echoing curses of threadbare Norman mercenaries called up memories of Pèire grousing about the last crusade with King Richard and King Philippe.

"Normans and Angevines like Richard Lionheart are the worst of the crusading brigands and thieves that floated like trash on the tide to Jerusalem."

She glanced back to make sure Sebastián followed closely and therefore nearly collided with a shaggy giant of a man at the end of the alley. A dusty, trail-weary man who smelled of horse and leather and clean sweat from exercise, the way a man should smell.

"*Ça va?* Uh…Are you all right, donzel?" The giant spoke the common tongue with a heavy French accent. He had ice-blue, piercing eyes. His probing inspection seemed intelligent rather than threatening. "Those fools didn't disturb you?"

"No, it's fine." She twitched a smile, which she didn't usually offer strangers, except he spoke kindly. Bearded, untrimmed—unlike most French fighters—he had the bearing of a knight, but a knight who'd endured a harsh journey.

"Do you know where…" The giant sought words, not fluent in the local tongue. "Where can I find a doss house? Or a brothel that lets pallets for the night?"

She did not know, despite living in Toulouse more than six years. "Ask in the St-Sernin market square."

He murmured thank you, in French, and then drifted down the alley toward the market.

Isabella and Sebastián crept through the narrow, deserted alley behind the stables of the Montcava villa. The high brick walls cast deep shadows, even in the glare of morning sun. They loitered beside a narrow alcove that even the most attentive passerby saw as just another reinforcing arch.

Pèire insisted that in the Outremer, the crusader-conquered lands across the Great Sea, every fortified citadel built an escape route, so crusaders who came home added secret passages to their villas. In the months after Sebastián was born, Isabella snooped through every corner of the Montcava villa, seeking such a passage, finding it in her husband's room. It served as the only access to freedom she had in Toulouse.

Sebastián stomped on the cluster of anise at the alley's edge.

"If you destroy their fields, they must become your slaves."

"Sebastián, stop that. A soldier of the cross who's a man of honor doesn't destroy without provocation."

She pushed aside the dusty veil of blue clematis and pawed through the tendrils of the vines that hid the entrance in the wall.

"Into the breach!" Sebastián croaked in a whisper.

He scrambled into the tunnel, but she reined him in to follow her into their enemy's house. For the last time. She was going to take them home, to their real home.

·

When Isabella exited the passageway and entered Nicolau's room, Renoud was pounding at the barred door and calling her name. She had one heartbeat to throw a robe over her traveling leathers and answer, pretending to have been asleep.

"You only hide to punish me, Isabella."

Renoud towered over Isabella just as his brother, her husband Nicolau, had done, telling her without saying the words: *I can make you do what I want.* Renoud, tall and with a lion's mane of tawny hair, he'd come home from Constantinople, where Nicolau died. The flower of the southern lords, that's what women in town called Renoud. But Isabella considered him vermin. The Montcava emblem embroidered on his sleeve suited Renoud: a scorpion with a red crescent moon.

"Isabella, *cor dolç,* this isn't a nice homecoming for a crusader like me, with you hiding and my poor mad mother turned heretic."

He moved so close that she could smell wine on his breath. He touched her chin and cheek the way one comforts a child, which repelled her. He'd come home with a cross tattooed on the back of his hand, little crescent moons picked out in red at each point of the cross. It was a badge of brotherhood among crusaders, he said, but none of Renoud's comrades resembled the dignified crusaders who served her grandfather Pèire Leteric.

"I am worried about you, dear sister." He caressed her shoulder, which always led to worse.

The pale, vexing wraith that was Renoud's mother, Senhóra Eloïse stepped in front of Isabella, blocking her way.

"You mustn't touch her," Senhóra Eloïse said. "She's filthy. Dirty with sin."

She endured more chiding and fondling from Renoud in front of Eloïse and the gossiping servants and, worse, a silent and sober Sebastián. Isabella pleaded a headache to retreat, and then she sat with Sebastián to comfort him, feeling him quiver in his struggle not to weep.

Then she heard hammers echoing from the passageway.

There was no longer a hidden exit from the Montcava villa. It was being nailed shut. After long moments considering her choices, Isabella removed her dagger from the traveling pack. She and Sebastián would have to leave through the front door, impossible to do while Renoud lived. But there would be blood. She hated blood. She tried to imagine fighting her way to freedom without blood touching her.

Playing beside her, Sebastián sang that nursery rhyme.

> I saw the wolf before the wolf saw me.
> I'll kill the wolf before the wolf kills me.
> God take the wolf and God save me.

In the alley beneath the balcony, the Montcava guards called to each other; Renoud's voice rose above the rest, and her whole body tensed with hatred.

She whispered, "We're going now, Sebastián. Carry this pack."

Letting her tunic sleeve fall over the hand that gripped her dagger, Isabella slipped through the upper hall and down the stairs. The wraith Eloïse again manifested, grasping Isabella's forearm.

"When you call up the Dark God, he comes." Eloïse wrenched away, raking Isabella with her claws.

Renoud's servant, Miró, held open the main gate. Renoud stood in the courtyard, raising his arms as if in supplication. She came behind him, preparing for what she had to do to escape.

"Who'd believe it!" Renoud shouted. "We never expected to see you here in Toulouse, senhór."

"God in the golden heaven with all the sobbing angels, why wouldn't I be here? Every other goat in town died but you."

Isabella called Sebastián to her side. She wouldn't have to touch blood to be rid of Renoud.

Her grandfather, Pèire Leteric, had come to bring her home.

END PREVIEW • ACCIDENTAL HERETICS

Read all the tales that Isabella told Taresa.

Accidental Heretics Series
Lost in the Languedoc Crusade

Book 1: *Bone-mend and Salt*
Book 2: *Trebuchets in the Garden*
Book 3: *Crux Lunata*
Book 4: *Song of Valerós*
The Madwoman of La Catalane, A Novella
The Blue Door and More Heretics Tales

www.eastewartauthor.com

Glossary

A – C

Angevines: The Plantagenet dynasty that ruled from Ireland to the Pyrenees. The Angevine empire grew through the marriage of Henry II and Eleanor of Aquitaine.

arrèsta: Stop.

aventail: A chainmail curtain to cover the neck and shoulders.

balefire: A bonfire or pyre.

belette muet: Mute weasel.

beneeixi: A blessing.

benvingut: Welcome.

bon amic: Good friend, or boyfriend.

bon día: Good day.

bonfraires: A brotherhood.

bonhommes: The so-called Cathar community's term for itself; Good Christians.

booty: Treasure; during the crusades, the primary way crusaders financed their armies or to pay their mercenaries. That is, rather than "looting" as we now think of booty, these cultures considered booty as legitimate plunder. ("To the victor go the spoils.")

brioix: Bread.

bruixa; bruja: Witch.

cabres: Goats.

canço d'amor: Love song.

canço d'guèrra: Song of war and warriors.

Catalan: In the Middle Ages, a language, not a political entity.

cavaller: Cavalier, knight.

cor dolç: Sweetheart, an endearment.

crucesignati: Crusaders.

crux lunata: Lunate cross, featuring lunar crescents at each terminus; a pagan symbol; war tokenism imported to Europe by returning crusaders, adding the Islamic crescent in heraldic and other symbols.

D – L

desencusa, desencusatz: Sorry.

domus: Household, meaning the larger economic household of a titled landholder.

don: A courtesy title for a gentleman from the landed classes.

donzel: A young gentleman, in training for knighthood.

fadrin: A lad, a term of endearment.

Franks: At the time of this story, a reference to western European people.

fustian: A heavy cotton fabric.

gai sauvatge: Wild jay.

goodmen, goodwomen: A reference to the people whom the Church called heretics; now commonly called Cathars.

gos: Dog.

gràcies: Thank you.

holá: Hello.

Jhezu del tron: Jesus in heaven.

jongleurs: Medieval minstrels who sang the troubadours' songs.

J'rigole: I jest.

Knights Templar: A monastic crusader military order, the most elite of the crusader armies.

M – R

ma dòmna: My lady.

marquis, marquesa: A lord (and his wife) whose land is on a frontier border, and so must be a capable defender.

mercé: Thank you.

misericòrdia: Mercy.

mon amics: My friends.

Monsenyor: An honorific, such as for a king.

montanha negra: Occitan for Montagne Noire, a mountain range in central southern France

Moors: People from northern Africa who settled on the Iberian peninsula under Muslim leadership. Colloquially, a person of mixed heritage or dark complexion.

Normans: Descendants of the Viking Northmen who settled Normandy, and later invaded Britain and also conquered the Muslims in Sicily in the eleventh century.

òc: Yes.

Outremer: The lands across the Great Sea, where the Crusader States were founded and other territory seized by Christian invaders.

paratge: A world view from the time of the troubadours, with multiple connotations about honor, civility, nobility, grace, and tolerance, defining a culture's view of "right living."

peccador: Sinner.

punxor: Prick.

renrén: Fool.

S – Z

Saracen: Colloquial term used in Europe for Muslims.

sarawil: Trousers.

seigneur: A man of rank who rules lands and a household.

senhór, senhóra: Titles of respect, equivalent to señor, señora.

Sodalitas, fidelitas, virtus: Latin motto of the *bonfraires*: fraternity, fidelity, virtue.

sòr, soeur: Sister.

squire: In the southern lands, a fighter of rank between knights and foot soldiers, for his lifetime. In the southern world, squires did not rise to become knights.

surcoat: A long coat worn over other clothes or armor.

viscount: A European noble rank, above a baron, below a marquis.

vivètz: Live!

woad: A plant used to create a blue dye similar to New World indigo; grown as a cash crop around Toulouse.

Place Names

Valerós and Montcava exist within the world of the Accidental Heretics, but nowhere else.

Acre: A city on Haifa Bay in the Outremer, now part of Israel. At the time of this story, it served as the capital of what was left of the Kingdom of Jerusalem.

Aquitaine: A duchy in what is now southwest France that was a key portion of the Angevine empire under Henry II and Eleanor of Aquitaine.

Aragón: In the mid-thirteenth century, a union of the Kingdom of Aragón and the County of Barcelona established the dynastic Crown of Aragón, with tributaries across the Languedoc at the time of this story.

Barcelona: A territory on the Mediterranean, now approximately the political entity of Catalonia, for which Pedro II held the title Count of Barcelona.

Cahors: A town in the Occitanie region, north of Toulouse and on the connecting route to Paris.

Cairo: The seat of the Ayyubid dynasty that Saladin founded, with the third oldest university in the world.

Carcassonne: A fortified city in the Languedoc, which surrendered to the French crusaders in 1209.

Constantinople: Capital of the Eastern Roman Empire, sacked in the Fourth Crusade, becoming the seat of Norman rulers for the next fifty years.

Cyprus: An island in the Mediterranean, south of Turkey and north of Cairo. During the Third Crusade, its Muslim rulers were conquered by Richard Lionheart who sold it to the Knights Templar, who in turn sold it to Guy de Lusignan.

Girona: An ancient city in the northeast corner of Catalunya; part of the countship of Barcelona at the time of this story.

Iberia: The old Roman name for the peninsula now called Spain.

Jerusalem: Captured by the crusaders in 1099, recaptured by Saladin in 1187, traded back and forth for several decades until finally captured by the Mamluks and lost forever by the crusaders.

Minerve: A town in the Languedoc that sheltered refugees from the massacre of Béziers and was subsequently defeated by Simon de Montfort, and its own heretics were burned by the conquerors.

Montpelhièr: A walled city in the Languedoc, near the Mediterranean, with the second oldest university in Europe.

Morella: A town near Valencia, taken from the Moors by El Cid, lost later, then finally becoming part of Aragón in the Reconquista.

Narbonne: A rich Mediterranean port in the Languedoc that was the seat of the archbishop and home to a significant Jewish community.

Naxos: A Greek island in the Aegean Sea, alternately under Byzantine and Venetian rule.

Outremer: The Frankish Crusader States in the eastern Mediterranean; the land overseas.

Provence: A county on the Mediterranean, ruled by the counts of Barcelona; governed by Pedro's brother Alfonso at this time.

Roussillon: A region in the southeastern Pyrenees and foothills.

Toulouse: A county in the Languedoc, whose count owed allegiance to the king of France at the time of this story. The city, on a major trade route between the Mediterranean and central France, was a bishop's seat.

Urgell: A county in Catalan-speaking lands between the Pyrenees and Lleida.

Valencia: A region and ancient Roman port city on the Mediterranean peninsula. Seized from the Moors by El Cid in the eleventh century, then retaken a hundred years later and still held by the Moors in Pedro's time.

About the Author

E.A. STEWART is an American writer whose *Legends of Valeros* and *Accidental Heretics* series explore intrigues in France and Spain in the early thirteenth century.

Ms. Stewart lives and writes in Seattle.

To learn more about
the Accidental Heretics series, visit:
www.eastewartauthor.com

Acknowledgments

Thanks to Elizabeth Bjorkman, Jacyn Stewart, Susan Urban, and Laurie Cropp for critical and editorial reading. And thanks to Waverly Fitzgerald for Mondays and Thursdays at Liberty on Fifteenth Avenue East.

From Jugum Press

HISTORICAL AND CONTEMPORARY FICTION

Nzinga, African Warrior Queen by Moses L. Howard

Nzinga, in history and legend, is a brilliant leader during a time of violent upheaval. This fictional biography brings to life the 17th century Angolan culture in a flourishing African kingdom, now lost, where early explorers' maps of West Africa call out: "Here reigned the celebrated Queen Nzinga!"

Nine Volt Heart by Annie Pearson

He said, "I love you." She said, "You don't even know the real me." He said, "Great title for a song. Key of G? Can we try close harmony?" Jason and Susi meet by accident in Seattle. Secrets, songs, and stalkers quickly entwine their lives in unpredictable ways.

This Charming Man by Ajax Bell

A chance encounter with an intriguing older man inspires Steven Frazier with visions of a more rewarding life. A vibrant snapshot of Seattle in the early 1990s, this story captures the drama of coming into one's own as an adult.

PERSONAL VOICES IN HISTORY SERIES

Journey into Gold Country: Memories of a Forty-Niner

by Ralph Buckingham; foreword by Charles Barker.

Three wild years in the California Gold Rush, remembered sixty years later by a New England younger son who went to seek his fortune.

We Were Walimu Once and Young

Edited by Brooks E. Goddard

Stories from the Teachers for East Africa and Teacher Education for East Africa experience in the 1960s, describing student and village life, adventures with flora and fauna and food, and journeys to explore remote parts of East Africa.

Find print and ebook editions:
www.jugumpress.net

www.ingramcontent.com/pod-product-compliance
Lightning Source LLC
Chambersburg PA
CBHW030330200626

46816CB00006BA/1992